More Critical Praise for Olive Senior

For *Dancing Lessons*

- Short-listed, 2012 Amazon First Novel Award
- Short-listed, 2012 Commonwealth Book Prize

"Senior is particularly deft at exploring social class, maternal terrain, and distance. The territory she writes about could not interest this reader more . . . Senior skillfully depicts the space between mother and children . . . What's remarkable at times is Senior's subtle depiction of family tension, the prodding between mother and daughter, the apprehension of what the one does or mainly does not know of the other."
—*Globe and Mail*

"Senior's insights about gender, race, and class in Jamaica reveal her keen eye for details."
—*Canadian Literature*

For *The Pain Tree*

- Winner, 2016 OCM Bocas Prize for Caribbean Literature
- Short-listed, 2017 Association of Caribbean Writers Grand Literary Prize

"At every level of her stories' constructions, Senior works deftly . . . dealing with open palms in the deep wells of remembrance, ancestry, and a crosshatch of colonizing scars, this fiction looks face-upwards to the mountains of multiple Jamaicas for hope, home, and daily bread."
—*Trinidad Guardian*

"The magic of Olive Senior's stories is that they weather time with uncommon power. In these collected short fictions, published and broadcast in various incarnations from the 1990s forward, the concerns of class, language, identity, and refuge reign, explored in prose that is all the more commanding for its subtle navigations." —*Caribbean Beat*

"[Senior's] prose is supple and ornate . . . there is technique aplenty."
—*Quill & Quire*

PARADISE ONCE

BY OLIVE SENIOR

BROOKLYN, NEW YORK
Publishing books since 1997

Published by Akashic Books
©2025 Olive Senior

ISBN: 978-1-63614-227-2
Library of Congress Control Number: 2024949341

Akashic Books
Brooklyn, New York
Instagram, X, Facebook: AkashicBooks
info@akashicbooks.com
www.akashicbooks.com

CONTENTS

Semel vocauit inde semper excitam . . .

He called her but once and thenceforth she was always awake . . .

—Inscription on engraving of *America* (c.1600)
by Jan van der Straet

Author's Note

To assist the reader, a glossary of mostly Taíno words used in the book can be found at the back. It has been collated from numerous sources but is not intended to be in any way the last word. The effort to retrieve the Taíno language is still very much in process, reflected in conversations about pronunciation, meaning, and spelling variants. The retrieval of the Taíno language is part of a larger project to define a new Taíno identity, stimulated by the quincentennial in 1992 of Christopher Columbus's arrival in the "New World" and the challenge it posed to history with the implication of the "discovery" of peoples without history. The Taíno were so decimated by the discovery that over time they were declared "extinct"; this ignored the fact of their absorption into the multicultural Caribbean societies that developed. Though there was discontinuity in terms of direct lineage, recent revelations via mitochondrial DNA (through the maternal side) prove that a significant portion of Caribbean peoples do carry Taíno in our blood and Taíno language and cultural practices in our genetic inheritance. I hope my extensive use of their language will help to bring alive the vibrant Taíno society as it existed in the sixteenth century.

The children, seated in a circle around the poet, will ask: "And all this you saw? You heard?"

"Yes."

"You were here?" the children will ask.

"No. None of our people who were here survived." The poet will point to the moving clouds and the sway of the treetops.

"See the lances?" he will ask. "See the horses' hooves? The rain of arrows? The smoke? Listen," he will say, and put his ear against the ground, filled with explosions.

And he will teach them to smell history in the wind, to touch it in stones polished by the river, and to recognize its taste by chewing certain herbs, without hurry, as one chews on sadness.

—Eduardo Galeano, *Memory of Fire, Part I: Genesis*, translated by Cedric Belfrage

PART I
THE VILLAGE

There are those who will always say it was Feather the Trader bringing the foreign bird into the village that caused the first shedding of blood that unleashed the flood that ended in our destruction.

We all know there was discord long before, from the time of our kacike Omeyra's murder in a foreign land and the quarrels over his successor. Discord that split the village into two factions—one led by Matron Greenstone, the other by the new kacike Runs Swiftly and his retinue, which included Councillor Maura, Runs Swiftly's uncle and brother to the formidable Matron. They didn't talk to each other.

But it was far, far more than a family feud.

We should really say it all began long before, from the time the foreigners sailed to our shores and split our world in two. There were those who avidly leaped to secure the talismans of modernity. And those who wanted to cling to the rules laid down from First Time, regardless . . .

And there are still those who say the model of our turbulent existence within the duality of light and dark, good and evil, feast and famine, was ordained long before that, at First Time, with the birth of the twins Boinayel, Son of the Dark Serpent Bringing Rain, and Márohu, Bringer of Fair Weather, warring opposites even before they left the cave of their mother's womb.

It happened. Once.

So it was, so it always will be.

Chapter 1

As swirling mist swallowed the last notes of the holy man's Greeting to Sun and shreds of sacred *tabako* floated from his outstretched palms, Maima village exploded into life.

Girls puffed their cheeks out as they blew on the fires to make balsam tea and warm up *ajiako*, pepperpot stew that sat in a covered *olla* at every family hearth.

Servants hurried off to the *kaney*, the large rectangular building facing the main plaza, the dwelling of the nobles.

Pet birds, lap dogs, monkeys, iguanas, and small children alike were scrambling in and out of the houses and screeching. Men and boys tuned up their panpipes and whistles on their way to the river for their first bath of the day. Men headed upstream, women downstream in a bantering exchange of laughter and greetings.

Only the women on the farm roster were quiet and purposeful as they got ready for the trek to their fields, baskets on their backs with their knives, digging sticks, and water calabashes. Some had a cotton spindle and thread already in hand for spinning as they trotted single file to the *konuko* along a path still slippery with dew. Small children of nursing mothers peeked out from cradle boards.

Night Orchid, on her way to her uncle's workshop, accompanied her mother as far as the crossroads where Pebble joined the other women heading for the *konuko*. As she watched them vanish in the mist, Night Orchid wondered, not for the first time, how soon she would see her first blood and be able to join the ranks of women.

Shark Tooth watched from the bushes as the girl Night Orchid passed below where he sat on a boulder. Small and plain, not yet a woman, he observed. Little did she know what power she would wield in time. But he knew, for he made it his job to watch and listen and learn, which is how he had overheard the biggest secret of all. So big that it made him decide to make a marriage offer to her uncle now, for when she came of age. He knew there would be objection from the girl's family. But it had already been sanctioned by the *kacike* no less, and his word was law.

Shark Tooth smiled at how easy it was to manipulate Runs Swiftly, the young man who had surprisingly succeeded to the leadership with the sudden death of Omeyra. He knew the high-ranking *kacike* had tolerated his presence in Maima because he had arrived as a Lucayan refugee and deserving of hospitality. But never would he have allowed him to approach the inner circle.

Truly, thought Shark Tooth of Omeyra's death, the powers smiled on me. Once the girl came of age and was married, the present office holders would be the only obstacles to his total control of Maima village. The old woman would die soon anyway, and removing her daughter before she succeeded as the keeper of the most sacred object in the nation could always be arranged. He thought of the magic darts that had been embedded in his body when he pledged his soul to the Shark God of the underworld—Bagua Guamacajayo. Darts that left no record of their journey.

Smiling, he struck his flint to light his *tabako*, and almost toppled off his perch as an eerie laugh penetrated the silence, seeming to come from nowhere and everywhere. *Ai ai ai.* It sounded unpleasantly like the Old Man of his youth who had both blessed and cursed him and whose spirit seemed never to let him go.

He jumped down and picked up a stone but dropped it, knowing it was useless against spirits. Bursting with anger, he set off for his medicine hut. It needed serious work to counteract this omen.

Chapter 2

In the men's section of the river, boys were joking around, soaping up, diving in and out of the water, wrestling or noisily splashing each other.

"*Kanoa*!" Flint shouted, waving his arms and pointing.

All eyes turned downriver where a narrow boat hugged the bank. The canoe was piled so high with goods the paddler was not immediately seen. When he was, the boys whooped with delight, calling out "Feather, Feather," as they sped down the gravelly beach to meet him. They arrived just as Feather lifted the conch shell to his lips to signal his arrival.

Flint got there first. The young warrior Heart of Palm, feeling he should be first in everything, tried to grab hold of him so he could get ahead, but Flint twisted his slippery body out of his grasp and splashed on, determined not to be outdone.

Heart of Palm screwed up his handsome face into a scowl as he splashed behind him, because Heart of Palm was not only *ni-taíno*, but he was also, at seventeen, already a proven fighter, the best wrestler in the village, the best stick fighter, and captain of the junior *batéy* team for the whole region, while Flint, Flint was nothing, the least of the boys gathered there. Flint was not even full Taíno. Flint was the ugliest boy in the village, with a long head, pronounced cheekbones, and with the slanted eyes of his Ciboney ancestors. Just like his ugly mother Crab Claw. Ignorant savages who lived on the island before the Taíno came and taught them how to live like decent people. So thought Heart of Palm now, but only because he was fuming. Most of the time, Flint was seen just like any other villager.

Flint had inherited his father's keen sight and good lungs. His endurance as he ran messages between villages or tracked small game in the bush was as strong as his sense of sight and sound. But Flint had little time to polish up his skills for competition, for his natural abilities only made people work him harder, sending him on all sorts of errands.

"It is because you are a reliable boy. People know they can trust you, Flint," his mother Crab Claw often said as she rubbed *bixa* paste into the part in his long straight hair to ward off evil spirits, or painted his body with his guardian *cemíes* that protected him in the bush. Her heart filled with both joy and sadness whenever she thought of her only son who always seemed so sober and older than his years.

His uncles had given the boy his first toy spear and axe from the time he could walk and had taught him the ways of the bush. So now, at thirteen summers, Flint was almost as respected a woodsman as they.

Flint knew his own worth as well as his station in life and never complained, though he would have liked to have more time to play ball or practice the stick fights. For though he was sinewy with a body built for speed and he lacked the bulk of Heart of Palm who was built like a tree trunk, he would have dearly loved the challenge of beating him at something with the whole village watching.

But now, all was forgotten as they turned to greeting Feather with shouts of joy, for this was everyone's favorite trader of all the traveling merchants who made their way to Maima, situated on a bluff overlooking the bank of the beautiful Abacoa river. Where, every morning as the girls added new wood to revive the dying embers of the fires that burned in their houses to protect them from the cold night air, the beautiful scent of the burning copal resin rose on the air like a benediction.

The landing stage became a scene of joyful melee as Feather ran the canoe onto the hard river sand. Boys rushed to place the rollers to haul it up the beach and secure it to a post. Feather swung lightly to the ground and stuck two fingers inside his medicine pouch of exotic black seal skin and offered *tabako* to the twin brothers, Winds of the Four Quarters, turning to each direction as he did so. He ended up facing the water, where he made an offering first to Attabey, Mother of River Waters, who had allowed him to travel safely here, alone in his small *kanoa*, then to Yukahú, Lord of the Seas, who had permitted his safe arrival on the coast in his large pirogue manned by a crew of twenty, now docked at Maguaca village two days to the south. Finally, he offered up the holy herb to his spirit familiar.

Only then did he turn and take notice of the men and boys and the snot-nosed urchins standing awestruck and silent as he surveyed them with piercing eyes under bushy eyebrows which, with his huge nose, made him seem like a bird of prey on long sinewy legs. Glaring at the little children to scare them even further, he nodded at the older boys who rushed to the boat to unload it.

The strange bird was not noticed at first for it was inside a beautiful covered basket of fine twill weave. But everyone could see that the basket contained something precious, from the way Trader carefully lifted it from the boat. He looked around and, spying Flint, signaled him to step forward.

"Here, hold this carefully, and don't go running off now. Wait for me."

Flint couldn't stop grinning widely. Inside the basket which he held close to his chest, he could feel something alive and moving. But he could see very little through the weave.

Feather lifted from the *kanoa* his large carrying basket, heaved it on his back, and adjusted the straps and the tumpline across his forehead. Taking up his *koa* to help him navigate the steep path to the village, he set off, Flint closely following in his footsteps.

Chapter 3

Flint's mother Crab Claw was on her way to the *kaney* to attend to Matron Greenstone as she did every morning, with her calabashes and reed tubes filled with medicine and towels of the finest cotton over her arm.

Her undyed cotton *nagua* reached halfway down her thighs and her calves bulged from the tight protective bands of woven sisal that rose in layers below her knees and above her ankles, like the ones that also banded her wrists and upper arms. Images from a roller stamp covered her shoulders and her bare breasts down to her waist, overlaid by red *bixa* paint. Her medicine bag hung around her neck, along with her vomiting spatula and a small carved stone amulet of Great Mother Attabey.

The only refined and seemingly valuable object on her person was an intricately carved conch shell pendant of unusual design and exquisite workmanship which hung from a string covered in miniature white shell beads and pearls. Although the pendant's pattern had tantalized her fellow villagers for decades, none could give an accurate description of what it portrayed. It was as big a mystery as Crab Claw was.

Matron Greenstone nodded as Crab Claw greeted her with a low bow before kneeling on the woven rush mat at her side. She carefully placed her equipment on the mat and laid new coals on the fire in the pottery brazier. Then, dipping her hands in the salve of precious turtle fat and winter-green in her calabash, Crab Claw rubbed her palms together and made ready to soothe her mistress's aching limbs.

Matron Greenstone wondered, not for the first time, if it was the anxiety of what was already happening during her nephew's brief rule as chief that was bringing on the worst pain she had ever felt in her life. Or were the *cemíes* using it to punish her for some infraction or warn her of a greater pain still to come?

Her mind was wandering along this maze and she was dozing off when the sound of the *kobo* brought her fully awake. The cries of children and adults, the whole village it seemed, rushing down to the landing place at the river announced more than the notes blown on the shell that Feather the Trader had arrived.

Matron Greenstone wondered excitedly if he had finally brought her what she most craved—the amulet blessed by IxChel, Lady of the Rainbow on the island of Cozumel, patroness of medicine, weaving, and love—which he had failed to bring her for so many seasons.

"My dear lady, your humble servant is desolated," he said each time, his imperfect Taíno overlaid by the slight lisp in his flowery tongue as he touched his forehead to the ground before *kacike* Omeyra's sister. "But things are not as they were before. Since the coming of the Panols, all the trade routes have been disrupted . . ."

Those accursed paranaghiri!

Crab Claw could feel her mistress stiffening up and wondered which angry spirit had invaded her souls. She sent a silent message to Attabey, *cemí* of easy passages, to untie the knots. And then, as she always did, she touched her amulet and offered up a prayer to Bokura, the spirit of the Old Ones who were her ancestors. In these times of peril, one could never have too much protection.

* * *

At the far end of the *kaney*, the *kacike* Runs Swiftly was submitting to his morning grooming and trying hard to curb his impatience. It would not do, he knew, for the chief of Maima to rush off at the first sound of the *kobo* blown by a trader. Though this was not just any trader, this was the legendary Feather and his stock of goods was always exceptional.

In the past, Runs Swiftly would have been down at the landing place like the others crowding around Trader's boat.

"Don't worry, Nephew. As chief, you will have the first choice of everything Feather has to offer." Maura's silky voice breaking into his thoughts was like the buzzing of an annoying fly, until his uncle added, "Besides, he is sure to bring you a magnificent present to celebrate your elevation."

Runs Swiftly had no idea his impatience was showing, and his uncle's overcultivated voice at the best of times made him want to grit his teeth. Maura's side of the family was the one with pretentions and he seemed to have consolidated them all in his person, just the kind of man Runs Swiftly and his pack of bully boys in the past loved to provoke. Given their rocky relationship, Runs Swiftly was surprised at Maura's backing of his chieftainship. If it weren't for Maura, in fact, he probably would have declined in favor of Falling Water, Matron Greenstone's candidate.

But Maura would do anything to provoke his sister and retain the powerful role he had enjoyed as Omeyra's chief administrator. And he had won over Runs Swiftly by laying out all the advantages a powerful chief could enjoy. "Power is one thing," he had said, but there were also (ticking them off on his fingers): "the chief's warehouse full of choice goods, his elaborate traveling *kanoa*, invitations to travel to other islands, the possibility of acquiring an exalted wife or wives, gifts from visiting dignitaries . . . everyone bowing and scraping." The list seemed endless, with no mention of the duties.

It was Maura's promise to "keep things going" that had convinced Runs Swiftly, for in truth he was afraid of the responsibility. With Maura in charge of everyday matters, Runs Swiftly would be free to continue with his life as before, especially his ball playing, and at the same time exercise the power of the chief. All he had to do was not let the silly man irritate him beyond belief.

Runs Swiftly sat up and straightened his back. The ends of his long cotton breechclout fell between his powerful legs planted on the floor and he placed his hands on his knees and sat still as a statue while the women painted and dressed him, his broad forehead and hawkish profile all adding to his seeming invincibility, as if he were built for the role. Only his dark eyes which flitted constantly here and there and his small, bow-shaped mouth which betrayed his connection to the Blue Heron family, revealed signs of weakness.

Runs Swiftly looked down at his splendid necklaces and touched his *guanín* pectoral, symbol of the high office he had gained, and grinned, showing even, though slightly wolfish teeth. He was third in line of succession, so never dreamed it would happen. But his eldest cousin, Matron Greenstone's son, had drowned in a swollen river as a youth, which left his own brother Amanex, who had been in Omeyra's party that was slain. Blessed! The *cemíes* had smiled on him.

Dignity was everything now. But the sound of Trader's shell blow made all that fly out of his brain. He was thinking that with Chief Omeyra and so many of the other senior nobles no longer around, he would have the first pick of the treasures that Feather brought. Even before Matron Greenstone herself. A thought from which he took a great deal of satisfaction.

Chapter 4

Matron Greenstone was relaxing under Crab Claw's gentle hands and welcomed the peace and quiet at last, but she couldn't stop the tears that welled up every time she looked around the partly empty and often silent dwelling. At this hour, it should have been abuzz with activity as the nobles and their families prepared to start their day.

But nowadays, except for Runs Swiftly and his retinue, much of the building was empty and the rest occupied by older single people like herself who remained saddened and silenced with even their servants creeping around like ghosts. A lethargy had encompassed the entire village, now that their head had been so cruelly cut off. A fate that seemed to be overtaking all of the Taíno, Matron Greenstone thought, except for those traitors who were prepared to bow. Worse, to join the *paranaghiri* in the slaughter of their own. What was happening to the world these days?

Her beloved brother Omeyra would never have bowed his knee, of that she was sure. Nor would any of the fifteen trusted chiefs from the other islands summoned to a parley by Grand Chief Guarabo at his fabled home on the island of Borikén. A family compound in which exotic animals and birds imported from far-flung places wandered the grounds or roared in large bamboo cages and water fountains played over the extensive gardens that had been created by the nation's finest artists. Matron Greenstone would not have believed some of the wonders there if she had not seen them with her own eyes.

Omeyra, *kacike* of Maima and overlord of nine smaller villages in the mountains, accompanied by nobles, war chiefs, and advisers, as well as their ladies and a retinue of servants, had traveled in his lavish seagoing *kanoa* to Borikén.

The true purpose of the meeting, Omeyra had confided to his sister, was to formulate a policy once and for all to drive the Spirits of the Great Water from their lands. But the grand fiesta to which they were invited was ostensibly to arrange marriage alliances, including a match with Grand Chief Guarabo's own granddaughter to Omeyra's heir, Amanex. What a mark of favor that was!

And what a lot of trade goods that particular alliance took to accomplish. The thought of the negotiations, not to mention the emptying of the family warehouse to satisfy that greedy man, made Matron Greenstone shake her head even now. But such an alliance with one of the most powerful *kacikazgos* was a brilliant one for the illustrious but obscure Blue Heron family.

Omeyra had brushed aside any mention of the drain on their resources by the negotiations. "Especially now we have a regular market on the mainland for the red heron feathers. Six *kanoas* in the last season alone."

"The Xamaycan cousins aren't displeased we are cutting into their trade?"

"No problem there. They can't keep up with the demand, Yamarex assured me. The appetite for the feathers from the temple builders is insatiable and we in the islands have a monopoly. But we are concentrating on the newer markets to the north. Feather the Trader informed me after the last trip that there are anxious middlemen waiting to carry our trade west and north."

"Not that Guarabo isn't an old rascal for demanding so much."

Omeyra laughed. The grand chief was well known for his cupidity. But for the ladies he was full of charm and the men recognized his leadership as a war strategist. His brilliant conquests were sung in the *areitos* and the strategic marriages of his numerous daughters by eighteen wives—to the defeated *kacikes* usually, if they showed great courage—had allowed him to cement an astonishing network of connections up and down the islands. He had shown no inclination to submit to the *paranaghiri*, which is why those who wanted to resist were placing all their hopes of victory in his hands.

But all to no avail now, everything was lost.

The *paranaghiri* must have planted a spy in their midst, for without warning they fell on the party the second night of the fiesta before the celebrations had even got underway and butchered them all. Down to the youngest child present, a three-month-old granddaughter of the grand chief. What kind of savages were these? How could people have ever imagined they were divine?

Despite her brother's assurances, Matron Greenstone knew when he left he was as troubled as she was by the news of destruction that traveled the length and breadth of the Taíno nation, up and down the islands. To the point where some chiefs were forming alliances with the Kwaib who had begun to send mercenaries to bolster the dwindling Taíno forces.

When the *kacikazgos* of their allies were being destroyed, the Maima villagers had first sent help, then withdrew into themselves as the best policy of not attracting attention; they had increased their watchfulness and intercessions to their *cemíes*. But the *cemíes* seemed to be deserting them too, for eighteen moons ago the barbarians had returned to their island of Cuba with the objective of conquest, and had already cut a swath of murder, terror, and enslavement across the southeast. Though the hill folk had so far been spared, it seemed only a matter of time before they too were discovered and enslaved. Armed resistance was going to be a key topic at the grand conclave.

What were Maima's war plans? What weapons had they to fight with?

She couldn't help smiling as she remembered her brother's parting shot. He had come to take tea with her as usual and they had quietly discussed the upcoming meeting in Borikén. She again voiced her reservations about leaving Runs Swiftly in charge as acting *kacike* with Maura as administrator. Maura was a good manager she had to agree, as long as he could raise himself out of the *hamaka* of the latest young wife and break his habit of betting on everything in sight. But . . .

Omeyra laughed. He was far more tolerant of their younger brother. As for Runs Swiftly, who would be acting in the role, "It will be good for the boy to have some responsibility beyond being the best ballplayer we've seen for many generations. Besides, he can't get into any trouble for it's the slowest time of the year. There are no major celebrations planned. Nothing to do, really, but supervise the work rosters. We'll return well in time for the spring planting. And a major fiesta to celebrate Amanex's wedding."

He had turned and smiled at his sister, a mischievous grin that softened his usual stern expression so that she could glimpse again the beloved playmate of her childhood.

"Of course, my dear, we know who is really in charge here, at the best of times." And he gave her a meaningful look. "I leave everything in your capable hands."

Matron Greenstone smiled whenever she remembered her brother's remark. Well of course! Men had their roles, but descent was through the female line. Female household heads controlled the family names and totems, interpreted the rules and regulations, and had an equally strong voice in the village councils.

Female *kacikes* were not unknown, which is why Matron Greenstone had felt confident in putting forward Falling Water to succeed Omeyra; she was a wise and intelligent woman of some twenty summers who had impeccable credentials as she was next in line after her mother to be Keeper of the Bundle, the nation's most sacred possession. Matron Greenstone thought most of the council was behind her, to the point where she hadn't imagined there was really any contest between her candidate and Runs Swiftly.

"Well, I guess we totally underestimated the adulation people have for their sports heroes," was Falling Water's wry comment after the vote.

Unlike Falling Water, Matron Greenstone could not leave well enough alone. She knew her nephew's tenure would not end well; the omens were clear. Something had to be done. As Crab Claw was manipulating her right ankle, it came to her: the answer to their problems. *Ha,* she thought, *let's see who can outmanipulate the manipulators.*

She waved her hand at Crab Claw to cease.

She had ruminated on the problem long enough and finally knew just what needed to be done to turn the situation around. Power had to be righted in Maima village. Signals had to be sent. The *cemíes* demanded nothing less.

Chapter 5

When Feather huffed and puffed his way up the steep hill into the village and stopped to catch his breath and look around, he was most surprised to see the new *kacike* seated among the crowd milling about in the plaza in front of the *kaney*. In the past, Runs Swiftly would have had a silly grin on his face, but now he sat straight and unsmiling, his powerful chest thrust forward so that the *guanín* pectoral glistened golden against his skin.

Approaching him, Feather carefully laid down his pack. He raised his palms and bowed all the way to the ground in greeting. The *kacike* nodded and signaled for refreshments to be brought. Feather unpacked his offerings.

Flint saw it as soon as the trader opened the basket. First, the baleful eye staring at him, the crown, the claws on the one foot that it flexed, and last of all the feathers, glowing iridescent red and gold, shimmering and glinting in the colors of Sun.

There were audible gasps at the auspicious colors as Feather lifted the strange bird on high so everyone could see it before placing it on the ground. The bird staggered a bit, then righting itself, hopped inside the semicircle of onlookers, lifted its wings, and flapped. And then, to everyone's amazement, it raised its head and emitted from its throat the most astonishing sounds ever heard from a bird: *Cock-*

a-doodle-do. Over and over, in varying tones, *Cock-a-doo-dle-do.*

People clutched their amulets and backed away and the timid screamed and fled. As if pleased at the effect it had, the bird lowered its head and pecked at the handful of *mahíz* Feather had placed on the ground, nodding before swallowing each corn grain. Though its angry eyes never wavered, it allowed Feather to pick it up, hold it under his arm, and stroke it, before he bowed again and offered it to the *kacike*.

Runs Swiftly nodded, and his assistant Dark Water stepped forward and received the bird in his arms. He too tried to stroke it, as he would a parrot or a dove, but the bird suddenly exploded and scratched him, its claws leaving bloodied marks on his cheeks and chest. Dark Water gasped and let go of the bird, which fell to the ground and skittered about, its wings flapping. Those nearest backed away, though the braver ones laughed as the trader did. The *kacike* had not moved a muscle. He looked questioningly at Feather.

"This is the Bird of the Morning of which I have heard?"

"Yes, the ones brought by the Panols to rouse them from their *hamakas*."

"Their holy men do not do that?"

"No, *Guama*."

By this time, the trader had taken hold of the bird again and he was stooping in the circle, the bird on his knee. He was stroking it and feeding it corn kernels. The bird closed its eyes and seemed calmer; its feathers became luminous as Sun climbed high enough to send its rays to strike the plaza.

Feather knew just how to grab and hold the attention of the crowd. He was speaking to the *kacike*, but now he raised his voice: "This is the bird they use to pull Sun from its watery bed every morning. See its red crown, its wattle. See it dressed in the colors of Sun?"

Everyone looked, for although the village, their entire world, was filled with beautiful birds, they had never seen one like this. Many in their hearts thought their own Sunbird, the macaw, was far more beautiful, and nothing could compare with Kolibri the hummingbird, for he was *guanín*, one of the sacred powers. But all could feel this bird bursting with power too, the power of the Other, the ones who had come from far.

The fact that Feather had brought this strange bird into the village filled many with another kind of fear. Their beloved chief Omeyra had joined the ancestors, yet such was his aura that everyone present knew what he would have said about the gift, for Omeyra had banned anything that came from the *paranaghiri*. But such was the fascination with the bird, no one wanted to think of that now.

"Shall we keep him tied up?" Dark Water asked, anxious to get away and be cleansed.

"Just for a few days until he gets used to you. He will fly up into the trees and the housetop, but he is a domestic bird, he won't run away. He has no intention of looking for his own food."

"Won't he attack us? Or our animals?" Dark Water asked, for he had already noticed how the rooster had his eyes fixed on the little dog that the *kacike* had cuddled on his lap. All the villagers had pets—dogs, tame birds, iguanas . . . and if this warrior bird would attack humans, what would he do to a small animal?

"Nooo."

Feather said this with such assurance that they breathed out a collective sigh of relief. After all, hadn't he traveled alone, up and down the coast for many moons, with birds like these ever since the *paranaghiri* brought them and their mates from far over the seas and the native women had learned how to raise them from their eggs which the *paranaghiri* liked to eat? So it was said. But then, everyone knew the traders were crazy men who bought protection in every village they went. It was because they had so much protection that they could live forever, people said, shedding one life and simply taking over that of another, as long as they kept moving. Like the boa that was their totem.

Chapter 6

The women on the farm roster were on their way by dawn and too far away to hear Feather's shell blow, so they worked in their field unaware of the excitement in the village.

"Ha," said Sun Woman, tugging with her digging stick at the *yuka* root to loosen it before pulling out the whole plant with both hands. She chopped off the growing top with her axe and scraped away much of the dirt from the root before throwing it into the carrying basket. "I hear they wear the same clothing as their women do. Long black robes covering their entire bodies. And they don't have wives either." She said this last bit in a falsetto voice, rolling her eyes and suggestively wiggling her hips under her thigh-length *nagua* made of woven palm fiber stained red with *bixa* and now brown with dirt.

The women within hearing paused in their labors, wiped their sweaty brows, and laughed, and Squash Blossom derisively threw a dried-up sweet potato in Sun Woman's direction.

"Sounds just like our Silver Fern," said Root Girl, for their holy man sometimes dressed as a woman. Root Girl was expecting her first child and her waistband, which had a short reed apron attached, was stretched to its limits.

None of them had ever seen a priest, or even a single

Panol. The older ones could remember the stories of the foreigners arriving in the east floating on the water and the people taking them for gods. For hadn't the elder and prophet Guacanagari of Borikén had a vision of the coming of the *guamikena*? After one span of time they had left. Then they'd returned, bringing death and destruction.

The *kacike* Omeyra had not wanted the village to be tainted by the strangers and had ordered confiscated any of the gifts that made their way there. So the children had no little tinkling bells, the women no foreign beads and shiny mirrors, and the warriors no red woolen hats. Also forbidden were the strange animals and the new plants.

Yet, as if nature itself was unafraid to defy the *kacike*, where a seed fell from contraband fruit, new plants were springing up all over the fertile valley, in the woods and out of sight, though people increasingly cut through the vegetation in search of them, for they were magic. On the other islands—Quisqueya, Ayití, Borikén, Xamayca—the animals the *paranaghiri* brought—pigs, goats, cattle, horses—multiplied and ran wild and soon would overwhelm their own island of Cuba. It was as if the New World was being overrun by nature's fecundity as the native peoples were diminishing.

No one told the hill dwellers that fruit trees and animals from their lands, even some of their own people, were being taken to the land the Panols came from, where they too would be seen as exotic or magical.

Despite their fear of the ghostly strangers, the women at the *konuko* could not resist showing off.

"Look," Sun Woman said to Root Girl, "look at what Burning Spear brought me."

Root Girl moved closer as Sun Woman fished a foreign metal object from her medicine bag.

The women took the object and studied its shape, smelled it, turned it this way and that, and passed it from hand to hand.

"What is it for?"

"I don't know. He traded a fisherman from Plumtree village two spear points for it."

"Two spear points?" They were impressed. Burning Spear's points were the best.

Sun Flower, a young girl who had recently joined the ranks of women, said quietly, "You are not the only one," and brought out of her bag a beautiful bead of a startling blue.

All fell silent in awe, even Sun Woman, for this eclipsed the buckle.

"Did your husband give you that?" someone asked.

"Yes, he traded a wooden *cemí* from Corncob's workshop to a man in Baracoa."

"What? Those fishing folk are making a mint. I bet you he found that somewhere."

"He says it was blessed by the *paranaghiri* priest. It's to protect me from pain in my joints."

"You don't have pain in your joints."

"See. That's why."

Sun Woman rolled her eyes.

As if the blue bead had opened up a new world, a blue ocean beckoning, each woman suddenly felt the need to reveal her own foreign acquisition which she had hidden on her person or describe those among her personal possessions at home. As if ownership of some object that had been touched by the *paranaghiri* was the newest marker of status.

By now, several other women had drifted over. Among them was Pebble, an older woman known for her placid nature. She listened without speaking, until the pregnant Root

Girl reached into her medicine pouch and triumphantly pulled out a small mirror.

Everyone gasped, though before they had a chance to say anything, Pebble darted forward and grabbed it. "No, no," she said, and to everyone's astonishment, she threw the mirror on the ground and used her heel to push it into the soft earth, then picked up a rock and pounded it.

The action was greeted by gasps and sharp intakes of breath.

"Oh oh!" Root Girl put her hand to her mouth and started to wail.

There was uproar from the rest. Pebble moved forward and tried to reach out to Root Girl as the others drew away.

"I'm sorry," she said, "I didn't mean to. The spirits—"

"What will I tell Arrow?" Root Girl wailed. "He promised so much trade for it."

"Hey, shush," said Sun Woman, pointing at Clover, the senior matron striding toward them.

"What's going on?"

"Oh, these first-time mothers," Sun Woman declared with a smile, and the others nodded agreement.

Even Root Girl stopped sobbing long enough to nod. "I'm all right, Clover."

"Don't worry, we'll take care of her."

"Time for a break anyway." Clover smiled at Root Girl as she went back to where some women were already sitting down with babies at their breasts.

Without saying anything, the small group of women including Pebble went and sat in the shade of a ceiba overlooking their *konukos* which covered large squares of undulating fields on the gentle slopes below. The fields were divided into raised beds in which the holy *yuka* flourished, along with sweet potatoes and other tubers, *mahíz*, pumpkin vines, pineapples, and more fruits and vegetables in exuberant array. The women closed their eyes and inhaled deeply, giving thanks for the blessings of their ordered world, before they settled down to hear Pebble's explanation for her extraordinary conduct.

Chapter 7

ebble was very much like her name—everything rounded: her body, her face surrounded by a cap of short hair, her eyes; even her lips were rounded. Only her nose was straight, and somehow lent balance and dignity to a face that would otherwise seem clownish. Unlike the hardness of a pebble, though, the message her smiling face sent out was one of comfort and warmth, and she was a favorite of everyone, always willing to lend a hand or give advice. Which is why her behavior so shocked the women.

She made a point of seating herself beside Root Girl, who was still heaving with small sobs. She thrust Pebble's hand away when she reached out. "What will I tell Arrow?" she wailed.

"I'll give you more than enough trade to make up for it," Pebble assured her. "I didn't mean to, truly the spirits moved me, but"—and she said this defiantly as the other women stopped eating and stared at her—"I'm not sorry I destroyed it. I know what it will do to your baby, you see."

She had everyone's attention now. Root Girl drew in her breath and laid her hand on her belly.

Pebble sighed as if to give herself courage to go on. "I had one of those, long ago when I was carrying my baby Night Orchid. Candlewood says that is what attracted the evil spirit to her. And her guardian spirit was too young to fight back. Don't you remember what Night Orchid was like?"

The older women nodded, remembering a child disturbing the village whenever she was racked by convulsions, but the young ones like Root Girl looked confused. Night Orchid was Pebble's youngest girl, and they only knew her as a quiet and hardworking carver in her uncle's workshop.

"You are too young to remember it," Pebble said, looking at Root Girl and Sun Flower, "but Sun Woman and the others can tell you what we went through."

Root Girl said, "I don't understand."

"Let me tell you a story I never told anyone before. Then perhaps you'll forgive me." She smiled and handed Root Girl one of her specially flavored corn cakes. Root Girl took it reluctantly but soon was chewing as she listened.

"From the time Mockingbird and I were first married, we took a trip every year to the coast in the *kacikazgo* of Guanabo where Mockingbird has kin. We went to collect Marginella shells as this was good trade. Mockingbird still goes every year but I have never returned since I saw them, the *paranaghiri* and—"

"What? You saw them?"

"And you never told anyone? Tell us, what were they like?"

"Is it true that . . . ?"

The women were so excited by this news they were all talking at once.

"I was too frightened," said Pebble. "I'm frightened even now when some eleven summers have passed and Night Orchid is nearing her womanhood."

"So what happened?"

"Well, I used to enjoy those trips. We'd spend a few days

with kin and leave the children with them. Then we'd find some quiet spot on the beach. Beautiful white sand. Like crystals. Not like our black river sand."

"So we've heard."

"It's true. I saw it. We'd camp and spend a few days collecting the shells. Anyway, this time I was making another child. The fourth. A few moons along. We beached the *kanoa* and were walking along when suddenly I saw something out at sea coming toward us. Like a huge white bird with wings skimming the water. But big. *Big.*"

"What did you do?"

"I was so frightened my feet stuck fast to the sand. Mockingbird grabbed my hand and pulled me: 'Sails. Spirits from the Great Water. We must hide.'"

Pebble paused and Sun Woman pressed, "Then what?"

"I wet myself."

Everyone laughed.

"Seriously. I could barely stand up. My breath was coming and going like a drum. Mockingbird dragged me up a high bank and we hid. The strange men came ashore and lifted big jars from their *kanoa*. They filled the jars from the spring and called out to each other in their strange voices. A cloud passed over the sun. It gave me chills. *O Mama Attabey, protect me and the baby,* I prayed."

There was absolute silence.

"I closed my eyes, for the *paranaghiri* were even uglier than people said, with long matted hair and blotchy red and white scaly skin, and I didn't want my baby to come out looking like them. Mockingbird nocked his spear and kept watch until they finally loaded up and paddled back to the big *kanoa*. We hid until they went off."

Pebble paused and took a sip of water. "It was when we were walking back down the beach—I tell you, my legs were trembling so much I had to hold on to my man—that we saw this strange thing shining in the sand . . ."

Root Girl froze with food halfway to her open mouth and Sun Woman couldn't hide her impatience. "What, what, woman?"

"Mockingbird bent down. When he came back up, something in his hand reflected a flash of sky and right away I knew it was one of those mirrors we had heard so much about. Mockingbird laughed and held it out to me and I took it and brushed the sand off, but . . . I can't explain my feelings . . . I wanted it, but I didn't want it. I took it and stuck it in my bag without really looking at it. To tell you the truth, I felt ashamed to be going against our *kacike*'s wishes yet thrilled to have something that the *paranaghiri* brought from afar."

Pebble stopped talking and no one spoke, for each owner of a foreign object had had the same conflicted thoughts.

Pebble continued in the same pensive voice: "As we paddled along, I felt sad. I was thinking that in taking the mirror, I had lost a bit of myself to those people in exchange. That is how they were conquering us, little by little."

There was silence as the women chewed this over, and several of them nodded.

"When I told Mockingbird this, he asked, 'But how does that differ from the things we get by trade from far-off lands? Where would we be without salt from Kaikos or greenstone from the lands of Guiana or copper from the southern lands?'"

"Quite right," said Sun Woman. "Have you seen Matron Greenstone's new pearl-encrusted belt?"

"Or Maura's harpy eagle feathers?"

Several women laughed.

"But that's different," Pebble said. "Those are things we

get by trade with people like ourselves. They don't want to come and turn our world upside down."

"What about the Kwaib? They're always raiding."

"Yes, but we trade with them too."

"Some were even fighting on our side among Hatuéy's warriors."

"The great Caonabó was half Kwaib himself."

"Lots of people are—like that Tiguri who is married to Nightingale."

"And Willow Leaf's brother-in-law."

The women all started to argue and talk at cross-purposes until Sun Woman clapped her hands. "Come on, let Pebble finish her story."

Pebble swallowed the last of her corn cake and took up the story: "When we got to Bayamo, everyone was talking about the monstrous *kanoa* that had sailed close to the shore but hadn't stopped. Mockingbird and I had decided that we wouldn't tell anyone about the mirror or seeing the *paranaghiri* who had come ashore."

She paused, as if struggling to get the words out. "I don't know why, but we were still feeling touched by just the sight of them, something exotic and alien intruding into our world, and it rocked our souls. We vowed to get purified as soon as we reached home and we never talked about it again. After a while the memory faded, as if it had never happened, though the little mirror stayed there in my medicine bag, like a beating heart."

The women stayed silent.

"Night Orchid was born with a caul, so we knew right away she was special. But Heavens! She cried and screamed nonstop, and then as she grew she started to have these fits."

"Oh boy, I remember," said Sun Woman, who was also of the Mud Fish family and slept in the same *bohío*.

"Candlewood said she was born with warring souls that had to be put right," Pebble continued. "We arranged everything for the ceremony . . ."

Tears started streaming down Pebble's face as she went back to that evening in their family *bohío*. The children had been sent to stay with neighbors and the adult family members vomited to purify themselves. All were painted with black *jagua* so they appeared as silhouettes against the fire that burned in the center. The child was lying cradled in a basket on the ground, for once quietly asleep.

The *behike* Candlewood had also been painted black, but he wore his headdress with the harpy eagle feathers, and tufts of white feathers were stuck into armbands near his shoulders and around his calves. He entered purifying the area with smoke blown from his foot-long cigar and shaking his *maraka*.

He chanted and danced around the child in the space they had cleared for him, the collective family surrounding them in a circle, arms around each other's shoulders as they moved from side to side in step and chanted *Aya* at the end of every line until they lost track of time.

Suddenly, Candlewood shouted, then stood as if mesmerized before he spun around and dropped to the ground. The circle moved back to give him space as he thrashed around, arms flailing, just as the little girl had when seized by the spirits. Only he was making grunting noises, which gradually changed to a guttural voice speaking in a language they did not understand, while other strange voices poured into the hut from all directions. The voices built to a screeching crescendo, then changed tones so it sounded as if Candlewood—now on all fours—and the spirits were trading questions. This dialogue went on and on, while the dancers kept the rhythm going.

Then the voices stopped and the dancers halted in their step. In the dead silence, the onlookers were afraid to even breathe. Candlewood lay on the ground for a while, his breathing labored as if recovering from a long journey. When he finally stood up, he was trembling in every limb, but they could tell he was furious from the way he was shaking his rattle at the ceiling, and his hand trembled as he blew smoke from the cigar his assistant lit and handed to him. He had puffed and mumbled quietly to himself for a while and then spun around and planted himself in front of Pebble.

"I remember," said Sun Woman. "We were shocked. Candlewood stopped and held out his hand, palm up, as if he wanted something."

"Yes, that is how it was," Pebble resumed. "His eyes were glazed and he looked ghastly, like a spirit himself. I was confused at first. Frightened. I was trembling so much I couldn't think straight. Then it was as if someone gave me a blow that turned my head around and I knew what he wanted. I dug in my medicine bag and took out the mirror and placed it in his hand, wanting to die of shame. Candlewood took it and blew smoke to purify it, then he passed it over the child who had gone into one of her seizures. He passed it over again, back and forth, as she thrashed from side to side, foaming at the mouth and rolling her eyes—"

"And suddenly," Sun Woman smiled as she took up the story, "Candlewood tossed the mirror into the air and clapped his hands together and caught it, and the child instantly became still; she looked at him and smiled. Ai ai ai, none of us could believe it."

"He'd brought her warring souls together and there they have stayed ever since. She fell into a deep sleep. When she woke, he made her drink tea made from dried hummingbird tongue and he alone knows what else. She was never bothered with convulsions again. But Candlewood was so angry. Remember, Sun Woman?"

"Well, no more angry than usual."

"Oh yes. He took the mirror up, threw it in the air again, caught it between his hands, and then *poof!* There was a lot of smoke and a strange smell. When he opened his hands, there was nothing there. After that, he had to cleanse the whole *bohío*, all of us who were there, to get rid of the evil."

"I'd forgotten that. Our entire house had this strange smell for days."

Pebble grew tearful again. "Mockingbird paid Candlewood with gifts from our family, but me—he made me pay by making me cry and pray for four days and nights. He said that adults get fits because they have done something displeasing to the spirits but it is adult carelessness that causes it in children. I have never forgotten that—or forgiven myself."

"Well," said Sun Woman, trying to cheer up her kin, "say what you will about old Candlewood, he certainly fixed your daughter right. Night Orchid is the most sensible girl in all of Maima. And at her age too."

"Yes, that is what her uncle says," Pebble responded. "She has the steadiest hands he has ever seen with a chisel. You know, when she was small she didn't want to stay with me or the other women, she always wanted to go to the workshop. Her uncle let her stay for she was quiet and she played on the floor with bits of stone and wood and watched everything he was doing. He got so accustomed to her presence that he didn't even realize she was using the tools, until one day when she was seven she presented him with a wooden owl she had carved. He said it was so perfect tears came to his eyes, and he knew he had found his successor."

The women nodded or sighed or smiled at Pebble's story for they all knew Night Orchid, the only girl in her uncle's workshop and one who had carved several of the *guaízas* they each owned. They saw her as different from the other girls her age, too serious perhaps, and they couldn't help wondering how difficult it might be for her uncle to find her a husband when she came of age.

Chapter 8

"**A**i ai ai." It wasn't her usual elegant response but a cry ripped from the innermost soul of Matron Greenstone. The *kaney* was still deserted except for Crab Claw, who had just now rushed into the longhouse in a fashion that was totally out of character, trembling with excitement as she imparted the news that had so upset the lady. Had Matron Greenstone been able to rise from her *hamaka*, she herself would have witnessed the astonishing spectacle from the *kaney*'s porch overlooking the main plaza.

"Ai, that foolish boy! As for that Feather, he should know better. He knows Omeyra wanted nothing to do with the foreigners—or their goods. He has never dared to bring anything from them before. Ooh, thank you"—this to Crab Claw, who was lightly placing a warm pad on her knee.

That is what Crab Claw had been doing earlier when the sounds from below signaled that Feather had arrived, and Matron Greenstone had sent her off to find out what was happening. When Crab Claw came rushing back, her customary placid mask had slipped and speech flooded out of her the way it had never done before.

"I know that boy is silly. But I thought he would have more sense that this," was Matron Greenstone's response to the news. "Where was Eldest Uncle to advise him? Why isn't he doing his job?"

She glared at Crab Claw, who silently bowed her head and resumed the task at hand. "He should not have been out there to greet the trader like any common person. If he had waited for the trader to be brought to him, as Omeyra would have done, all this ridiculous scene could have been avoided and Feather's gift would have been privately given and discreetly set aside, with no hurt feelings either way. Then we wouldn't be treated to this ridiculous scene as the one you described. Imagine, Dark Water at his age, to be scratched by a Bird of Evil Omen and made a public spectacle." She shook her head and cheupsed a sound of disgust.

The news Crab Claw brought placed Matron Greenstone in activist mode. Her mind was already on a war footing, so she missed some of what Crab Claw was saying. But her ears pricked up when she heard:

"He is so big and puffed up with himself, my lady. I have never seen so much pride."

Her mistress's sharp rap with the fan and querulous voice asking, "Who? What?" made Crab Claw realize she hadn't been listening.

"I was talking of the bird, my lady. People are already saying that he is the child of Sun itself, born to pull it up from the dark cave each morning. That is what the *paranaghiri* use him for, to summon the dawn. And that is what Runs Swiftly will now use him for. People are saying."

"What? Blasphemy! Witchcraft! And they have brought it here!"

The laws that regulated the appearance of Sun each day were the most sacred of their laws, having been laid down from First Time.

Matron Greenstone so forgot herself that she swung both legs out of the *hamaka* and instantly regretted it.

Crab Claw lifted her feet back and straightened her *na-*

gua. As Matron Greenstone twisted her bare upper body to settle back into a comfortable position, her many expensive bead necklaces made clicking and tinkling sounds as they fell between her breasts. She began again masticating the wad of sweetly cured *tabako* that she had stuck in her jaw after her morning prayers, a sign that she was thinking.

The chewing stopped abruptly and the famous eyebrows were now pulled together in a frown, her rosebud mouth screwed up tight as she contemplated the troubling news. "Was Candlewood there?" she finally asked.

"No, my lady, the *behike* was absent. The priest was not present either. But"—she hesitated "—the man . . . Shark Tooth was there . . ." Her voice dropped and trailed off, for she knew Matron Greenstone's feelings about this man. "I—I think he was the one starting the rumors . . . about the sun bird . . ."

"Hmm." Matron Greenstone fell back to chewing again and Crab Claw's hands went still, so as not to disturb her. Then, her mind obviously made up, she tapped Crab Claw with her fan. "Please go and find Candlewood. At once. Ask him to favor me with his presence. And when he comes, return to sit at the door that I might not be disturbed."

This is serious business, thought Crab Claw. *Yes, indeed.*

"I need time to think." Matron Greenstone turned around in her *hamaka* to face the wall. She reached for her medicine pouch and offered it to the Four Quarters before pulling the string and pouring the sacred powder into her palm. She painfully stretched and sprinkled the powder liberally over one *cemí* among three that lined a low bench of carved mahogany, closing her eyes as she invoked its blessings.

Crab Claw had risen to her feet as soon as Matron Greenstone gave her instructions, but she lingered long enough to see which *cemí* her mistress chose to appeal to. She was not surprised. The invocation was to Guabancex, Lady of the Winds and destructive forces. Her lady was on the warpath.

Chapter 9

Trouble was coming. In fact, it had already arrived. Crab Claw knew it in her bones and shivered as she trotted to Candlewood's *bohío*. She tripped—a bad omen.

She threw out her hand to break the fall and a small sharp stone punctured her palm, drawing blood. She righted herself and held out her palm to look at the damage and drew back in horror, for what she saw in the marks made on the broken skin was the face of the skull, Maquetaurie Guayaba, Lord of the Dead.

Crab Claw moaned and clutched at her amulet. It appeared to be a well-known representation of Attabey, a talisman worn by all the women. Only Crab Claw and others like her, if there were any, would have known its other meaning.

For when the wearer looked at the image upside down, what they saw was Bokura, guardian spirit of the Old Ones, the ones who were there from the beginning, the ones before the Taíno arrived. The ones to whom Crab Claw's soul belonged. No one knew how vivid the dreams were that came to Crab Claw in times of trouble. For no one was ever told. Only to Bokura did she whisper her fears, for it was he who came to her in dreaming.

Crab Claw tried to still her beating heart as she skirted the plaza, avoiding the crowd, taking the road to the west and the setting sun where in the northwest quadrant was

located a smaller square adjoining the burial place of the ancestors, the ball court, and the temple. In this quarter on the
very edge of the cemetery, Candlewood had his *bohío,* as did
the holy priest Silver Fern. The two men could not have been
more different.

Silver Fern was *ni-taíno,* of noble birth himself, but from
an early age had been set apart as the one chosen by the gods.
But of late, ever since the arrival of the Lucayan Shark Tooth,
Silver Fern had been wasting away and performing his duties
with less vigor. More and more, power was passing over to
Shark Tooth, and no one seemed able to stop it.

No one, that is, except Candlewood, the old *behike* whose
power resided in his ability to cure the souls of individuals
and hold together the weave of the social fabric falling under
his care. The power of *behikes* varied but Candlewood was
acknowledged far beyond the boundaries of Maima as more
powerful than most.

Crab Claw was still shaking and could feel her bones
begin to ache, all over her body, as she approached the *behike's* hut. Her bones never lied, for they had a pedigree that
stretched back way beyond that of Matron Greenstone and
her noble family, well before the people that arrogantly called
themselves Taíno—the Good People—were even thought of.
It was Crab Claw's ancestors who were the first peoples of
the land—that she knew. *Ciboneys,* they called them now, an
insulting name that had no meaning for the Old Ones.

Their coming to the islands had been lost in the mist of
time, but Crab Claw still remembered the stories the Old
Ones told at night in the cave, before a roaring fire.

The best storyteller was Alavik, a fiery old man who
came fully alive when he recounted the histories handed
down by the ancestors. Alavik literally threw himself into his
stories. His eyes would shine with an inner light as he leaped

and pranced around the fire, roaring and shaking imaginary spears as he mimicked the action with his skinny old body red with ochre, his conch shell necklaces jumping in time to his rhythms and his bird feather crown casting grotesque shadows in time to his movement.

"*They* are people of the south . . ." he would say scornfully. Everyone knew *they* were the Taíno. "*We* are people of the north. Snow People we were. A long, long time ago."

No one knew what snow was, except that it was very, very cold, from the way Alavik wrapped his arms around his body and shivered, before finally, with hands outstretched, finding saving warmth in the fire. They also understood from the way he stretched out both his arms and turned in circles, leaning from one side to the other as his feathered headdress danced, that "a long, long time" had neither beginning nor end.

The Snow People, Crab Claw remembered, had first braved the burning winds and white mist to cross over from the top of the world where the Great White Birds of Dawn had deposited them.

The Snow People had given their souls to the spirits of White Bear, to the Mammoth and Raven that had blessed them and carried them onward while they mastered the new lands, spreading to cover the earth. On the mainland they were fierce hunters, battling against animals ten times larger than they, animals that would take twenty men to kill, so the ancestors said. Uncle Bear and Father Mammoth were their parents that provided the ancestors with all they needed—food, clothing, shelter, weapons, and amulets for protection.

The island youngsters to whom the stories were handed down had no idea that these were more than fabulous monsters about whom the old people made up tales to put them to sleep.

For those descendants of the Snow People who had drifted to the islands found there no threatening weather, no drought or cold, no large animals there to hunt, no dangerous beasts; and the warm turquoise waters that teemed with its bountiful harvest of conch and shellfish that could be gathered from the shore made lotus eaters of them, until they forgot all of the old ways. And that was their downfall.

For when successive invaders came in waves, they had no gods to summon; they had abandoned the Old Ones and had forgotten to cultivate the new. They worshipped no other deity but the conch that provided them with all they needed. It was easy to hunt small game with simple traps and spears loaded with conch-shell points, to pluck fruit and berries from the forests, paint their bodies with stone-ground red ochre to ward off evil spirits, and shelter in caves from wind and tropical rains. They had neither gardens nor pots. The bountiful land gave them everything, including gourds that could be hollowed out.

They were peaceful and happy, at one with the rhythms of life. Happy, that is, until the invaders came from the south, the ones who brought *yuka*, who fished in the ocean floating on the buoyant trunks of dead and hollowed-out trees, the very same that had carried them hither.

At first they came in small groups, these explorers who called themselves *Taíno*—the Good People. They greeted the Old Ones as friends, and the Old Ones showed them the bounties of the land and taught them many things and were happy for the company. But their numbers grew and more and more kept coming, and they began to settle down in villages. And as they grew in might and power, they changed toward the Old Ones, treated them cruelly, drove them off until they found refuge only in the farthest reaches of each island. So Crab Claw remembered.

Some of the young attached themselves to the newcomers willingly and their bloodstreams merged. Here and there on the islands, a few remnants of the Old Ones refused to change, clinging to the old ways. The newcomers become proud and arrogant enough to make up all sorts of rules to mark them off as The People, and—as far as the Old Ones were concerned—adopted a spurious genealogy. Now, they claimed, they had been born on that very island, had emerged from underground as The People from the Cave of the Jagua. See, there it was, that cave. That one there. High up in the mountains at Cauta.

Those descendants of the Old Ones who were eventually forced to live in the villages of the Taíno—like Crab Claw—were never allowed to forget their inferior bloodlines and bore the mark of their status. For they could intermarry with the commoners, but they were never permitted to bind the heads of their newborn children so as to acquire the shape of beauty, the broad forehead that signified The People. They were marked forever as outsiders, robed in their own natural ugliness—for so they were made to feel.

And it was ugly that Crab Claw was feeling now, in both mind and body, as she stood at the door of Candlewood's *bohío* and beseeched him to attend to her lady on a matter of the greatest importance.

Chapter 10

C rab Claw trailed behind the *behike*. As soon as he entered the *kaney* and was greeted by Matron Greenstone, she served them tea and a basket of corn cakes flavored with wild honey and pumpkin seeds that Candlewood loved. Then she went and squatted in front of the doorway to ensure their privacy. Not that anyone was around. The whole village still seemed to be in the plaza milling around Trader and the rooster.

Crab Claw sat back on her heels and rested her hands on her ample lap, allowing her thoughts to wander. She thought back to the day the hunters found her. She had not been abandoned or lost. Her father had left her to be found. Everyone else had died from the sickness. Her mother had gone. Her father was ill. She never understood why she hadn't been ill too.

That day her father had risen from his sickbed and dressed his only child in all their wealth—numerous strings of shell beads finely crafted. He took her to a trail and told her to wait under a tree for the hunters who would take her to their *yukayeke*.

She said, "I am afraid. The hunters will eat me."

"No," her father responded, "sometimes we are friends. We trade. Say, '*Taiguey*—good day!' when you see them," he instructed, and made her practice. "Then say, '*Bara*,' and point to our cave. That means *dead*. They will take care of you."

He vanished and she was alone.

She sat there and never moved, for how long she had no idea, for her mind drifted away to a land that was full of huge animals that were friendly and talked to her so she did not feel alone—Uncle Bear, Father Mammoth, Brother Raven.

When the hunters came, she said "*Taiguey*" and "*Bara,*" and they took her to their village. All she remembered was that Matron Greenstone was the one who had taken off her necklaces. "I will put them in a safe place for you," she had said.

Crab Claw never moved a muscle as the lady removed them all, until the smallest one remained, a little circlet with a pendant carved in a strange shape. The child didn't know it was the finest one of all. When the lady attempted to remove it, she cried.

She didn't tell her that her mother had taken it from her own neck and put it around hers when she was a baby, just as all their mothers had done, going as far back as anyone remembered. That much she knew. It was the only record she had of her own history.

The lady seemed to understand because she left the necklace with the strange pendant alone, smiled, patted her on the head, and popped a sweet into her mouth. The taste was strange but it comforted her.

The lady summoned a woman of the Red Bird family who had no living children and handed her over. She had joined the kin group in their *bohío*. The other children teased her unmercifully and she wouldn't speak. *Couldn't* speak, for she didn't know their language. But that didn't stop her from carrying out her duties, day and night.

The father, Dark Rain Cloud, soon got sick. No one could help him. Crab Claw (for so they named her) went and stood beside his *hamaka*, as she sometimes did, and wiped his face with bast dipped in water. He hardly noticed her, so far gone was he. But some impulse made her look deeply at him, as if seeing him for the first time, looked so hard she could see right through him, and so located the blockage that was the source of his illness. And a voice that spoke in the language of the Old Ones gave her a song.

She sat on a low stool by his *hamaka* and sang the song all night and into the next day. She could feel the tumor struggling against the power of the song, but finally with a great wrench it broke away and dissolved, and her singing ceased as abruptly as it began.

Dark Rain Cloud opened his eyes for the first time in days and smiled at her. "Thank you," he said.

Everyone saw and heard these things, for the girl's singing had attracted first the residents of the house and then, as news traveled, those from other *bohíos*. They seated themselves in a circle around the girl and the sick man by the fire and found themselves swaying their bodies and humming along with her song. The little girl never faltered once in her singing, repeating strange words in a kind of enchanted loop that swirled around them and came back to the place where it started and took off again.

But once the man opened his eyes and said, "Thank you," she fell over from the stool on which she was sitting and didn't wake up from the *hamaka* they laid her in until late the following day.

Far from integrating her into the family or the village, the incident only emphasized her strangeness, especially when they saw Dark Rain Cloud walking about as if he had never been ill when they had long given him over for dead. Now people's attitudes were not scorn or pity but became tinged with fear. Crab Claw never knew the difference, she only felt her own sadness.

After this, others would come and ask for the outsider girl to come and sing to their sick. She did not pretend to be anything but what she was, a simple girl with a gift for healing. On the advice of Candlewood, Matron Greenstone apprenticed her to Wading Bird the old healer, who had already seen forty summers and who passed on to the willing girl everything she knew, leaving her with knowledge, medicines, and instruments when she died.

Crab Claw still did not know what magic she had in her hands or in the waking dreams or in the song that the Old Ones had given her. No one else could sing the healing song. Others secretly listened and tried to capture it, she knew, but the song was meant for her alone. It was the only thing she possessed and it became more powerful each time she sang it.

When Crab Claw became a woman, Matron Greenstone herself sponsored her Coming Out. She showed her the necklaces which she had kept for her and said they would provide her with a good dowry. She herself liked the necklaces that were in the old style and no longer available and would give fair exchange for them. Unschooled in the ways of the world, Crab Claw didn't know if that was a good or bad thing, but she saw the greed in Matron Greenstone's eyes. The lady offered to trade the necklaces for other goods of the same value that a husband and his family would prefer. Shyly, Crab Claw said yes, but she chose two for her daughter—or daughter-in-law. She didn't have a daughter so in time she gave one to her son Flint to wear.

Matron Greenstone wanted to keep her in the village and had found her a good man in Marou the hunter. She provided them with what they needed for the household they established in his family's *bohío*—water pots, cooking pots, mortar and pestle, *hamakas*, mats, and for Crab Claw a fine sealskin bag for her medicines. Crab Claw knew in her heart that Matron Greenstone had been more than generous, but she still wished she had all the necklaces, for they were her only link to the old ways.

Several moons ago, she'd come up with an idea, and she'd traded a bag of medicines for two queen conch shells from the coast. In her spare time she began cutting them into the shell beads that were the mark of her people. She was awkward and clumsy with the tools at first, but the slow, careful cutting of each bead from the shell, the grinding down with river sand, the polishing, the drilling of the hole, comforted her somehow. At the rate she was going, it would probably take her a lifetime to complete one necklace, but each bead was a journey taking her back to who she was.

When it came to her son Flint, Crab Claw wanted him to move totally into the present and told him nothing about her past. She desperately wanted him to belong the way she never had. His mixed blood would be a mark against him when it came time for him to marry. He would have to acquire credit in other ways. Crab Claw knew it was up to her to find a path for Flint to make something of himself.

Really, it was not her job to worry about Flint's future, it was that of his father Marou and his uncle Dancing Water, in whose *bohío* he was raised. But what really counted after all was the mother's bloodlines, for it was the women who held the wealth and the power in the family. And what was a mother to do who had no recognizable bloodlines?

She had been adopted into the Red Bird family of the Land Tortoise Clan, it is true, and to all outward appearances was treated respectfully by all. But who knew what storms raged in her heart and what wounds that would never heal, for losses that could never be assuaged? Flint was her only route to redemption, his success the only tribute she could offer her ancestors, the vanished Old Ones.

Crab Claw had never learned the Taíno tongue fluently, so she hardly ever talked. But she was proud when she heard Flint speak. He sounded just like everyone else, and if she had her way he would become like everyone else—no, he would become so famous and move so high, they would be bound at last to recognize him. Just as the whole world had been forced to recognize the great warrior Caonabó even though his father was Kwaib.

As she listened to the sounds coming up from the plaza, she wondered how she could discover the route by which her son would make his name.

Then, just like that, the idea popped into her head. She couldn't wait for Candlewood to leave so she could plant the idea in Matron Greenstone's mind. It would take careful handling. She knew her lady well enough to know that the idea would have to appear to be all hers.

She would get Matron Greenstone to send Flint on a quest to obtain a treasure that would be irresistible to her, one she had so far been unable to obtain: the secret of a pain-free existence.

Chapter 11

Crab Craw had heard whispers from time to time of other people like her on the island, or at the very least, remnants of people who were there from Before Time. She hadn't paid much attention because she did not believe they were *her* people—her father had told her they had all died out, that her family was the last of their kind. Then one day, her husband's brother Dancing Water, who went seal hunting on the north coast every season, said: "I know where your song comes from."

She was standing at a lean-to under a tree preparing fish for their evening meal when he imparted this news. She dropped the knife in shock.

"I'm sure of it," he said, taking a seat on a fallen tree trunk and stretching out his long legs.

"Please, tell me. What do you mean?"

He smiled at his sister-in-law's anxious expression.

"You know during last year's hunt when that freak storm blew us off course?"

She nodded.

"We were near the cays and were able to tie up, but the wind and rain didn't let up. So we paddled deeper into the mangroves, looking for better shelter. That's when we came across these strange people."

Crab Claw's mouth was wide open as she listened.

"They lived in huts on stilts on a little island that rose above the mangroves and wore their hair long. The Macorixe, they called themselves. They clearly weren't used to visitors and they were as shocked to see us as we were to see them."

"Wh-what did they look like? Were they like me? Tell me."

"They weren't Taíno, they were more like you. They used ochre instead of *jagua* or *bixa* on their bodies. I mean, they were like us, but different. Like that other set—the Gauanahatebeys they call themselves—that live over in the west."

The Macorixe had given them a grudging welcome and offered food and drink and allowed them to stay in a hut away from the village until the wind abated and they could resume their hunt.

Dancing Water said he had not heard them sing but told Crab Claw that the language she used when singing sounded exactly like theirs.

Their *kacike* spoke Taíno and said their ancestors had come Before Time from the frozen north. Around the fire they built outside their hut that night, a wizened old man shared tales of strange fantastic animals called Bear and Raven and Mammoth as the chief sat beside them and translated. The way everyone reacted, these were stories they were used to hearing all the time, for they laughed and commented and urged the teller on.

The next time Dancing Water set off, Crab Claw begged him to find out more. When he returned, he reported that they kept to themselves but traded goods with the coastal villagers, including finely carved conch shell items. They had no healer of their own since the last one had died, but they allowed a Taíno *behike* from Turtle Village to come when needed and he had taken the *kacike*'s son as his apprentice.

Dancing Water left the best news for last—the rumor that

they had a magical healing tree which they closely guarded. They traded the leaves which were said to completely cure pain of the joints and perform other miracles. They never let the magic seeds out of their village.

The information lay dormant in Crab Claw's mind until she needed it, which was now.

The idea of a cure would be sure to excite Matron Greenstone, who spent her time and her trade constantly searching for remedies. But how to convince her that Flint would be the right person to go and fetch it? Perhaps she could suggest that she knew more than she did, Craw Claw reasoned: that the people were of old stock, like herself, and would only have dealings with someone of their own kind.

She already knew trouble lay ahead over the Bird of Evil Omen. When the storm broke, she didn't want anyone to remember Flint's part in physically carrying the bird into the village. If her plan succeeded, it would take Flint out of the way, at least for a while.

But what had she to trade that would be of such value to these people that they would be willing to pass along the secret of the magical tree? The only thing of value she possessed was her song.

She had to plan carefully. First, she had to seek the permission of the Old Ones. She had to share with Flint the secret of his birthright. What if he couldn't learn the song and the Old Ones became so enraged they took it away?

She tried to remember how she had acquired the song. It took a great deal of effort as she cast her mind backward to that night she had first sung it. She saw herself as a child sitting there and staring at the sick man, wishing she could take away his pain, and she had idly put the pendant her mother had given her into her mouth. She had never done such a thing before, and as the cold shell touched her tongue she felt a jolt and the song flew out of her mouth. Could it do the same for Flint and could he pass it on? Would the Old Ones yield the song and would the mangrove dwellers accept it as a fair exchange?

Perhaps all she had to do was give Flint the pendant to wear without telling him anything else and the song would be carried along with it. The rest would be up to the gods. It was a big gamble, but one she was prepared to take. She knew in doing so she risked losing everything—pendant, song, and Flint—forever.

Chapter 12

Crab Claw squatted outside the entrance to the *kaney* as Matron Greenstone had instructed, to prevent anyone from entering and interrupting her visit with the *behike*.

She heard the voices from within almost like chanting, Candlewood's low rumble alternating with the Matron's higher musical pitch, and it went on long enough to lull Crab Claw into dozing. But from time to time she was pulled awake and she tried to listen to whatever would make the two elders raise their voices. She could only grasp the odd phrase or sentence, not enough to make sense of it. But she strained her ears when she heard Candlewood say, "Can you believe he is planning to make a marriage offer for her? Backed by the *kacike*."

Who? Crab Claw wondered, hearing only, ". . . he has already approached her uncle."

"But why her?" Her lady's voice was distressed. "She . . . hasn't even come of age yet."

"She's Owl Clan."

"I always thought he had far too much interest in the Bundle. That's why he came here."

The Sacred Bundle. The most holy relic of the nation, which was always in the keeping of the priest and a senior matron of the Owl Clan. Crab Claw knew now they were talking about Shark Tooth, for she had overheard Matron Greenstone on the subject.

"But how would he know we matrons have decided on Night Orchid as Falling Water's successor? . . . Her sister Bright Star is the oldest girl of her generation, but really . . ."

". . . wise . . . Night Orchid . . . more special than any of you realize."

Shark Tooth. Night Orchid. Crab Claw savored the news. News she would never share with anyone. She kept everything to herself. Knowing was the important thing.

The voices in the room dropped to a low murmur for so long she fell back into a doze. Raised voices pulled her back to alertness. Matron Greenstone was bidding Candlewood goodbye. She moved to the side of the doorway expecting the *behike* to exit, and he must have been standing just inside as his voice came clearly, "Don't worry, my lady, all will be well."

"No one but the two of us?" The Matron's voice was anxious.

"You have my word."

They were still speaking in low tones but now could be heard clearly through the straw matting that covered the doorway.

"The loss will be powerful but it will bring the people of Maima to their senses." Matron Greenstone's voice was stronger now, and Crab Claw could almost see her stiffening her spine. "They will see it as poor leadership. Runs Swiftly will be thrown out and we will get the *kacike* we deserve. A noble successor to Omeyra."

"The act is justified. You are right. We cannot continue as we are."

"Taking it isn't offending the *cemíes*? The powers will sanction the deed?" Crab Claw detected a new note of uncertainty in her lady's voice.

"I will take *kohoba* and consult with them. I would not risk it otherwise. It will be the most dangerous thing I have ever done. But I will ensure its safety."

"Our plan will be the saving of Maima." She sounded back on firmer ground now. More like her usual self. "Our people will see the light. We must present a strong front against the *paranaghiri*."

There were sounds of final leave-taking and Crab Claw hastily moved away to stand at the side of the building where she wouldn't be seen. She wasn't sure yet what she had overheard, but she knew it wasn't meant for her ears. Was Candlewood going to take something? Hide something? But what?

Candlewood departed without looking in her direction and she waited outside for a short while to catch her breath, wondering why her hands were trembling and her souls were tumbling about so unsteadily.

A movement on the other side of the *kaney* caught her eye and when she went to look, keeping close to the wall so she wouldn't be seen, she saw a figure disappearing. It was the man Shark Tooth who was last seen in the plaza with everyone else. What was he doing creeping around outside the house of nobles? Had he been there long, spying? Had he seen or overheard anything? Should she say something to her lady? Crab Claw decided not to, thinking of the uproar it would cause. Besides, she had enough troubles of her own.

Chapter 13

Burning Spear leaned against a post holding up the roof of Corncob's workshop, watching his cousin put the finishing touches on an immaculate ebony bowl, its handles carved in a representation of Yukahú. He always took pleasure in observing the master carver at work, just as others watched with admiration whenever Burning Spear crafted his stone spear points.

On the worktable were spread out more of Corncob's best wares—smaller bowls, effigies ranging from one splendid carving of Baibrama, the fertility *cemí*'s power summed up in his erect penis, to *guaízas* pierced with holes for strings to be worn around the neck. These were tiny, intricate carvings of owls, bats, raptors, and lizards, representing the sacred powers, the gemlike images the work of Corncob's niece Night Orchid, the quiet girl who was sorting the finished goods at the other end of the table and who stopped only long enough to greet the visitor. She was wrapping the goods in *maho* fiber and tying them with string before placing each into woven baskets lined with raw cotton to protect the delicate objects.

"Feather's?" Burning Spear nodded at the display.

"Uh-huh."

"He's taking some of mine too."

"But driving a much harder bargain this time around. Have you noticed?"

Corncob kept his voice low, though at that hour they seemed to be the only ones about in the quarter where the workshops were located.

"He claims all the trade routes are disrupted now that the *paranaghiri* are in control. Most of the *kacikes* are wiped out or virtual prisoners. Not too many are in a position to trade at this time. And the *paranaghiri* are savages who simply take what they want without any idea of value."

"Yeah. He says not even traders are respected anymore. He's changing his routes, he says, because the old ones have become too dangerous. He has stories of traders vanishing without trace or their goods taken as soon as they touch port. There's no point in complaining. The foreign devils will slash your throat and toss your body to their vicious dogs, for good measure."

"Are these things even true?"

"Well, Feather is given to exaggeration, but I have never known him to lie."

This was greeted with a huge guffaw from the wood-carver.

"He claims he won't be going back east, not with the *paranaghiri* in control. From here he's heading south for Xamayca, and from there straight across the big sea to the land of the temple builders. He thinks the islands are done for, and he's also looking to the big lands to the north of us. The *paranaghiri* will want to develop a different kind of trade. All they want now is gold and more gold, pearls and precious stones, hardwoods for building their *kanoas* . . ."

"He's too old, Feather says, to stoop to them."

Burning Spear laughed. "The old devil. He'll bow to anyone who will buy his goods. Did you see his greeting to Runs Swiftly? I almost died laughing."

"Well, he is the chief."

Corncob shook his head. As a young man, he had spent

time in the fabled islands to the east and seen the splendors of the grand chiefs in such places. He listed them aloud now: "Borikén, Quisqueya, Aiytí, not to mention the sacred isle of Mona. Our cousins in Xamayca . . . all overrun. How is it possible? And so quickly. What magic do these *paranaghiri* carry?"

"Their magic is called murder!" Burning Spear said it so explosively that he startled Night Orchid, whose hands stopped working though she never raised her head.

"Murder, my friend. Theft of our lands. Rape of our women. Enslavement of our men. They are not men, they are animals who are so cowardly they hide their bodies behind metal shells so not even our finest spears can pierce them . . ."

"Hatuéy gone with our last hope of resistance. Now they march across our precious land of Cuba. Are we the next to be crushed?"

"We wouldn't be if our dear chief would make up his mind to put us on a war footing."

"Well, War Chief Conch is trying. He has the young men practicing maneuvers every day."

"It's that witch who has the ear of Runs Swiftly though, preaching his poisonous message of greeting them with open arms." Burning Spear was getting louder and angrier. "What does *he* know? Wasn't he one of those who had to run from them when they captured and enslaved the entire population of the Lucayan islands? Isn't that how he ended up here?"

"Shh!" Corncob put his finger to his lips and looked over at his niece, who hadn't raised her head from her task, and signaled for Burning Spear to follow him outside. He led him some distance away and sat on a big flat rock. Burning Spear eased himself down on another rock across from him and looked questioningly at his friend. Corncob was wearing a heavy work apron that was stained with dyes and he wiped his hands on it now.

"Look, I need to talk to you about something." Corncob paused and adjusted his headband, buying time, then looked back at the workshop where a shadowy Night Orchid could be seen in the gloom of the hut. He nodded in her direction. "Shark Tooth . . . he's made a marriage offer."

"*Guay!* For Night Orchid? Are you crazy?"

Corncob signaled Burning Spear to calm down, wishing he would go back to polishing his spear point, as that always kept him on an even keel. He wet his lips, finding it hard to talk, so there were long pauses between his words. "It's a very handsome offer . . . The thing is, you know I'd like to keep her here in the workshop. To keep the family line going . . . We are renowned by now . . . She'll take over one day . . . It won't be easy to find her a husband who will want to move here. You know our women go to join their husband's family . . ."

Burning Spear was still shaking his head. "Shark Tooth? That monster? Why? Did you tell him where to put his so-called offer? You'd want that mongrel in your family? Quite apart from anything else, we don't know the first thing about him. He tells so many lies, we can't even be sure of his blood-lines. What is he? Have you found that out?"

"The *kacike* has approved it," Corncob said quietly. "So there's nothing I can do."

"Yes, he has certainly wormed his way into Runs Swift-ly's ear."

"Besides, he's not exactly poor."

Burning Spear looked at his kin with something like hor-ror. "So you would sell your niece to that witch . . . that imposter . . . that . . . that . . ."

Corncob looked miserable. "Come now, that's harsh.

You know how it is. My sister's children are of our blood, so as their eldest uncle, I am in charge of bringing them up, finding them mates, just as my wife's eldest brother is in charge of bringing up ours. I have a responsibility to make the best match I can for Night Orchid—all Pebble's children. You know Bright Star is already spoken for and will be moving to her husband's village. Night Orchid is . . . well, Night Orchid is . . . special . . . you might say, finding her a husband won't be easy."

"Have you told Pebble?"

"Not yet. That's why I'm sharing this with you, Cousin. I need your help with that. You know what my sister is like."

Burning Spear laughed and held up his hands. "No, not me. I am not going anywhere near Pebble with this. Nor Mockingbird. You know they feel as I do about that man. Anyway, why now? She hasn't even seen her first blood."

"Sure, it will be two or three years before she can marry, but we will be looking for offers at the first solstice ceremony after she's seen her first blood, which might be soon. But I don't know why now . . ."

"Hmm." Burning Speak took up his tool and resumed buffing his point as Corncob ruminated.

"Why Night Orchid? I don't know what the attraction is. Our skills have given prestige to the family over the years. We are Owl Clan, yes, but we are not among the highest rank. Everything we create in the workshop belongs to the *kacike* anyway, and we are grateful for whatever he returns to us."

Corncob turned to look at the workshop where his niece could barely be seen. "Look at Night Orchid, a skinny little thing, sweet and hardworking but shy. No womanly airs about her—not yet anyway. There are other, far more attractive girls in the village closer to marriage age . . . I've really been turning this thing over and over in my head. But I can't go against it if it's our chief's wish. I tried to talk to Runs Swiftly, but he refused to discuss it."

"But Night Orchid and that *anki*? Every day since he arrived, I've asked those who fawn over him, what is his pedigree? What are his bloodlines? Where does he come from? No one knows. Corncob, you cannot let it happen." With that, Burning Spear stood and put his tools in their leather bag, his smile on arrival replaced by an angry scowl. "I'd rather commit murder than let that man have his way."

Corncob stayed seated and opened his palms in supplication. "What can I do?"

Burning Spear started to walk away but turned back. "Only one man can help you. Have you talked to Candlewood?"

"Not yet. I'll ask the *behike* to consult his *cemíes* on this matter. No one can go against whatever the gods decide. Not even the chief." Corncob smiled as he rose and went up to Burning Spear and put his hands on his shoulders. "Thank you, Cousin. As ever, your mind is as sharp as your points."

Chapter 14

Feather stayed until he had disposed of his goods and acquired enough for the return trip. He tamed the bird, sitting in the plaza with it beside him, one leg attached to a piece of string which allowed the rooster to roam and peck at corn. "Next time, *Guama*, I will bring you a hen," he called out to Runs Swiftly when he strolled by, "then you'll have a flock. They make good eating."

The day before he left, the trader set the rooster free, and it flew at once to the highest point in the village, the coronel which topped the center pole on the chief's *kaney*, and there it sat, preening itself, until the people got tired of watching. Feather left it to roam when he departed.

The next morning, just as Silver Fern began his chant to rouse people from their *hamakas*, the world split open with an ear-shattering sound: *Cock-a-doodle-doo!*

Those in the vicinity witnessed the bird on top of the roof, straining itself, its head thrust high, pulling up Sun from the depths, for they could see the first glimmer on the horizon that heralded the day. The bird was facing the rising sun and summoning it, they all saw. It drowned out the invocation of their priest.

Even when Sun was fully seen on its rightful path, the bird did not cease its calling. Candlewood came screaming into the square, scattering the onlookers, shattering the calm of the morning. He picked up a bowl and threw it. The bird leaped out of the way, paused, then returned to its perch to crow, as if taunting him.

"Evil! The trader has brought evil into our village—the bird must go!" Candlewood shouted.

"It is my bird, and I will thank you not to throw things at it." Runs Swiftly stood in front of the *behike*, his feet braced.

Candlewood did not move an inch. "Omeyra would never stand for this."

"Omeyra is no longer here and I am in charge now."

The young men who were about to accompany Runs Swiftly to the bathing place murmured their agreement.

"The bird must be destroyed. The village must be cleansed. The *cemíes* won't look kindly on this."

Runs Swiftly bowed to Candlewood and walked away, trailed by his retinue.

Candlewood stood there for a while and then marched off in the direction of his *bohío*.

The priest himself continued to say nothing, and every morning he competed with the bird to bring Sun up from the depths where it spent the night. But his voice began to waver and grow thin, as if he was no longer even aware of anything outside his own deep souls into which he seemed to be perpetually looking, asking what he had done to so fail the people. And the people began to notice that Sun itself seemed to wobble in its path.

Chapter 15

Although officially the property of the *kacike*, the sun bird was of an independent nature and seemed without ownership, strutting around the village. People stared, and some drew back in fear at its approach, but no one would touch it. It was as if the rooster had become a flash point for arguments and jealousies never publicly revealed. Disaffection became the norm in Maima village. In the past, conflicts would have been quickly dealt with by household heads or, if serious enough, the *kacike*, and settlement made or punishment meted out according to the rules laid down at First Time. Not anymore. Almost every day there were disturbing incidents, even among the young children.

Seemingly at the center of it all was one who strutted around like the bird—darting his nose into everything, like the bird pecking food, his enemies said, but he was not just consuming, he was sowing the discord and eating their souls.

Who could tell? No one spoke aloud; he had his followers, the powerful among them, for he had wormed his way into the *kacike*'s circle. Only Councillor Maura remained scornful, and now tended to hang out with the younger men who avoided Shark Tooth and defended the old ways, including Crab Claw's son Flint. Ranged against them were those who regarded themselves as progressive and proudly wore a new, secret tattoo. They called themselves the Rooster

Society, signifying their willingness to form an alliance with the *paranaghiri*, as Shark Tooth advised. He counted among his followers the proud young man called Heart of Palm.

Chapter 16

Shark Tooth was in his element. Things were working out even better than planned. Not that he'd had a plan when he jumped into that boat of Lucayan refugees escaping from the *paranaghiri*'s deadly harvesting of the islanders. When they landed in Cuba, knowing no one there, he had ended up with a group heading for Maima where they had kin. At first, he had wondered if he, a man of the sea, had made a mistake in coming here. But his time in the mountain village had rewarded him well.

He wished that his father was alive so he could show him his power and what he had turned into—his wealth, how people admired him, confidant of the *kacike*, no less; the same father who had so mocked him, denied him his birthright as eldest son, and would have ordered his death if he hadn't fled from home.

But now he smiled grimly—there was no home to return to, even to boast; perhaps his family were all dead, caught up in the *paranaghiri*'s nets. His twin brother Mucaro, the favored, was long gone, that he knew, for his *opía* had appeared in his vision from time to time but quickly faded, so he knew he had no power over him.

Shark Tooth never regretted for one moment running away from home. It was that or death. He had no illusion the *kacike* would have ordered his killing, once Mucaro told him what he had seen.

Mucaro had spied on him, he knew, just as he'd spied on Mucaro, always searching for something, some transgression to take the other down. It had been that way from birth; they grew up not loving as expected, but perpetually at war with each other. What hurt was that Mucaro, though the youngest, was the favored one, which meant he—Shark Tooth, though that was not his name then—was always the one who was blamed. The one born with *anki*, the evil spirit. So they said.

Shark Tooth couldn't understand the hostility, for everyone could see he was the one chosen by the *cemies*—he was better looking, more agile in speech, better at games, mastered all the lessons faster. He couldn't help it if he had to be constantly fighting to defend himself, for everyone was against him.

He knew the girl Blue Quit was forbidden for they were kin. But they couldn't help themselves, and who would know? She had seen twelve summers but hadn't yet entered the menstrual hut, so there was no question of their going any farther than they had. Furtive meetings. Warm embraces. Rolling on the ground. Tearful partings.

The girl had caught his eye, and she wanted it too, even though the first time he grabbed her and pulled her into the bushes, she had fought him off. But after her initial shock, he could tell she liked what he had done. She could not keep away. They both knew it was not forever and there were limits. Her uncle would be finding her a husband from another clan, just as his would seek for him a suitable wife.

On the day it happened, he had just parted from Blue Quit, a long, lingering embrace. As he came out of their hidden place and into the path, straightening his waistband and with his bun askew, he almost stumbled into Mucaro, whose glare told him everything.

He didn't even think before he hit him so hard that Mucaro dropped to the ground. As Shark Tooth raised his leg to give him another blow, Mucaro sprang to his feet, and to his shock, his usually peaceful brother, the soft one, grabbed a heavy stick from the ground and whacked him hard across his face. As blood spurted, Shark Tooth moved forward with murder in his eyes. But the pain slowed him down, as did Mucaro's words before he took off running: "I will tell. You have disgraced us."

Shark Tooth had stood still, shocked at how quickly events had escalated. Then realization hit him. He had committed a primal sin. There was no pardon for incest. Separation of families was the earliest of their laws, laid down from First Time. Wasn't that why Guacar the Moon now lived in the sky with signs of guilt spotting his face, forced to flee to the Heavens after he'd tried to rape his sister Earth one dark night and she daubed his face with *jagua* paint so he could be recognized?

He had no doubt Mucaro would tell. Which would mean death. Unless he killed his brother first.

He shook his head to clear his thoughts, but they had remained fuzzy and confused as he tried to wipe away the blood dripping from his wounds. He sat on a rock to stop the dizziness and center his thoughts. There was no way he could go home now.

Mucaro would talk. They would search every inch of the island for him and they would convene a meeting of the council. He would be condemned.

There would be no point denying it, for Mucaro would name the girl. She too would be tried. For just one moment, he thought he should go and rescue her so they could run away together. But then he dismissed the thought. He didn't want baggage; whatever he did for the rest of his life, secrecy was called for: he traveled alone.

Chapter 17

The only person who would learn anything about Shark Tooth was the Old Man, and the Old Man was a witch whose penetrating gaze could slice through one's mind like flint and suck all the truth out.

The morning after *Urakán* washed Shark Tooth ashore on another tiny island in the cays, more dead than alive after days in a stolen pirogue tumbling and tossing in rough seas, the Old Man had been nice to him. Raised him up and made him lean on him as they navigated the fallen trees and debris on his battered island; took him to his *bohío* where he tended to the festering cuts on his cheek and other gashes and bruises; built a fire and fed him warm tea and then small bowls of gruel, until he slowly revived.

It didn't take him long to realize the Old Man was the island's only inhabitant. And that he was, in effect, the Old Man's prisoner.

After several moons, he gathered up his courage and stole through the bushes to the highest point on the leeward side. He was surprised to see this island connected to a larger one by a narrow spit. Beyond was a low canopy of stunted trees. He strained his eyes and was rewarded when, at the farthest end, he made out a cluster of houses sloping down to a wide beach. People then.

Shark Tooth's spirits lifted, for he was tired of the Old

Man and their life of solitude; he was longing to be part of what he considered normal life: a *yukayeke* with all its joys and sorrows, fears and quarrels, stories and feasts, ball games and *areitos*, solstice gatherings and everything else that bound up the soul of his people.

The cays that his people the Lucayan occupied were strings of tiny islands, some barely above the surface of the sea, but most of them close enough that they could easily paddle from one to the next for social gatherings or trade. Although he always felt an outsider, still, it was the life he knew. Not this life of constant stress under the tutelage of someone who was even stricter than his uncles.

Soon after Shark Tooth recovered from his ordeal, the Old Man had looked into his eyes and said, "You are already there," and claimed him as his apprentice. He didn't know what he meant, only that the Old Man was forcing him to undergo worse ordeals. Shark Tooth wasn't sure if his restive spirit was really cut out for a life of such rigorous dedication to the world of the spirits.

Now, standing high on a sand dune looking at the distant village, he was filled with optimism. He could plan his escape—he would make his way to the village, he would take some of the Old Man's goods to barter for a *kanoa*, and he would paddle away as far as he could go.

In his escape from home, he had been so blown about by winds that he had no idea where he had ended up or even the name of the island on which he stood. When he asked, the Old Man had smiled his chilling smile and said, "*Mi cairi,*" which only meant, "My island." But he could tell from reading the night sky that he had traveled southeast from his home, which was one of the islands farthest north. So south he would continue traveling.

He was savoring the thought of freedom when he felt a

hand on his shoulder and heard the Old Man's raspy voice. "They wouldn't want you in their village when I tell them the nature of your offense. You won't find help there."

Shark Tooth gritted his teeth whenever he thought of how the Old Man had extracted truth from him and, using his own truth against him, had been able to bind him in a knot.

He should have known from his first sight that this was a man of power, but he was already helpless. He always thought of him as the Old Man; although he had told Shark Tooth his many names, he feared to use them, and he addressed him only as *Guama*—Lord, or Elder. That first morning, lying half-dead on the beach, he had come to consciousness with someone shaking a rattle over him and chanting in a hoarse but strong voice.

He had been too tired to even open his eyes until the chanting ceased and someone saying, "Come, boy, wake up," blew *tabako* smoke over him and prodded him with his foot. He had rolled over and then sat up wearily, trying to see through swollen and bloodshot eyes. And nearly died of shock when he got a good look.

The Old Man's skin was wrinkled as an old turtle, his stringy, unbound white hair hung down to his waist, and his sharp nose was pierced by an intricately carved circlet of *guanín*. His breastplate and sacred rattle announced his calling as a medicine man. But Shark Tooth hardly noticed, for his breath had caught as his eyes lighted on the huge necklace he wore—a stunning array of crocodile teeth.

He was too weary and confused to think further, for the elder was already helping him to his feet and he simply yielded to his care. But as soon as he recovered, he could tell that this was no ordinary *behike*.

Everything about him—his *bohío*, his lifestyle—shouted that he was one of the feared crocodile men, known along the islands more by reputation than actual encounter, so many thought they were not real but creatures of legend.

They dedicated their souls to the crocodile god of the underworld who granted whatever they wished as long as they were paid in human blood. *My blood!* Shark Tooth thought frantically. *So that is why he is keeping me alive. To fatten me up for sacrifice.* He couldn't help noticing the Old Man's filed incisors whenever he smiled his chilling smile.

The hut was a simple circular dwelling some twenty paces each way, like any Lucayan dwelling. But the interior told a different story—this was a man of wealth. In niches along the walls were sumptuous carvings of the leading *cemíes*—Yukahú, Attabey, Baibrama, Corocote. A special niche was reserved for the weather twins—Márohu and Boinayel—and the two legs and high back of his carved *duho* bore the representations of the crocodile.

Still, the Old Man's solicitous treatment kept him confused, until one day there was no room for doubt. As soon as he was strong enough, the Old Man took him on a hike to the other side of the island where a freshwater creek flowed through mangrove roots that colored the water mahogany.

As they moved up the creek and neared a sand bar, it took Shark Tooth awhile to realize that what he had at first thought were tree trunks bleached white were actually crocodiles sunning themselves beside a lagoon of clear water. Crocodiles of a size he never believed possible, smaller ones, baby ones. Some quietly lying still, some slipping in and out of the water.

So this is it, he thought, and the sight caused him to retch and hold on to a tree trunk for support. He could hear the Old Man chuckling.

"Fear not, my son," he said in his whispery voice. "Stay here. You are in no danger if you do not move."

With that, the Old Man undid his breechclout, dropped it on the ground, and with one graceful movement, dived into the pool of crocodiles. Shark Tooth closed his eyes, and when he opened them was amazed to see the Old Man happily floating in the pool and the crocodiles showing not the slightest interest in their human interloper.

He couldn't keep his eyes off the sight, pierced with fear again, wanting to shout a warning but voiceless as one of the larger beasts slipped into the water close to where the Old Man was swimming and opened its jaws wide—but like the rest, it acted as if the Old Man was not there. Or as if he were one of them. And indeed, he might have been. For one minute, he was in the water, and the next nothing but bubbles could be seen.

Shark Tooth looked down to the bottom of the pool, but nothing moved except for an enormous crocodile making its way lazily to the nearest bank. He fought the rising nausea and tried not to close his eyes in case he missed bloodied bits of the Old Man floating. But suddenly there was movement on the far bank where the crocodile was last seen, and in place of the animal he expected, the Old Man emerged.

Shark Tooth could not believe what his eyes told him, though he had heard of such things.

The Old Man came out of the water and used his breechclout to dry his dripping hair and body, then tied it to his waistband again. He laughed at Shark Tooth, whose shock and amazement were still showing.

"There is a secret to swimming with crocodiles," he told him. "But it is too soon for you to know."

The incident left Shark Tooth no less puzzled, though he no longer feared that he would be the sacrificial victim: the Old Man clearly had other plans for him.

He acted as a helper, taking care of the small kitchen

garden, hunting food, fishing, and tending the fire and the pot, also carrying water from the spring and searching for the plants or objects the Old Man used in compounding his medicines.

It was these medicines that he traded with the *kanoa* men who met him at his hut on the beach, for he had a reputation as a healer. It was they who brought in exchange things the Old Man did not grow: his *tabako, yuka,* bread, and *kasaripe.* They also brought the trade items that the Old Man added to his store of wealth.

He must be really famous, Shark Tooth thought. *To be given so much.* And it was the possibility of gathering such a fortune himself that made him endure for many seasons the rigorous and painful process of becoming a medicine man himself.

Chapter 18

It was the Old Man who named him Shark Tooth, after he conducted his inquest on him shortly after his arrival. They were sitting on a bench outside the *bohío* when the Old Man said, "And what is your name?"

By that he meant the boy's real name, known only to his priest and family, for he had already introduced himself by his traveling name. Shark Tooth was taken aback—one was never asked, for handing over this name meant handing oneself to the other. But it was as if he was already in the Old Man's power, for he blurted it out.

"And your clan?"

"Seal."

"Family?"

"Yellow Bird."

"Island?"

He lied.

"Come now," the Old Man said lightly but with steely eyes.

He told him.

The questions went on and on to establish his pedigree. Nothing unusual there among strangers. Shark Tooth began to relax. Until the old man said, "Outcast?"

Shark Tooth opened his mouth but said nothing.

"Death sentence?"

He bowed his head and maintained silence, trying to force back the tears.

"Murder?"

He shook his head.

"Incest?"

He nodded. "We didn't . . ."

The Old Man shushed him with a wave of the hand. "The thought is as good as the deed. Besides . . ." and he leaned closer to Shark Tooth and peered at his face where he had sewn up and treated the wounds that had festered from his brother's blow with the stick, "you are marked for life. Just like Brother Moon." And he gave a great cackling laugh.

The Old Man never referred to the conversation again—other than his threat that day on the hill as they looked toward the distant village. But Shark Tooth knew that as long as the Old Man lived, he would never escape the past, and fear of exposure quashed all desire to flee.

When the Old Man gave him the shark-tooth necklace he had never removed since, it was tacitly understood that he was the chosen apprentice. *Chosen* was the word the Old Man used, for he said he was the one responsible for the young man's arrival.

He was a powerful weather worker, Shark Tooth was to learn, for he could stir up winds or calm them, send rain as needed or beg the rain to cease. And it was he who sent the powerful *urakán* that had brought him the right person.

Some time after the crocodile incident, the Old Man took him to the windward side where sharks could be seen swimming close to shore. Shark Tooth had no idea why the Old Man handed him a bamboo tube and insisted that he should rub the contents—an ointment with a fishy smell—all over his body, until he pushed him toward the water, saying, "Go make friends with them."

Shark Tooth dug his toes in and refused to budge. He was used to hunting young sharks for food, but from the safety of a boat and with a harpoon in hand. Nobody walked into a sea full of vicious adult sharks.

He had no more time to think as a powerful shove sent him sailing over the edge into the middle of the sharks. He came thrashing up to the surface, expecting to be attacked and torn to bits. But just as the crocodiles had ignored the Old Man, so the sharks continued feeding on prey in the seagrasses. One or two came up to him as if checking him out, then continued on their business.

After the initial shock and surprise, Shark Tooth found himself playfully diving and swimming among them, feeling content for the first time in his life, as if this is where he really belonged.

Once the test confirmed his choice was right, the Old Man put him in a *kohoba* trance where he traveled to the house of the Shark God Bagua Guamacajayo which occupied the innermost core of the subterranean sea.

He awoke days later with a new name, and painful tattoos on his back and stomach that paid homage to his new spirit master. He knew that the exchange for any boon he requested of the god had to be paid with a human life. Embedded in his body were four spirit darts that he could use one at a time to accomplish this. He was warned not to be greedy in using them up; once they were gone, his own life could be forfeited. It was a warning he easily forgot. Just as he forgot how sharks were sometimes prey for crocodiles.

Shark Tooth did not begrudge time spent with the Old Man for he knew how rare it was to learn so much from a powerful medicine man who opened up more and more pathways of knowledge as time went by. He could heal as well as he could harm. But he couldn't see a future for himself and he yearned for more. He knew now the Old Man had no intention of sharing with him the most powerful secret of all, the secret of controlling weather. Not perhaps until he was an old, old man himself.

The Old Man performed his weather magic alone at night in a separate hut near to the crocodile pool. The creatures came awake and bellowed with the voice of thunder in response to the Old Man's own bellowing. Even from far away, Shark Tooth could hear the dreadful noises that summoned the rain gods or ordered them to stay away. That much he knew, and trembled alone in the darkness when he heard the steady drumming from on high, as the rain gods stamped their feet, or pissed, but he would never learn how they managed it.

He yearned for other companionship, he ached for a woman, he yearned for a place of his own, he yearned to possess his own wealth, for the Old Man shared none of the gifts he received with him.

Above all, he longed to have adventures like those the Old Man related. How, while still a youth, he had come face-to-face with creatures from another world. They appeared from the skies—without warning they were there, great white birds sitting offshore, rocking gently in the swells. Only later did the secret watchers hidden behind the dunes realize that they had in fact come floating upon the ocean, monstrous *kanoas* with sails.

"I was living on Guanahaní then," said the Old Man, "a youth like any other. My life was uneventful except that at an early age I was chosen. I had just finished my apprenticeship and received the tools of office from my master who was the chief *behike* when the great white sails appeared."

The Old Man never told a straightforward story. It zigzagged among his memories as they sat in front of a fire at night, and so it too zigzagged into Shark Tooth's mind until the stories became his own.

The Old Man told how he was alone in his boat one day and was plucked—*kanoa* and all—into the *guamikena*'s ship. He spoke their words from time to time, but so garbled, Shark Tooth could only capture fragments, yet these he also stored in his memory to be regurgitated as his own.

On the shrine in the *bohío* hung the red hat, the necklace with the *paranaghiri*'s cross, and a tiny bell of strange metal. These were the Old Man's proudest possessions for they were touched with power. He seemed to have stayed on the boat while they surveyed the coasts of nearby islands, he their translator and the great admiral's pet.

But when the strangers were gearing up to return to their faraway place, a yearning for home gripped him, desire so strong that one night he let down his *kanoa* from the deck where they had stowed it and silently paddled away.

It took him many moons to work his way back home, the Old Man said, but he'd had enough of travels. "I wanted to share my adventure with my people. So on arrival, I put on the Christian's necklace and the red hat and tinkled the bell to impress them. That was a mistake."

Instead of being welcomed, he found he had already been mourned as dead and his reappearance caused nothing but consternation. "I was *opía*, they said—a living dead." Worse, one wearing the symbols of the white-skinned *guamikenas* that some believed came from the land of spirits.

Since his departure, he learned, his promised bride had been married to another, and his mother, father, uncle, the *behike*, and several others from his village had died mysteriously— all of which they attributed to the arrival of the birds from the skies. He was contaminated and untouchable. So great was the hostility that he believed he'd be killed by the angry mob that surrounded him.

"I became angry myself," said the Old Man, "to receive such a welcome. The new *behike* had always been jealous of me, and he was behind it. I didn't even have time to offer *tabako* to the spirit of my parents. Blinded by my tears, I untied my boat and set off, with no sense of direction and no idea of where I wanted to go."

Shark Tooth couldn't help thinking how the Old Man's story paralleled his own, and for the first time experienced a feeling of kinship. Another outcast, then. But the Old Man had other surprises up his sleeve.

"Time uncurled slowly. Hungry and thirsty, I drifted. I waited for Opiyelguobirán, Death's messenger, to come and ferry me across the threshold. I prayed to the Christian's *cemí* the Black Robe had hung around my neck to take me to their Heaven that was full of white robes singing.

"I remember nothing until I came awake lying on a beach. When I heard singing, I thought I had been taken up to this Heaven, but I was surprised that the song was one I recognized, accompanied by a rattle. I opened my eyes. A strange *behike* was standing over me, and the first thing I noticed was his enormous necklace of crocodile teeth. I was instantly afraid. 'You have come, finally,' he said, and revealed teeth filed to points."

Over time, as the Old Man revealed fragments of his story, Shark Tooth realized that while his teacher had taught him everything he knew before he passed on, his Old Man had been stingy with him, withholding so much. His anger grew to the point where he desired more than ever to be free. And he began to take a few of the Old Man's treasures— small objects that he hid in his medicine bag. He was owed, after all.

The only hint he ever had of the *behike*'s displeasure was his saying, "Your spirit is too entangled in greed; unless you can untangle the knots, you will never be truly free."

Sometimes he would cast his glance at the weather spirits, Márohu and Boinayel, twins who were always warring. "One cannot exist without the other, my friend. Just as night needs day, rain and sunshine must seek balance, good cannot exist without evil. A broken gourd cannot find its center."

Such statements reminded him too much of his family and the things they used to say to him, comparing him to his twin. One day, he vowed, he would show them.

Chapter 19

Shark Tooth's freedom came sooner than expected, for the Old Man sickened and died. Lying in his *hamaka*, he wasted away by rejecting all food and drink while calmly giving instructions for the disposal of his body. Shark Tooth was relieved that the decisions were made for him, as a *behike*'s death was a frightening thing.

He wrapped the old man in his *hamaka* and lifted it, surprised at how little he weighed, and walked unsteadily down the path to the crocodile pool where the Old Man wanted to be interred.

Shark Tooth stood on the bank and heaved the body in. The splash attracted a horrendous din from the pool's denizens that curdled his blood, and ended in bellows like those he used to hear from afar when the Old Man summoned the weather spirits.

He backed away with his hands blocking his ears, and didn't open his eyes until all noises ceased. He was afraid to look, but when he did, the water was calm, crystal clear as it always was.

Yet what should be floating serenely on top but the Old Man's necklace of crocodile teeth. It came closer and closer to Shark Tooth, assuming a shape disturbingly like a mouth, and he picked up a stick and reached for it, as it was clearly meant for him.

When he stretched to grab it, the Old Man's cackling laughter came from all directions, filling the air and sending chills down his spine. He pulled back in horror, the stick fell from his hand, and he watched as the necklace bobbed on the surface, seeming to smile a crafty smile, then disappeared with a loud plop as the water swallowed it.

Shark Tooth turned and ran, back up the path, throwing himself down on the ground when he was halfway to the *bohío* in order to catch his breath and still his beating heart. He lay there for a long time. Well, that was it. The Old Man was mean until his dying breath. But—and Shark Tooth laughed out loud as he came back to himself—he couldn't take with him the treasures in his *bohío*, that were now rightfully his, payment for all his time in servitude.

Ai ai ai. Shark Tooth threw his head back and laughed loudly as he walked, pumping his fist in triumph, his laughter coming to a dead stop as he crested the rise that gave a view of the *bohío*.

There was no *bohío*.

He gazed in astonishment, wondering how he could have taken the wrong path. But he hadn't. The kitchen garden was there, so was the bench under the tree; the outdoor shed was there. Everything surrounding the house was as always, except that they were now littered with fragments, strips, bits and pieces from a hut that could only have exploded. As if a whirling funnel had picked it up and shaken it and dropped the pieces back to earth. Very small pieces.

Shark Tooth took his time walking slowly around, burning with a hatred as deep as anything he had ever known. Why had the *behike* done this to him? Worse, when he thought of it, what had he done to bring this on himself? It was the latter thought that galvanized him into action—he needed to get away from the accursed island as fast as he could.

He combed the ground for anything he could salvage, and was pleased to find intact the little bell, the holy cross and chain, some blue beads, and a few other trinkets from the Old Man's travels. There was also the red hat, but when he picked it up a swarm of moths flew into his face and the hat fell to pieces in his hands. Very little else was salvageable and he didn't have time to wonder why the foreign goods were the only objects impervious to the Old Man's malice. He was left with nothing, not even a *hamaka* or a water gourd.

As he ran for the boat, he wondered if that too had been obliterated. But the *kanoa* was there, with gourds which he filled before pushing off and jumping in. Once again, he was leaving an island in a hurry, no better off than when he came except for the wealth that he always made sure to carry safely on his person.

And that remained the pattern of his life from season to season as he zigzagged from island to island, successful as a healer, mating with women, producing children, acquiring followers and wealth, and then each time, witnessing his initial success turn to ashes—the kind of failure that forced him to take off for paths unknown to start afresh.

Such failure was never his fault, Shark Tooth told himself each time. Always, the *cemíes* turned on him, for a reason never revealed, except for the curse his father had no doubt laid on him. Not even a consultation with the Shark God had elicited any information. Bagua Guamacajayo always said, *Half of you is too much in shadow. Unless you can bring it farther into light, I can read nothing there.*

Shark Tooth had no plan when, many islands later, he jumped into the boat laden with people who would eventually take him to the mountain village of Maima.

Alone in a *kanoa*, he had been paddling his way south and had just landed on a little cay, hoping to stock up on food and water and perhaps spend the night. He'd secured the boat and unloaded his pack and started walking toward a small cluster of fishing huts when frantic screams and shouts erupted. He stood stock-still as about two hands of people came screaming out of the dunes behind the huts and rushed toward the beach without even noticing him, the men urging on a small flock of women with shouts and helping hands and collecting the children.

Others were removing the rollers from a large seagoing canoe and getting ready to launch it. Shark Tooth looked around to see what caused the panic, and he panicked himself when he saw the white sails out to sea. What everyone was talking about, up and down the islands. The *paranaghiri* who had returned and were ravaging the cays, scooping up whoever they found and taking them who knows where. Many of these low-lying islands were flat and almost treeless cays, creating a sturdy people who lived more on the sea than on land and had nowhere to hide when the slave hunters came. They were as easily crushed and gathered up as the sand grains on the beach. Those who tried to escape were cut down. Those captured were stuffed into the *paranaghiri*'s boats like crabs and were never heard from again.

They said the bodies of the dead thrown overboard marked a trail of death that could be followed by the movement of sharks and the scavenger birds. Only the bravest or the luckiest were able to escape. The captives, they said, were being sent to the gold mines on the other islands where the inhabitants had already been killed off, or to the pearl fisheries far away to the south.

The sails were headed in their direction and Shark Tooth didn't hesitate—he took off after the others. The boat was casting off but several hands reached down and hauled him in. There was no time for speech as he grabbed the nearest paddle and picked up the rhythm to join the others as they pulled away. They paddled south all night, and it wasn't until the next day that they were able to seek shelter and rest on another island and take notice of the stranger in their midst.

What they saw was a well-shaped man of perhaps thirty summers, his handsome, symmetrical face marred by a badly healed Y-shaped scar on his cheek and a smaller, moon-shaped one on his forehead.

He was of medium height and powerful body with the broad, sinewy shoulders of boatmen and fishing folk, and he was tattooed all over, with the main image of a shark circling his upper body. That and the shark-tooth amulet he wore were enough for some to keep their distance as they whispered of connections to underworld powers. But Shark Tooth only laughed and claimed they merely showed he was a man dedicated to the sea.

Ending up in Maima, far inland from the sea, was the best thing that could have happened to him, Shark Tooth knew. The balance of power was slowly shifting in his favor. With his betrothal to the girl Night Orchid and marriage when she came of age, nothing would be beyond reach.

Chapter 20

A few days later, the simmering tensions in Maima came to full boil in the plaza. After that, nothing was ever the same, as disaster upon disaster piled up.

While some blamed Feather for bringing the bird, it was Shark Tooth who encouraged the *kacike* and others in the foolish beliefs surrounding it. The bird noisily crowed at the same time as the morning blessing and people had gotten into the habit of coming out of their homes to watch. Candlewood protested the blasphemy, but the *kacike* refused to banish the bird.

Candlewood could stand it no longer. This day, as soon as the morning blessing ended and the monstrous bird continued to crow, he marched into the plaza where the bird was allowed to climb up to the topmost pole of the *kaney*. In an instant, the *behike* had climbed the pole himself—or had flown, as many who witnessed it swore, for how could the old man have gotten onto the roof so quickly? Before anyone could even react, he had seized the bird, wrung its neck, and flung its body at the feet of the *kacike*.

Everyone watched in horror as a thin trickle of blood flowed from the broken feathered body at their feet and proceeded to meander around the plaza in circles while the terrified witnesses screamed and tried to run out of its way.

Flint was always to remember how his eyes happened to

be on Shark Tooth when the bird plopped virtually at the man's feet, and the look of triumph on his face when the blood started to stream from it. Flint could see that Shark Tooth was tightly squeezing the *paranaghiri* cross that he wore openly now.

He chose that moment to stare directly into Flint's eyes, and the boy's blood ran cold from the malevolence he saw there.

Candlewood flew down from the rooftop and, landing on his feet, stopped long enough to curse the village at the top of his voice before storming off.

Flint didn't want to think of all the things that started to go wrong the minute Candlewood abandoned them. Everywhere they saw signs of the *cemies*' anger.

Not long after, Flint awakened with no idea that this day would mark the start of the greatest adventure of his life. He was headed home after his morning bath, looking forward to his pepperpot, when his mother waylaid him.

"Flint, please attend to Matron Greenstone. Now."

He often ran errands for the lady and was not surprised by the summons, but he was surprised by the state his mother was in. She was clearly agitated, but pleasantly so, for a rare smile broke up her normally inscrutable face.

Flint looked at her questioningly, but she only squeezed his arm and said, "Later, my son."

When Matron Greenstone told Flint that he had been selected to undertake an important journey on her behalf, all the way to Turtle Village on the north coast, he trembled in shock but could not wipe the smile from his face.

"Your mother will see that you are fully prepared and will fill you in. I myself will give further instructions before you go. I would like you to leave in three days."

Three days! Flint bowed to the lady and left. Once out-side, he turned cartwheels as he traversed the plaza, much to the shock of onlookers who had never known him to be a boy given to high spirits.

Chapter 21

Flint had already departed Maima when spine-tingling wails from the holy man's quarters alerted residents to a new disaster.

Silver Fern was unable to speak coherently at first, though soon the news was taken up and passed from one end of the village to the other.

"The Bundle. It is gone. It is the end of time."

"The end . . ." was repeated and echoed around the hills. The weaker ones fainted, others fell to their knees and clutched their *cemíes*. The rest ran to the quarter where the temple was located.

The Sacred Bundle was kept by the priest and brought out for the holiest celebration each year—the grand *areito* that marked the first harvest of the sacred *yuka* at the summer solstice when Sun was at its zenith.

The Bundle contained the most sacred relic: the triangular stone that had been handed down from the first ancestors.

Every year the priest and the Owl Clan matron brought the Bundle from its secret place to the temple where the *kacike* and the elders washed it with *tabako* smoke as it was reverently opened. A piece of the first *yuka* plant reaped that year would be added to harness the power of Yukahú the Father of *Yuka* and Attabey the Earth Mother, and so ensure fertility over the coming year.

The Bundle was carefully rewrapped and taken to the plaza where the people had gathered for the *areito*, to serve as the sacred reminder of their origins, before it was returned to its hiding place.

Once every four years, it would be brought in solemn procession along the sacred path to Cauta, the holy mountain, for renewal in the Cave of the Jagua, the place of emergence of the Taíno. This was the year.

Maima's Bundle was special because it was the holiest not only in the village but in the entire *kacikazgo*. It had been entrusted on First Day to a female of the Owl Clan—the first to emerge—and thereafter was in the keeping of the eldest female and traveled with that matron wherever she resided. Although women most often moved to their husband's homes after marriage, for several generations now, Owl matrons had resided in Maima, their power attracting husbands from afar.

The Bundle's disappearance was a crisis of immense proportions. The leading family—especially Matron Pimento and her daughter Falling Water, the entire Owl Clan, faced certain disgrace unless they could quickly recover the object before the news spread. But who could have taken it? Someone from a rival village? An enemy within?

Matron Greenstone and her clique immediately pointed to Shark Tooth, but then concluded that even he would not have been so bold.

Chief Runs Swiftly was enjoying a ball game when the news reached him. He immediately ordered the closing of the four entrances to the village and for guards to be set there. An immediate search of every building, every nook and cranny, revealed nothing.

At the council room, he found the family heads and elders already assembling and the mood was loud and caustic with accusations being thrown; his enemies seeing in it a test of his rule.

Several voices cried out for the *behike* Candlewood to be brought back as the only one who could be trusted. Others could be heard accusing Candlewood of the theft, though no one claimed to have seen him since he had cursed the village and left.

"But we all know he can fly."

"He can make himself invisible," others claimed.

"He can transform himself into any animal he wishes and you'd never know."

"He can turn into a leaf, a tree."

"An ant."

Never before had so many attributes been given to Candlewood.

The meeting ended in uproar and disorder. The village leaders only dispersed when the *kacike* announced he would take *kohoba* and consult the gods.

But the *kacike*'s trance following ingestion of the holy powder resulted in disturbing visions and no satisfactory answer, as the news was conveyed to another assembly. The vision yielded no sign of the Bundle. Worse, the supreme being Yukahú did not appear; instead, he sent destructive forces such as Guabancex and her heralds of thunder, lightning, and flood. Guataúba and Coatrisquie took over, foretelling winds and whirlwinds. Maquetaurie Guayaba, Lord of the Dead, was accompanied by the dog Opiyelguobirán, the guardian of the gates to the underworld.

The vision also revealed monstrous animals with fiery eyes bearing on their backs strange creatures encased in shell, and a procession of skeletons entering the very bowels of Mother Earth to dig and ravage in search of some alien substance.

Many again called out for Candlewood as the only one capable of interpreting the visions and taking countermeasures, but no one knew where the *behike* had taken himself.

While the elders wrestled with the disaster and how to deal with it, there came an explosive new announcement: the *paranaghiri* were on their way to Maima village.

Arriving that morning were six Taíno from the coast who bore white talking leaves that they attached to a tree trunk. Looking at the leaves, one spoke aloud what they said: *"Caciques and Indians of this land, hark ye! We notify you that there is but one God and one Pope and one King of Castile who is lord of all these lands. Give heed and show obedience . . ."* The strange Taíno went on for some time, and though no one understood what it meant, they were awed to witness the talking leaves of which they had heard so much. The visitors also said they brought instructions from their master, Comandante Narváez, and the holy man, their priest: In three days the priest would arrive to baptize the children. A dwelling apart from the main village was to be prepared for him and the other visitors. The rest of the men would follow, led by Comandante Narváez. They came, repeated the herald, with good intentions—not to injure but to convert them.

The village went into shock, fear, anxiety, and, for some, pride that they were thought worthy of a visit. They were the ones who vowed that Maima would not be outdone in their level of hospitality.

The women got busy with reaping and preparation of *yuka*. In every family work hut, the girls' fingers were raw from passing the root back and forth over the graters of sharp coral stones embedded in cedar. The grandmothers were packing each lot of grated *yuka* into a *cibucán*, a long snakelike woven tube which was hung by a loop on a post. Into another loop at the base, a long pole was inserted. The young children were summoned from play to come and sit on the pole to compress the snake and squeeze the poisonous juice out. Once boiled, the juice lost its poison and became *kasaripe*, an important ingredient in the pepperpot. The *yuka* mass left in the *cibucán* was dried and used to make *kasabe*—the thatched roofs were already covered with the flat bread set out to dry. The intoxicating *yuka* liquor *kasiri* would be a vital contribution to the expected fiesta.

Builders and thatchers were erecting a new visitors' lodge in the southwest quadrant away from the village, and hunters and fishermen went off to secure extra food. The craftspeople were busier than ever, for almost everyone wanted to secure extra guardian *cemíes*.

And then, as if that was not enough, in the midst of the preparations for the visitors, Pebble's daughter Night Orchid saw her first blood. This was a matter of public concern, for the occasion had to be marked according to the rules laid down at First Time, the rules that guided the coming into womanhood of every girl of the Taíno nation.

Two married men were hurriedly dispatched to cut the poles and lianas to be used in the erection of her hut, the *guanara*. Before the first sod was cut to plant the center pole, the priest blew *tabako* powder through a forked tube to invoke the blessings of the heavenly pair, Yukahú and Attabey, patrons of procreation and fertility of plants, animals, and humans. And then, chanting and blowing *tabako* smoke all the while, he drew the insignia of the Winds of the Four Quarters on the ground to indicate exactly where the posts should be erected.

The builders raised four poles and crossbeams that met in a point at the top. Married women came to lay the thatch that covered the roof and walls right to the ground and tie it down tight with lianas. Even though the tiny hut would be destroyed at the end of Night Orchid's stay there, it had to be erected with the same care and attention as the very first house that was given to the first people: the model of Turtle Woman's shell.

Matron Greenstone's blood was boiling at fever pitch. Her souls were warring dangerously close to breakdown. *How dare they*, she thought, when she first heard the news. Yet her other self couldn't curb the excitement she shared with the rest of the villagers at the chance to see these strange creatures for the very first time. She strove to regain her balance. O where was Candlewood when one needed him most? she moaned. Where was that boy Flint in all of this? Shouldn't he be home by now bringing her the balm her aching limbs craved?

She steeled herself. One thing was certain: never would she be part of any welcome, even if it was her sacred duty to uphold the spirit of generosity for which her people were renowned. Hadn't the *paranaghiri* themselves changed the rules? Exchanging cruelty for kindness, answering generosity with murder and theft? No. No. Her mind was made up. She would face the consequences once the visitors departed. She and her kin would take themselves off to the communal longhouse for the duration, along with any other dissenters who cared to join them. She'd send the word out. Even if the move killed her, she would not remain in the house of nobles which faced the main plaza overlooking the spectacle of a welcoming party. She would not be a part of it. Never.

Chapter 22

In the excitement of her own preparations to enter the *guanara*, Night Orchid temporarily forgot about the *paranaghiri*. Her long silky hair, which would be ritually cut to signal her new status once she emerged, was unbraided and fell below her waist. She was stripped of all jewels and ornaments except for the protective insignia of My Lady that her mother painted on her cheeks in black *jagua*, to signify the death of her childhood self.

She was naked as usual, except for a menstrual cloth of soft *maho* lace bark which was attached to her beaded raffia belt. To protect her from the cold at night, she was given a white wrap with shell beads worked into the fringes at the four corners, like her soft *hamaka*, previously unused. Both were of the finest cotton from Xamayca, for which her mother had traded an exquisitely carved *duho* years earlier, and had put aside for just this occasion. Afterward, the cloths would be burned along with the hut and anything else worn or touched by Night Orchid. She would emerge from the *guanara* completely naked and free of adornment, like a palette waiting to be painted, and prepared for her Coming Out.

Night Orchid had looked forward to her ceremonial promenade through the village. Dressed in her finery, she would be the focus of all eyes. There would be feasting and dancing in the plaza while she sat at the place of honor beside the *kacike*, receiving gifts, the greatest day in every girl's life. But now she knew in her heart that her Coming Out would have to wait until order was restored in their universe. Up to the day she entered the *guanara*, the Sacred Bundle had not been found. And the village was in an even greater turmoil with the expected arrival of the dreaded *paranaghiri*.

Night Orchid twisted uncomfortably in the *hamaka* suspended from two of the posts that held up the hut that was so small there was almost no room to swing. Alone and hidden away from Sun for the duration of her bleeding, she marked time only by the arrival of her elder sister Bright Star, who stooped down outside the hut several times a day and saw to her needs. Through the thatch palm leaves that completely covered the hut, she whispered of everything that was happening in the village.

Night Orchid wished her sister was there all the time but knew she shouldn't complain. Her ordeal was meant to teach her to endure pain as the lot of women. But at times she found the quiet, the darkness, the loneliness almost too much to bear. The *jiu, jiu, jiu, jiu, jiu* which signaled that Siju, her little owl guardian that hunted both night and day, was nearby, uplifted her. But when Siju was unheard, she was tempted to tear aside the palm fronds and run screaming back home to her mother's arms.

She swung to and fro and tried to remember some of the grandmother tales, or the words of all the songs she knew, or all the playground chants. She whispered them softly so as not to attract unwanted spirits.

She practiced in her head designs for the patterns of the short cotton skirts she would weave for when she got married; Bright Star had promised to help her.

She would go with her sister into the forest, perhaps with her age mates to make a day of it, and collect the plants she would use to dye the cotton *nagua* she would weave for her wedding. Then they would gather fiber to make the aprons for everyday wear. Maguey leaves dried, combed, and spun made a very fine thread. Or palmito when young. Bark cloth was more delicate but held the dyes. Henequén was strong too. She needed blue for Attabey—they would have to find the berries which gave a fine indigo; cochineal for the red. Perhaps the boy Flint could be persuaded to bring her some special coloring material, something no one else had; she would tempt him with the promise of a carving, whatever image he desired.

Once she had her Coming Out, she would wear her jewelry again, and have the tight ligatures tied to her arms and legs to make them look fat and beautiful and protect her from evil spirits.

She realized her thoughts were wandering again. The sounds of the tree frogs surged in to fill the little hut and surround her with company: *Toa, toa, toa.* Little *kokis* that couldn't stop crying for the mothers who had abandoned them, for they had once been human children. This made her sad so she turned her thoughts to the visitors.

Here they were, coming to Maima—the dreaded Panol— and here she was, missing it all: the grand reception and the fiesta and no doubt a ball game, the greatest event ever to take place in Maima village.

Jiu, jiu, jiu, jiu.

Chapter 23

It was hard to tell time in the windowless hut. Night Orchid's attendants pushed food and water through a small flap at the bottom, careful that no light should penetrate; if even the faintest glimmer of sunlight fell on her, the entire village would be visited with catastrophe. Such tales of disobedience and its consequences were bred into every Taíno girl from the time she came to know herself.

Night Orchid tried not to think of the incident with the door flap and the sunbeam that for just one moment had pierced the hut and briefly touched her. It was the second day. Bright Star had pushed the flap too hard and instead of swinging back immediately to close, the coarsely woven thatch got caught up on the other side, exposing a triangle of light. Night Orchid, who was kneeling, pushed it shut, but not before Sun had peeked through and seen her.

It happened so quickly that Bright Star didn't seem to notice, for there was no break in her chatter. But Night Orchid was immediately seized with a severe pain which left her unsure if it was a menstrual cramp or Opiyelguobirán, the dog messenger of Death already tearing at her gut. She had fallen to the floor, hands wrapped around her body and teeth clenched in agony.

As soon as her sister's voice faded, she had staggered over to lie down, not even touching the fresh water and gruel. She was so tense with fear she could hardly move, but the pain gradually faded as she chewed on willow sticks. When nothing further happened, she decided that the moment had been too insignificant for the *cemíes* to notice. It would be best to pretend it never happened. But the incident kept nagging at her every time her stomach cramped. Suppose all the tales were true and she brought disaster to Maima?

She tried to focus her mind on something pleasant, the grand *areito* at the summer solstice more than three moons away, the one day of the year when the families of all the villages around came together for a grand fiesta. Time when marriage contracts were made and partners sought outside one's own village and clan. When she herself would become an eligible bride. Negotiations would take place between families, a suitable bride price would be agreed and a date set for sometime in the future when the exchange would take place.

Bright Star was lucky. Her great beauty had won her a handsome young man, the nephew of a chief; they would seal the contract at the next gathering and Bright Star would leave to go live with him.

Night Orchid worried about her own situation and who might offer for her. She knew instinctively that she did not have her sister's worth, for Bright Star was not only beautiful and charming but an excellent weaver. Though Night Orchid could weave and make pots and do whatever was required of her as a wife, she knew her skills were barely passable; her mistakes would not escape the eagle eyes of a prospective mother-in-law.

The next day, when the main body of the *paranaghiri* was due to arrive, a garrulous old woman named Cedar Wax came instead of Bright Star. Night Orchid was flooded with disappointment when she heard the voice calling out, but remembered her manners.

"Greetings, Grandmother," she whispered through the palm leaves. "You slept well?"

"I slept well, my daughter. But now I am wide awake, for there are so many new things in the world to be seen by these old eyes."

"Tell me, Grandmother."

Cedar Wax needed to catch her breath after the walk, so it took her some time to begin. While Night Orchid ate the gruel, the old woman repeated many of the wonders Bright Star had already spoken about. And then she said, "Your sister, my dear. Your sister Bright Star is so honored. She is one of the six maidens chosen to attend to the *paranaghiri* in the visitors' lodge. The six that had their Coming Out last year and are not yet married. Their priest, the Black Robe, is there too. She will have so much to tell you. Aren't you a lucky girl. Straight from her you will hear it."

Before Night Orchid could respond, Cedar Wax moved on to talk about the robed priest and the summoning of the children to be baptized. The priest and his companions had arrived on horseback ahead of the main party, accompanied by a young Indian on foot bent almost double from the large wooden box he carried on his back. Shark Tooth said it contained holy water to be sprinkled on the children against disease brought by the evil eye, but many of the parents objected. Cedar Wax said the Taíno guides accompanying the *paranaghiri* were from Xamayca and spoke with strange accents. "They garble their words, my dear, so you can hardly understand them." But most remarkable of all—and she had deliberately saved this for last—accompanying the priest was a totally black man. Night Orchid perked up. How had Bright Star not told her?

"You mean he was covered with *jagua*, Grandmother?"

"No-oh. Though that is what everyone thought. When he rode up on his horse, he was covered head to toe in some stuff like a shell. But afterward, when he took that off, his skin looked so funny—his face and hands and everything. People went up to rub their fingers on his skin to see if the color came off."

Cedar Wax cackled and paused. "I touched his cheek, though he is so tall I had to stand on tiptoe. Warm. Human like us, despite it all. His hair . . . well, that was the most remarkable thing. It was short and curly, like dried berries stuck all over. His features are not like ours. More like the *paranaghiri* except his mouth is larger and his nose . . . But handsome, my dear, once you get over the strangeness of it all."

Cedar Wax was silent for so long that Night Orchid almost interrupted her, but her voice came again, full of excitement: "He smiled a lot, too, and played with the children. Came right off the horse, and when he took off that heavy stuff he was wearing and laughed, it was as if he was in love with life. Much nicer than the ghostly ones. My dear, they smell! The Black Robe never washes. We were all trying to be polite and not gag, but it was hard. We hear that is how they all are. But the black man now . . . Anyway, I must go. Your sister will have so many exciting stories . . ."

Cedar Wax's next few visits were much shorter. The main body of men were on their way and she didn't want to miss a bit of it. She did say some of the families had outright refused to have the Black Robe sprinkle holy water on their children. Runs Swiftly didn't know what to do with himself. Matron Greenstone and her faction had decided they would not be a part of the gathering. She had moved with her kin and their followers to the communal longhouse where they planned to stay as long as the visitors stayed.

Night Orchid swung listlessly to and fro in the *hamaka*. She thought of the man who was black all over. Cedar Wax had said he was tall, tall and straight as a cedar tree. "Sekou," he had told the children his name was, pointing to himself. "Sekou, Sekou," they repeated, following him everywhere.

Night Orchid listened to the faraway sounds from the village and was surprised that she hadn't yet heard the booming of the holy *mayohuakan*, the slit drum made of a hollowed log that would have been brought out on such an important occasion.

Chapter 24

To his dying day, Sekou would be haunted by the rasping sound of metal on flint as a precursor to disaster. He himself had made that sound when his little party had stopped at the river crossing a half day away from Maima, a sound that was music to any swordsman—finding whetstones that were perfect for sharpening their weapon.

Only when he cantered into the village and saw the brown faces full of smiles, wonder, and fear did he have his first twinge of anxiety. But he forgot it as soon as he took off his armor and emerged from the visitors' lodge to be swarmed by people who had never before seen black skin. He was used to it. That day he was dressed in his leather trousers and boots and a linen shirt under his jerkin, the everyday dress of the Christians of which he was one, legally baptized and not a heathen, he was proud to say. The cross his mother had placed around his neck when he was torn from her in Sevilla at age six affirmed this, despite the color of his skin and his ownership by another.

As he was swept up by the villagers, admired and touched, offered food and drink and gifts, Sekou forgot his earlier dark thoughts and the sounds of sharpening. He had to tear himself away each time to do his job of looking after the priest.

Yet the dark feeling kept returning. He knew that the main body of men led by Comandante Narváez would do exactly what he had done by the river: take the opportunity to sharpen their swords. And in his time in the Indies he had seen what those swords could do to the native peoples, along with clubs, lances, pikes, arrows, guns, dogs, horses, fire. Often, just the sight of the Christians was enough. Which is why the comandante had ordered his men to arrive dressed in full armor. Those mounted on horses didn't have to do anything or say a word to force submission.

Sekou felt a twinge of shame each time he recalled how proudly he had sat on his horse as he entered a village square, fully encased in the steel shell of a Spanish caballero—visored helmet, heavy breastplate, arm and leg greaves, a metal skirt, a gorget for neck and throat, armored boots, and gauntlets. Not to mention his proudest possession: his sword of finest Toledo steel. The horse, the armor, and the sword were all new acquisitions, the gift of his owner, Comandante Narváez.

The comandante had ordered him to accompany the priest, and Sekou was happy with that. In his heart he knew: he was not cut out for soldiering.

Narváez had bought him off his previous owner, a rancher in Xamayca, because he could read and write and calculate sums. Sekou had become his valued assistant, nimbly carrying out his orders and keeping track of things. They had crossed over to Cuba to aid Don Diego Velázquez, who'd been authorized by their king to subjugate the Indios on the last remaining large island not yet settled by the Christians, and one, it was said, full of gold. Sekou's status as the comandante's errand boy made life easier for him as his army companions could scorn him for his difference but dared not physically harm him. In any event, after his eventful early life, he could more than take care of himself.

In the Indies he had also learned to harden his heart at the Christians' treatment of the native peoples. He had made friends with the Indios at the ranch and had gone with them to their village when they were allowed home. He was forced to turn aside and often felt physically ill when he witnessed their torture, well aware that their lives were valued as nothing compared to his. They were unfree *encomiendos*, assigned by their *kacike* on pain of death to serve the Christians as free labor and be brutalized, starved, maimed, or killed. His value derived from the large sum the rancher's widow had paid the ship's captain for him, as she constantly reminded, so she treated him well, as did the comandante in his turn. Sometimes he thought about these things, but they made no sense to him and since there was no one he could discuss them with, he pushed them to the back of his mind.

Not so the sound of metal on flint. Even now, awaiting the arrival of Narváez and his men, the strokes kept repeating in his head. What he had witnessed of this army's passage through the land so far had made him fearful in a way he hadn't felt since he'd been carried away from Sevilla.

Chapter 25

The day the *paranaghiri* soldiers arrived, Heart of Palm was glad his training in early youth had taught him to remain still for long periods of time. For this waiting was long. Almost a full day.

The *kacike* and *ni-taíno* had dressed themselves in their finest from an early hour and seated themselves on their *duhos*, chewing *tabako*, fingering their *sibas*, or talking softly among themselves. But most remained silent, seemingly lost in thought or dozing as they awaited the shell blow that would signal the visitors' arrival.

The main plaza was filled with the newly scrubbed and painted children and those adults who had rushed to fulfill their duties for the morning, all bathed and dressed in necklaces, feathers, and shell noisemakers, their bodies painted and stamped and adorned with their most beautiful and powerful images. They squatted, quiet and orderly, shifting down to make way for latecomers, with none of the usual noise and banter and joking. From time to time, little groups would form to touch up each other's paintings that began to melt on their sweaty bodies as Sun climbed across the sky. Huge mounds of food and drink awaited the visitors, to be laid out on mats in an orderly fashion, adorned with flowers and fruit.

Heart of Palm stood at ease behind the *kacike* and nobles in a group of young warriors, two hands of them, all kitted out, the *ni-taíno*—like himself—wearing their feathered capes. Hidden beneath the left armbands of several—like himself—was the tattooed insignia of the new Rooster Society to which they had secretly dedicated themselves. It was, Shark Tooth said, the mark of progress: *Adapt to the new or die.*

Another line of warriors, mainly the ones who were stuck in the old ways, were standing on the opposite side, arms folded; the two lines of young men spent much of their time glowering at each other.

They snapped to attention at a roaring sound, a rumbling like Mother Earth turning over in her *hamaka*, tumbling rocks and uprooting trees. The sound rolled closer and soon became a cacophony like nothing ever heard before, the drumming of horses' hooves on the ground, bells tinkling and harnesses jangling, and their riders' voices urging them on.

Into the plaza cantered a group of monstrous creatures, almost trampling those seated there and causing the rest to scatter. Trumpets sounded as horses snorted and pranced under riders who looked not human but alien creatures dressed in heavy metal from head to toe. Only their mouths betrayed them as they whooped and laughed and shouted and waved their swords while the horses wheeled and turned and whinnied. The square erupted in screams, shouts, and wild confusion.

The young warriors never broke rank. They stood expressionless, their hands hovering over their weapons. And yet it seemed as if a great tremor was running through all of them and it took awhile for Heart of Palm to realize it came from the collective trembling of their bodies. None showed the slightest sign of fear or any indication that they thought the sight extraordinary, even as the pandemonium rose to a crescendo.

The riders didn't dismount, Heart of Palm never knew why, unless it was simply to prolong the terror. They ranged themselves in a rough semicircle, with some foot soldiers milling around, laughing and chatting and looking about with a self-satisfied air. The one man who seemed to be their leader sat on a red horse, seemingly apart to one side. It was to him that Shark Tooth led the *kacike* and the nobles once there was a lull, the Lucayan having appointed himself their interpreter.

Heart of Palm could not hear what was being said but Shark Tooth seemed to be doing a poor job of translation, for an older Taíno who was holding the reins of the leader's horse intervened and thereafter took over, seeming to angrily rebuke Shark Tooth, who slunked away.

Heart of Palm was relieved that the awkwardness soon dissolved. While the horsemen never dismounted, the noise died down and the villagers moved about, offering water and fruit, smiling at the wild-looking men, touching their horses. Within a short span of time, the village squares and walkways became as crowded as a fairground as the foot soldiers and their Taíno servants joined them.

The priest was still busy baptizing the last of the children at the makeshift font in the visitors' lodge. Matron Greenstone and her followers, including some families that refused to have their children baptized, had established themselves in the communal longhouse overlooking the smaller square. The priest's messengers had been sent packing by the formidable Matron and her supporters. The priest planned to go himself as soon as he had a moment. He paused to shake his head in sorrow. How could these heathens be so cruel as to deny their children entry into Heaven?

Chapter 26

Heart of Palm pushed his way through the crowd and climbed to a slight rise on the outskirts to relieve himself. From there, he had an excellent view of the village spread out below, now pulsing with color and life. He was standing there, enjoying the spectacle, when bloodcurdling screams erupted from the main plaza. He turned to look and wished he'd never witnessed the scene: a bloodied head rolling, a body fallen, and blood splashing from the sword a soldier swung to cut down a body that was too stunned to flee.

Heart of Palm would never forget the unbelievable sights unfolding below in every part of the village, and how quickly Maima was overrun—the great beasts in motion neighing and screaming as the mounted men entered the fray, whooping and waving their bloodied swords as they cut the villagers down, bloodstained pieces of arms and legs and cracked brains flying in the air. No one was spared, not the babes in arms nor the eldest trampled by the horses. For a moment he caught sight of the *kacike* and some of his retinue in the midst of the melee with no time to react as they too went down amid the slaughter, to be trampled with the rest. Their colorful bird feather capes and headdresses marked their resting places as the *paranaghiri* reached down to rip off whatever wealth they wore from their bodies.

Heart of Palm could not remember how he got into the

nearest tree or how long he sat there, his mind frozen and his body chilled. What weapons were these that could kill so swiftly, slice so effortlessly through the posts holding up the *kaney*, and what manner of monsters wielded them?

He only came back to his senses when his nostrils filled with the acrid smell of burning, and wisps of flying thatch landing on his skin signaled a new horror: the *paranaghiri* lighting torches and setting everything on fire, starting with the roof of the *kaney*.

He was momentarily distracted by a sound brought by the wind. Faintly it came, from the communal lodge it seemed, voices raised in song in the face of Death. Raised by Matron Greenstone, no doubt, for despite the distance, he could hear her soprano soaring above the rest, singing the song of defiance: *Golden Flower . . .*

Was it real? From such a distance? An anthem to the *kacika* Anacaona—Golden Flower—slain eight planting seasons earlier on the island of Española, along with eighty-two male *kacikes* who had perished with her. They'd been herded into a *bohío* that was set on fire. She was hanged.

Golden Flower, you live in us still . . .

The beauty of the moment seized Heart of Palm. To sing at a time like this. He tried to join in but fear seized his vocal chords. He swallowed air to stop his sobbing. He closed his eyes. But nothing could ever erase from his mind the screams and the smell of burning flesh from the longhouse where those who tried to flee were slaughtered, the trees catching fire and the flames jumping onto the workshops of the artisans and the *bohíos*. Those who escaped to the outskirts of the village were chased and run through with swords. With no one left to kill, the men began to drift in the direction of the visitors' lodge, which was upwind from the fires. And still in his demented mind, he could hear singing.

Heart of Palm was fortunate too that his hiding place was in that quarter. Not that this registered in his conscious mind. He had no idea how long he remained on his perch. Only when there was no more sound or movement below did he drop down from the tree. He did not stop to see if anything stirred in the debris and ash and smoldering fires. He ran off into the darkness, away from the carnage, the word *coward* not yet burned into his souls.

Chapter 27

Unexpected sounds from the village shattered Night Orchid's thoughts. Why was she hearing shouts, screams, wailing? She stood up and tied her cotton wrap above her budding breasts as she listened, desperately wishing she could go outside.

She stiffened as her nostrils picked up the smell of smoke and she heard what sounded like the crackling of fire. Blessed! Something was terribly wrong and she twisted her hands together in torment, trying to make sense of what was happening. Were the *paranaghiri* enacting some strange rituals? Was it part of the fiesta or some disaster?

There had never been a serious fire since Night Orchid's birth, but she had heard enough stories to know how dangerous fire could be, how quickly it could jump from hut to hut, fed by thatched roofs and wooden posts, how quickly even the huge trees of the forest behind the village could burn.

What was she to do? If there was trouble, she was sure someone would come. But the sounds, brought on the wind, were clearer now and were unmistakably screams and shouts and the crack of burning wood.

Night Orchid's souls flew to her throat at the sound of a voice outside, hoarse but commanding. A man's voice.

"Out, Night Orchid. Run!"

She was too shocked to move. No man should come

within sight of the menstrual hut. Who was it and what was happening? She barely had time to think before the hut shook as someone slapped a post and the door covering was whipped away. O Mama Attabey!

She must have closed her eyes, for when she stopped screaming she was stunned to be looking up at the stars. She shouldn't be seeing stars, she knew, and she turned her back. But a coarse hand had taken hold of her arm and was dragging her outside. She almost choked on the acrid smell of smoke and her eyes watered. What was he saying? She knew that voice! But could it be?

"Run, child!" he ordered. "Don't stop. Don't look back. The Christians have slain everyone. Maima is burning. Go and take this with you." He grabbed her right hand and thrust something soft and leathery in it. "Guard it with your life. Travel east. To Cauta and the cave. I will meet you there."

Cauta! The holy mountain. She closed her hand tightly over whatever it was and the next moment nearly died of terror when a hand passed in front of her eyes and she felt something touching her neck. *He's going to strangle me,* she thought wildly, and kicked out, hitting a bony shin.

"O be quiet, child, I'm not the one to fear." The mildness of his voice quieted her somewhat, though his new grip on her arm was firm. When she stood still, he let go and she could feel him doing something at the back of her neck. She realized he was tying on a necklace and she could feel the weight of a metal object on her breastbone.

"Mama Attabey will guide you."

She reached up to touch the amulet and breathed out as her fingers closed over the outlines of a little frog. The Mother! She clutched the image tightly, hearing loud rasping sounds that she didn't realize were coming from her own body. She could now clearly see the red glow of flames as the trees started to burn. She might have stood rooted to the spot forever if a push from behind hadn't given her the momentum to start running, and after that she just kept on moving through the night.

When she stumbled over a root or stone or fell from exhaustion, her terror made her pick herself up and carry on and never once let go of the package. After her first fall, she had looked around and realized that her rescuer was not following her; she was all alone in the night.

"Blessed Mother," she cried aloud, "protect me!" She looked back once and never again, for in the distance she could see the huge red glow that was like the end of the world. When she finally threw herself down on the ground, her tired feet refusing to take her farther, she folded herself into a little ball that whimpered and burrowed itself into a thick undergrowth of leaves, holding the mysterious package tightly to her chest.

Chapter 28

Sekou was also on the run, tripping over tree roots in the darkness, throwing himself down from time to time to retch and weep and catch his breath and begin running again.

He and the priest had hurried outside as the sounds of the slaughter came nearer to the visitors' lodge. In vain the priest had dashed to and fro in a fruitless attempt to stop it. Yet what shocked Sekou most of all and galvanized his actions was the sight of Comandante Narváez calmly seated on his horse in the main plaza, dead bodies lying all around him, making no effort to call off his men. Instead, he jovially shouted out to the priest as he furiously approached, "How does Your Honor like what our Spaniards have done?"

"I condemn you and them to the devil!" the priest had replied, spinning around and rushing back to the lodge.

Sekou, his mind in a turmoil, had had no plan of action until he heard the words of his master and his blood ran cold. He knew without thinking it that he could not stay.

He'd had the presence of mind to grab his pack from the baggage piled on the floor in the visitors' lodge while the priest argued with the soldiers so drunk with bloodlust that they had descended on the lodge wanting to kill the very Taíno servants who had accompanied them. It was as if they had to wipe every Indio from the face of the earth. To what purpose? Only the threat by the priest of excommunication had persuaded the soldiers to leave. But not before some took advantage of the confusion to grab the girls who had been assigned to the visitors' lodge and were under the priest's protection. They dragged them outside and ran to their horses. Each mounted and pulled up a terrified Taína before racing away.

Burdened by his pack and his aching soul, Sekou faded into the darkness.

Mine the heavy task to sing their souls to Koaibay—sing them everyone as the Star People wept. And why was not I so old and worn among them? Why did the cemíes *put such a cruel burden on me? Allowing me to dream the terror to come but without the means to avert it. I sang all night long and greeted Sun's rising next day and sang some more, naming everyone and singing their souls to Koaibay.*

I did not sing the four who are chosen for they are no longer in this place. They are the new burden placed on me. To ensure their passage to safety and the re-creation of the new age. To vanquish the Dark Power. Only then can your servant fly home.

PART II
SURVIVORS

Chapter 29

Flint had left Maima before the announcement of the missing Bundle and was equally unaware of the subsequent events. He'd reached Turtle Village with ten knots on his string—one for each day of his journey. The sentries were surprised at how far he had traveled and immediately ordered two youths to escort him to the *kacike* and then to Matron Bilberry, Matron Greenstone's kinswoman. Giggling children trailed them through the village. A few adults looked curiously at Flint's appearance but most wanted to know where he came from and what trade he carried in his pack.

Matron Bilberry was the first to see the goods specially selected by Matron Greenstone and receive the gifts she sent, as well as the instructions regarding the trade she expected in return. Flint was fed and told where he could hang his *hamaka* and encouraged to rest and relax for the remainder of his stay. He was happy to spend the next few days wandering around the fishing village, an unfamiliar and alluring environment.

Unlike Maima and its arrangement around a central plaza, Turtle Village undulated along several beautiful bays, the houses strung out on a slight ridge above the water. Farther inland were the temple, ball courts, and cemeteries. The cultivated fields seemed small compared to other communities; the villagers obtained much of their *yuka* from the interior in exchange for their seafood.

Flint's most exciting moment came when a friendly fisherman took him to witness a practice the hill folk had always heard about but few had ever seen—the use of remoras to capture the huge marine turtles. From his boat, the fisherman threw out the specially trained fish with a rope attached to its tail. The remora had a large suction disc on top of its head that it used to attach itself to the swimming turtle. It did not let go until the fisherman pulled the huge creature into the vast corrals built in shallow water where hundreds at a time were kept alive.

Despite the beautiful setting, Flint sensed the same kind of tension he had felt in Maima whenever the subject of the *paranaghiri* arose, only here, their presence seemed much closer. On the third day of his stay, a canoe arrived with families fleeing their home in the east. Just the latest of many such refugees, he was told. Some stayed only long enough to rest and acquire supplies before heading for the hills or offshore cays. The *paranaghiri* army, they said, had crossed over to Cuba from Ayití, endless *kanoas* of them, and had captured the noble Hatuéy by trickery and set him on fire. They were moving westward in starts and stops and putting down *bohíos*, murdering and enslaving. Others of their kind summoned from Xamayca were sweeping inland.

Everyone remained anxious and alert, with frequent war councils. Among them were warriors who had escaped when Hatuéy was captured. They were given the run of Turtle Village but they walked warily, their hands never far from their weapons.

Flint was consumed by a different kind of anxiety, uncertain how to accomplish the second part of his mission, the secret part.

He did ask questions about the Macorixe, the people who lived in the mangrove, and was dismayed at how dismissive the Turtle villagers were of them. They were backward and surly and kept to themselves, he was told, but they did meet for trade. They made excellent arrowheads and took *yuka* and peppers in exchange for their smoked *hutía* meat.

The only one allowed into the Macorixe village was the *behike* Haw, who exchanged medicine with them and had as an apprentice one of the *kacike*'s sons, Echo, with the permission of both villages. That was good news to Flint. On arrival, he was thrilled to discover that Haw had once been an apprentice of Candlewood. The medicine man had greeted him warmly, eagerly seeking news of Candlewood and others he had known in Maima. Haw was a busy man but he easily fell into the role of uncle and guide whenever he had a moment to spend with the visiting boy.

Flint knew Haw was his passage to the isolated village but he wasn't sure how far he could trust him. Should he share his reason for wanting to go there or simply ask Haw to take him to satisfy his curiosity? He chose to do the latter, but then Haw peered at him strangely and said, "You look a lot like them, Flint."

Flint immediately felt as if a burden had been lifted. "My mother, Crab Claw, is one of the Old Ones. They all died off, she told me, and she is the last of her kind."

Haw nodded. "I remember Crab Claw, the healer in Maima. We never spoke. I don't think she spoke to anyone. But she once gave me a salve for a bad wound. It worked too." He smiled at the memory.

"She heard about these Macorixe on the coast and asked me to find out more. She thought we could be the same people."

Haw said nothing for a while, then nodded. "I go in three

days. I will take you. But only their *kacike* can decide if you will be allowed into the village. It could be a wasted trip."

That was good enough for Flint. He set off with Haw feeling wildly optimistic as their *kanoa* headed straight for the string of islets that looked completely untouched by humans, dark green lumps surrounded by mangrove stilt roots barring the way.

As they entered a channel between the cays, they rested from paddling and drifted along in a completely peaceful world, save for the occasional squawks of herons startled into flight or a crocodile floating along, only the ripples revealing its presence.

Flint was shaken out of his somnolence when Haw suddenly steered the *kanoa* straight into a seemingly impenetrable bank that—at the very last moment—opened into a narrow passage, the boat almost touching the sides as they glided through.

He had another surprise as they entered a large and still body of water. On the farthest bank, midway up a cliff face, a long chain of wattle houses perched on stilts, as if they'd sprung organically out of the mangrove roots.

Haw steered them to a sandbank and blew the shell. A response came eventually and Flint could tell he was asking permission to come ashore with a stranger from Maima village. There was another long period of silence, so long that they ran the boat onto the sand and sat in the shelter of a lone sea almond tree.

Haw seemed perfectly relaxed as he leaned his back against the trunk and took a knife and a piece of wood he was whittling out of his bag. He smiled at Flint. "It will be a long wait." Flint passed the time making string figures that became more and more complicated until his fingers began to fumble with the strain of waiting and he gave up in disgust. Many hands of time passed. Sun was on its way west when a boat pulled out from the other side with a single paddler on board.

"Sandstone," Haw said, "their *kacike.*"

Sandstone's black hair was streaked with white and he wore it long and flowing; he was stately rather than handsome, with pronounced cheekbones and a high forehead, large eyes, and a generous mouth. His expression was grim but his greeting to Haw was friendly.

Haw introduced Flint, who bowed to the newcomer, and then to Flint's surprise, both men began to speak in a language he did not understand, the name *Candlewood* among the few words he was able to make out. Sandstone was clearly asking questions and more than once scrutinized Flint in a way that seemed more observant than rude.

From time to time, too, he noticed Sandstone gazing with a puzzled expression at the necklace with the carved conch shell pendant that his mother had removed from her neck and put around his own as he left home. "The gods of the Old Ones go with you, my son. Never let this be taken from you," she had whispered before bursting into tears and running off.

Whatever Haw said must have persuaded Sandstone, for he suddenly picked up his paddle and gestured for them to follow.

Flint had the strangest feeling as they reached the top of the ladder which led from the landing stage into the village. It seemed that all the inhabitants had turned out to see the stranger and were lining the path that followed the houses along the cliff.

No one smiled or said anything as Sandstone led them into the longhouse. He invited them to sit. A girl appeared with refreshments and withdrew. Sandstone and Haw continued their conversation quietly in the same strange tongue, and the day wore on as men and women came and went, sometimes joining in. Flint, ignored, found himself sweltering in the hot and dark dwelling, so unlike the high airy *bohíos*, the only light coming through the chinks in the wattles and a smoke hole in the low thatch roof. Soon he found himself dozing off and awoke with a start when Haw touched him, and he saw that night had fallen.

The same girl—whom Sandstone had introduced to Haw as Pearl, his daughter—brought more food, a delicious feast of seafood that Flint enjoyed, despite his nervousness and the strange surroundings.

"We will spend the night here," Haw said, showing him where to hang their *hamakas*.

Haw fell asleep immediately, but it took a long time for Flint to join him. He was unable to read the mood of the place and couldn't help wondering, *What will tomorrow bring?*

Chapter 30

Flint had so much to tell his mother, but he would skip over the next two days when he moved among the Macorixe people. They were neither friendly nor unfriendly, they just seemed silent compared to the gaiety and laughter of Taíno villagers, and most averted their eyes as he passed. Only the children—and there were six of them—laughed and played as children do, and they laughed even more when the stranger joined them in their games.

He was not welcomed by the boys his age. A gang of youth led by the *kacike*'s son Pear Blossom seemed openly hostile, following him about and making remarks in their strange language. He was sorry now that he had come, for he couldn't see how he would ever obtain what his mother sought.

Things came to a head the third night when Flint accompanied Haw and Sandstone to the *hamaka* of a sick woman. Not even the medicine Haw administered gave her ease. Flint had to bend low to enter the round curing hut that was set apart from the other dwellings and was hot and fetid, filled with the sound of the woman's groans. A fire in a clay brazier gave the only light, but added to the heat. In the close air, Flint felt faint and his head started to spin; he thought with longing of the comfort of his uncle's *bohío*, and unconsciously lifted the necklace and put the pendant in his mouth.

He had no recollection of what happened next, but the curing song burst out of him, the song his mother had brought from the Old Ones. In a trance, Flint sat down on the low stool beside the woman's hammock, covered her thin hand with his own, and let the sounds pour out, a chant as old as time. He chanted on and on, beyond consciousness, and had no memory of when Sandstone joined in, chanting in the same language, the same rhythm, the same cadence, the very same chant that Crab Claw had learned from the Old Ones without knowing what it meant.

Soon their voices floated out into the night, and one by one the villagers gathered and, squatting outside the hut, could only marvel at the sound. No one had heard the chant since the last healer, Sandstone's grandmother, died. Now, here was their own Sandstone and the odd boy pulling it back to earth, pulling it back from where it had been hiding with the Old Ones and calling on them to help.

People started to move around the hut, men and women, hands to shoulders of the one in front, moving clockwise in a rhythm to the strange chant coming from inside, moving all night, those dropping out for a rest replaced by others, later rejoining the circle, stamping the rhythm into the ground with their bare feet and exhaling it with their breath so the healing chant would be bound fast and never leave again.

All this Flint only knew afterward when Haw told him—how the patient's fever had broken at dawn and she sat up and asked for tea. How the villagers had carried both Flint and Sandstone back and laid them in their *hamakas,* where they'd slept well into the next day.

Flint felt refreshed when he woke. He could hardly believe what Haw told him, but as he left the house he noticed a change in the atmosphere of the village, which seemed uplifted from the dreariness he had first encountered. People seemed friendlier, nodding in greeting. A few of the older ones took his hands briefly in their own and bowed, though no one said a word. The children stared at him with big eyes and ran away when he tried to play. His feeling of elation fell, however, when he realized that Pear Blossom and his gang seemed more hostile than ever.

When he and Haw returned from their morning bath, Sandstone met them and held Flint's hands in his own and gazed into his eyes as if waiting for some mystery to be revealed. "Your mother is right," Sandstone said. "We are of the same people. We are family."

Flint bowed his head in acknowledgment, trying not to break down and cry.

"We always heard there were once others like us," Sandstone continued. "Here and on the other islands. But then the Old Ones said they heard they had all died off. No one came looking for us and we went looking for no one." He gazed around at the boats, the fishnets hanging, the baskets of dried fish and clams, his cozy little village hidden from the world, and added, "We like it here," though Flint couldn't help noticing the sadness in the man's eyes.

Haw sensed they wanted to be alone and excused himself, and Sandstone led Flint to sit under a tree on the slight rise behind the village where the wind blew cool and steady. Flint told Sandstone what he knew of his mother's history and her people. He showed him the necklace handed down by his ancestors and told how the pendant carried the healing chant. Sandstone smiled and opened his hand and Flint gasped, for he was holding a necklace identical to his own.

"It belonged to my grandmother," Sandstone explained, "the last of the great healers. With her dying breath she gave it to me, but her souls flew away before she revealed the mystery." He had never worn it, had in fact forgotten about it, until he saw the same necklace on Flint when they met—the reason, he now confessed, that he had allowed him to enter the village.

Sandstone put on his necklace and they sat in silence, absorbing it all, while life went on in the village below. When Sandstone asked what gift he could give in return, Flint almost burst with joy. He told Sandstone of the healing tree they had heard so much about, and the desire of his mother and Matron Greenstone to acquire some of the leaves, perhaps some seeds?

Sandstone stayed quiet for so long that Flint squirmed in embarrassment at the thought that he had made an outrageous request.

"Of course," Sandstone finally said. "We guard the secret of our trees carefully, but we would likewise expect you to guard the secret of the ones we will gift you. A secret to be handed to you and to no one else except your chosen successor when the time is ripe. To do otherwise would be to break the laws laid down by the Old Ones, at your peril and that of your village."

Chapter 31

When Sandstone took Flint to show him the magic trees, Flint was disappointed to see they were hardly distinguishable from the mangroves, striking only by the different shape of their canopy and their leaves.

The seeds were borne in long black pods that hung down in clusters from the top of the branches and all the pods were closed so no seeds were visible.

"It takes four years for the trees to bear a first crop. Then they bear once every year thereafter," Sandstone told him. Harvesting them was forbidden to everyone but an elder who knew just when the time was ripe to sit at the feet of the trees, day after day if need be, and listen and hear them talk when the pods were ready to break open. He alone was allowed to collect the seeds and some of the healing leaves.

Strict ritual handed down from the time of the Old Ones had to be observed or, it was foretold, the trees and their people would die out.

Sandstone shook his head sadly. "More and more of the trees are dying and new ones do not thrive." With a wry smile, he added: "You might have more luck, Flint, perhaps yours will grow and thrive."

Flint was disappointed that Sandstone did not hand over seeds then and there. Later, he led Flint to sit again under the almond tree on the high and dry ground at the back of the village. No one was in sight. Flint nevertheless had a strange feeling of being overlooked, yet saw nothing when he glanced around and Sandstone showed no sign of unease. But then, Sandstone was not his usual wary self. He sat in the sun looking relaxed and smiling, different from the stern and serious man Flint had met on arrival. It was as if Flint's coming had breathed new life into him and his people, alone and isolated for so long, just as Crab Claw had felt isolated until she heard of the possibility of more Old Ones on the other side of the island.

Flint remembered how her eyes sparkled and years seemed to drop from her as she whispered her secrets to him. Her behavior had stunned him, for it was the first time his mother had ever uttered more than a few brief sentences at a time to him or anyone else. He had left home vowing to spend his life helping her to sustain that joy.

Now he noted that Sandstone's expression was serious again and his eyes showed pain as he talked about the future of his people.

"We are dying here, Flint," he said. "The young ones don't want to learn the old ways and they have to go outside to look for spouses. There are so few of us left."

Flint knew what he meant: relatives could not marry each other.

"Once the young ones leave, they never return. I've apprenticed Echo to Haw in the hope that he will return and take my place as head and lead our people. Echo is a good boy, but who knows?"

Sandstone was silent for a while, then he spat. "As for that Pear Blossom, my heart breaks for what he has become. He is the eldest, but I will never name him. His souls have been disarrayed from the start—some evil spirit lodged inside him that makes him do things that are foolish and disruptive. And now he has the younger boys following him. I am worried, Flint. Our gods no longer speak to us. When I pray, the future appears as smoke. Nothing that I sacrifice is pleasing. No answer comes. The gods of the Old Ones have gone silent."

Flint was amazed that a man such as Sandstone could choose him, a mere boy, to confide in, but he understood how there was no one else and he tried to assume a manly expression.

As he sat straighter, out of the corner of his eye he saw a flash of movement. A flock of birds squawked and rose into the skies as if disturbed, slowly wheeling back to settle down again. Sandstone turned at the sound but seemed not to make anything of it. Flint kept silent and wondered if Pear Blossom had been spying on them, and if he had heard what his father had to say. Worse, if he had witnessed Sandstone giving him seeds with whispered instructions for planting and care.

Flint touched his medicine bag in which he had placed the precious objects—four of them, now carefully wrapped, the brown outer shells as hard as rock, each rimmed by a shiny black circle around the edge which made them look watchful, like eyes. The seeds had felt warm as he took them in his trembling hand.

The thought of Pear Blossom knowing his secret made his stomach churn, for the boy and his bullies continued to threaten and harass Flint. In his old village, he had been teased and bullied and called names, but no more than others, and even the greatest bullies could turn into friends in an instant when they played and hunted together. Although he knew he was different, he never felt hated or threatened; most of the time he simply felt like everyone else, living a life that was secure and the rules known.

Here, though, it was different. Never in his life had he

felt evil directed at him as he felt coming from Pear Blossom. It turned him upside down, made him begin to question the world in ways he had never thought about before. The fact that he did not understand their language and whatever they spat out at him made it seem even more threatening, for he recognized a curse for what it was.

He did not know what made them so hostile, though Haw had explained they were simply ignorant, fearful of the outside and of strangers. Pear Blossom and the younger ones felt it was their duty to protect what they had.

But Flint knew that Pear Blossom's resentment had grown when he witnessed how Sandstone was showing such an interest in him.

Now that he'd gotten what he'd come for, he couldn't wait to leave.

Chapter 32

Flint was packed and ready for an early morning departure. At daybreak, he felt a hand shaking him and a voice in his ear whispering, "Flint, come. Before you leave I want to show you something. Something rare, that nobody ever sees."

Flint was surprised to see Pear Blossom of all people bending down with his hand to his lips for silence and, most amazing of all, showing his teeth in a smile. Flint was confused, but the boy's friendliness stifled his inner warning voice. Haw was still snoring in his *hamaka* and nobody else seemed to be stirring in the darkness.

He carefully eased himself up and stooped to pass under the low doorway as he followed Pear Blossom out.

Flint shivered in the morning cold. He was naked except for his breechclout and protective arm and leg bands and his medicine bag and *cemí* guardian that never left his body, along with the pendant his mother had placed around his neck.

Pear Blossom moved silently through the sleeping village, a faint glint of gold on the horizon heralding the dawn. Flint's fear started to melt because they seemed to be alone and he felt that no matter what the boy had in mind, he was two hands taller and much more agile and could handle any tricks Pear Blossom might play.

Pear Blossom was leading him to the only rocky part of the village, behind the almond tree where Flint had sat with Sandstone. A cliff ended in a sheer drop down to the sea, where the waves crashed ceaselessly and threw up white spume, a marked contrast to the gentle wash in the mangroves that lined the other side where their boats were anchored and steps led down to the water from the houses above.

Pear Blossom walked swiftly, turning occasionally to make sure that Flint followed. As they neared the highest point, Flint was startled by a sound behind him and spun around to see Pear Blossom's two bully boys, Water Bug and Sunshine, at his heels. They were laughing, and he felt his stomach clench with fear. Three against one—these two armed with *koas*.

He cursed his stupidity; his only thought now was how to get out of this mess, for he was in dangerous territory, hemmed in by seemingly impenetrable thorny scrub on both sides of the path and enemies behind and in front. Pear Blossom had stopped and was facing them, and his usual scowl had replaced the smile that had seduced Flint from his *hamaka*.

Flint thought of all the fighting he had done in Maima, seriously and for sport, and considered what his best strategy would be. Pear Blossom had a knife in a sheath on his belt. If he could disarm him and take the knife, he should be able to take down the other two.

He was momentarily distracted when Pear Blossom and the others started talking in urgent tones; it sounded as if they were arguing, and that gave him a glimmer of hope that their plans weren't to harm him. But Pear Blossom suddenly lunged at him. "Give me," he ordered.

Flint stumbled backward, thinking Pear Blossom wanted to rip his medicine bag from his body and take back the seeds. But a push from behind sent him almost barreling into the boy, whose intention became clear, for he reached out to grab the necklace Flint's mother had given him.

"No!" Flint thought, unaware that he had shouted it. Never. It was as if his life was bound up with the pendant, his soul reaching backward in time beyond his mother to the Old Ones who had created it, the ones who had breathed medicine and curing and song into it and ensured that he, Flint, was now its custodian. The very shell itself seemed to be crying out at the possibility of desecration, for his ears were tuned to another wavelength where the waters sighed and whispered and his souls seemed to be flying.

Another lunge at the necklace from Pear Blossom brought him back to earth and infused him with a fury he had never known before.

He threw himself at the boy at the same time that he reached to grab the knife, but Pear Blossom quickly blocked him and grabbed the knife himself. Flint pushed him to the right and, as he stumbled, fled past. Pear Blossom turned and slashed at him but it was too late, Flint's maneuver had placed all three of his antagonists together on the other side.

As he faced them, Pear Blossom holding his knife, the others with their sticks, ready to pounce, he knew he couldn't fight all three at once; he would have to find a way of separating them, and that meant moving off the narrow trail so they would be forced to spread out. For now, he had one advantage and he took it and ran, not knowing where the path led, ignoring the brambles and thorns tearing at his skin, praying for a way out, as the sounds of feet came pounding after him.

Flint started to rejoice as the path widened out and he hoped it would open up into a big enough space for him to face his adversaries, but hope died as he realized his error— the path ended at the cliff and a sheer drop to the roiling sea below. He skidded to a stop, looked down through the thorny bushes, and, stomach churning from the thought that he might have tumbled over, turned to face the boys.

They were standing close together and the smile was back on Pear Blossom's face, though it—like those of the others— seemed plastered on and menacing.

Flint had no idea how long he stood there, like a cornered animal, cursing his stupidity, while his adversaries calmly watched and waited, enjoying his plight.

He refused to show fear and held himself straight and proud, casting his eyes around to see if there was a branch big enough that he could grab and use as a weapon. A stone. Anything. But there was nothing, and one of the boys snickered as if reading his mind.

Pear Blossom broke the tension by ordering again in his harsh voice, "Give!" and holding out his hand. Flint ignored him and stared ahead as if looking through them, his thoughts churning all the while. He flexed his hands and twisted his body, limbering up for action, for he knew they would try to rush him and he was determined to take at least one of them down.

His actions seemed to perplex them. They chatted in a low tone that became louder as the other two began to argue with Pear Blossom. But they never shifted their bodies or took their eyes off him. Pear Blossom made one last attempt to get the necklace, adding some other words to "Give" that Flint did not understand. He continued to hold his head straight and ignored the boy, thinking that while they might try to hurt him, they wouldn't have the courage to push him over the edge.

In that he was mistaken—after what sounded like an order from Pear Blossom, they rushed him as one, Pear Blossom reaching his hand once again to grab the necklace. Flint leaned back to avoid him and lost his footing and suddenly he was flying through the air.

Flint was a good diver, accustomed to competing with other boys in daredevil leaps off a cliff into a deep blue hole in the Abacoa river. But now he was tumbling backward with no control over his body, which was forced down so deep his lungs almost gave out before he shot upward again. Alive but battered, he managed to swim toward the cliff and cling to the rocks, vomiting water. His head was hurting badly and the rest of his body felt shredded; he was bleeding all over where the sharp coral rocks had sliced his skin. His first coherent thought was, *Crocodiles! Or sharks*. He needed to get out of the water. His next panic-stricken thought was the pendant, relief coursing through him when he found it still around his neck.

He rested a bit more and took stock of his situation. He had to head back in the direction of the village where their boat was and hide. Haw would be certain to find him.

Every part of his body ached, but he forced his hands and feet to move and propel him slowly around the headland toward the landing. He stopped when he heard sounds from above and listened. The boys without a doubt, their voices high-pitched and anxious. Searching for him. *They cannot afford to let me live*, Flint thought. *This time they will really kill me*. No one would know since they had left before the village came awake.

Flint held on to a sturdy branch sticking out of the water and a sob broke from him. To have come so far, to have succeeded in his quest, and to be unable to return. *No*, he vowed.

The sounds came closer as the boys ran down the path which led to the landing place, probably intending to grab a boat.

By now Flint was in the thick morass, but if they steered close enough to the bank they would spot him. There was nowhere to hide. Unless he went under.

He looked around for a hollow reed to use as a breathing tube. They had done this many times in the river at Maima, hiding in the shallows, staying underwater and breathing through the tubes as they waited for the water birds to come to them so they could grab them by their legs. Their loud cries always made the boys laugh as they twisted their necks and tossed them into their baskets, their mouths watering at the thought of the feast. But now Flint was the prey and he had to move fast.

He found just the right reed and blew through the tube to dislodge sand and dirt before placing it in his mouth. Taking hold of a rock in each hand to anchor himself, he lay on his back with the end of his reed sticking out of the water, just as he heard the first stroke of the paddles coming around the bend. He heard the swish of the canoe cutting through the water and felt the wake as it passed, his air bubbles floating among the foliage.

As they moved out of hearing, he lifted his head above water and breathed normally. He shook his head to get rid of water in his ear but instantly regretted it for the sharp pain that sliced through. He touched his hand to his forehead and felt a large bump already forming. His entire body felt bruised.

The day was becoming lighter as Sun rose on the horizon and he whispered the morning blessing, adding a special prayer to his guardian spirit.

Sounds of the village coming awake drifted toward him—the screams of the children, the growling of the dogs, neighbors calling to one another, the music of panpipes, laughter and whistling, just like a morning at home. The smell of cooking added to his sadness and he couldn't help crying, tears and snot streaming down his face.

Within a finger of time he could hear the boys coming back, their voices urgent and angry. What conclusion would they draw from not seeing any sign of him? They would clearly be frightened. Would they say anything to anyone about what had happened? Flint doubted it.

He ducked underwater again as they approached, using the reed to breathe until their voices faded. He dragged himself up and rested the top half of his body on a flat rock sticking out of the water, letting the sun warm him, putting his head down and trying to calm his spirit, though nothing could stop the pounding headache. He wanted to rise and get to their boat, but he had no energy and sunk back into the water.

He must have fallen into a doze, for the sun was high when he was awakened by the swish of a paddler coming his way, and he ducked behind the reeds. He heard a voice calling his name and at first thought he was dreaming or that it was Plum Blossom trying to trick him. But as the sound grew nearer, he recognized the voice and drew himself up to peer at the boat approaching. Haw! Whose calling was getting louder now—he was shouting Flint's name.

Flint almost fell as he tried to move from his hiding place to where his friend could see him.

"Flint, is that you?" Haw called out as he steered the *kanoa* in his direction and leaned over the side to help him in. "Flint, my friend, what happened? I've been looking everywhere for you. No, don't talk. You've been hurt. Here."

In the boat, Haw helped him sit against some bags. Flint was shivering uncontrollably. Haw fished in his bag and draped a blanket around him. He gently lifted Flint's head to examine the deep bruise which was already turning dark.

"Flint, lean back there and try not to move your head. I'll make you a poultice later. Right now, take this, it will help to ease the pain." He poured powder from his medicine pouch into a spoon and handed it over, following it with water which Flint held to his lips as he drank greedily.

"My friend," Haw said as he settled himself to steer the boat, "try to stay awake. We'll make camp soon and I'll look at your wounds."

Within minutes, the swish of the paddles ceased as the boat glided gently downstream.

Chapter 33

Flint remembered little of the rest of the day and night. Haw took him to a fishing camp where fishermen helped him off the boat and into a *hamaka*. Haw tended his wounds and fed him fish tea, then gave him coca and lime to chew until he fell into a deep sleep. When he woke the next morning, the men had already left.

Although he rose at sunrise as usual, he could barely haul his battered body from the *hamaka*. Haw said they would spend a few more days there so Flint could fully recover.

The third day they were sitting by the fire eating roasted fish when Flint said, "I am truly sorry I was not able to say goodbye to Sandstone and thank him. What will he think of me?"

Haw smiled. "You might see him sooner than you think."

"You mean he's coming here?"

Haw was noncommittal as he tore into a piece of flesh. "Perhaps."

Flint had another worry. "But Haw, what will I tell him?" Although it pained him to talk about it, he had shared with Haw the story of his encounter with Pear Blossom and his bully boys.

"You will say nothing. Sandstone is the chief and a very astute one, though his people are so few. He will decide how this is to be handled. He will extract the truth. Pear Blossom might lie through his teeth but the other boys will crack. Whatever happens now is for the village elders to decide."

Earlier, Haw had described how when he woke the day before and saw that Flint was already up, he thought nothing of it, until the girl Pearl came rushing in and told him that she had overheard the boys quarreling with each other and talking about Flint as if he had gone over the cliff and drowned. "When Pearl told me that, I came looking for you. I'm sure she must have spoken to Sandstone too, but I made sure I packed my boat and got away without him seeing me. I didn't want us to get involved in a family quarrel."

"But . . ." Flint knew that leaving without asking permission of the chief was not common courtesy.

"When I left, I signaled to Sandstone that everything was all right and he understood that I had found you."

When they finished eating, Haw picked up his string bag and said he wanted to harvest *toona* fruit along the shore. Flint was alone except for the crabs scuttling into their holes and iguanas waking for their morning hunt. He was so lost in thought that he didn't see the *kanoa* until it was close to shore. Sandstone blew a greeting on his horn as he beached his boat.

He scrutinized Flint carefully as he spoke: "I see you, Flint. You are well?"

"I am well, Chief."

"And our friend Haw?"

"Haw is well, Chief, he is gathering *toona* fruit. May I offer you some tea?"

"Thank you."

Courtesies completed, Flint poured the tea into a calabash cup and handed it to Sandstone and refilled his own. As they sipped, the silence lengthened between them.

Finally, Sandstone reached for his bag, drew out a beautifully beaded purse, and held it out to Flint. "I am not staying, there are urgent matters at home to be dealt with. But Haw told me where you'd be and I wanted to say goodbye and offer you a gift for your mother. I hope one day, the gods willing, you will bring her to meet us. In the meantime, when you get home, tell her she has raised a good boy. One who I wished I had as a son."

Sandstone had tears in his eyes when he said this and Flint, too, felt himself tearing up.

After some time, Sandstone said, "My daughter Pearl will soon come of age. I would like to find her a good husband, someone outside the village who is not unlike us and who would introduce her to the world . . . Perhaps you will come this way again, Flint, when you have reached manhood and are looking for a wife?" Sandstone's eyes crinkled in a smile. Then he added, "But I sense in my bones that your *cemíes* might have a bigger destiny for you."

Flint grinned broadly as he recognized the offer, flattered that such an important man would think him worthy, but too shy to say anything. Not that anything needed to be said. He had liked the girl Pearl too. Whatever the *cemíes* decided, would be.

"You need never be fearful if you return to my village, Flint, as long as I am chief. Evil will always be rooted out."

Flint knew he was referring to Plum Blossom and his friends and wondered what kind of punishment they would undergo. If it were Maima, any punishment would be possible, including—for something that might be seen as attempted murder—a death sentence. He shuddered. To put the thought out of his head he picked up the bag Sandstone had brought as a gift for his mother and thanked him.

"Let us part as blood brothers, Flint," Sandstone said, reaching for the flint knife at his belt. "I will always be your protector."

He made a small nick in his wrist and held it out as the blood pooled and Flint did the same on his wrist. They put their hands together so their blood mingled and they exchanged names as *guatiaos*.

Nothing more was said as Sandstone drained his tea and placed the cup on the sand. He rose and Flint did too.

"Haw I will see again soon. I don't need to tell him goodbye."

With that, Sandstone jumped into the boat which Flint helped to push off. He stood up holding his paddle and waved it at Flint before sweeping it into the water. "Farewell," he cried.

"Farewell, *Guama*," Flint called out, with tears in his eyes and his heart overflowing with a happiness he would never have imagined coming so soon after the incident on the cliff.

Flint was silent as he and Haw paddled back to Turtle Village, the seeds still carefully wrapped and stowed in his medicine pouch that had survived his near drowning, the instructions for planting and care firmly implanted in his memory. He was sworn to secrecy, even from Haw who was Sandstone's blood brother and one of the few outsiders allowed into the village. Flint was ashamed to keep secrets from Haw, and he could almost feel the seeds hot and pulsating in the medicine pouch which lay on his chest.

Haw seemed pensive too, but their silence was companionable as they stroked together and their boat skimmed over the waves.

When they pulled into the landing stage at Turtle Village, Haw spoke: "I will tell no one of what happened, Flint." He paused in the act of unloading his gear and looked Flint in the eye. "I am glad I met you. I see sorrow and darkness ahead of you, but you have the gift of song. You will mend souls that are broken, including your own."

With that, Haw stowed his pack on his back and walked away.

Flint stood there, stunned. *I am too young for sorrow,* he told himself. Then dismissed the thought as he straightened his back and followed Haw. *I am almost a man. Why so much talk of darkness?*

The village children helped push these thoughts away as they rushed to greet him.

Chapter 34

O nce he had what he'd come for, Flint had been anxious to leave for home, though Haw insisted he stay until he pronounced Flint fully recovered from his ordeal.

Now on the last leg of his homeward journey, he felt like flying down the mountain path, but he slowed his pace, mindful of the pack on his back almost as big as he. The tumpline across his forehead which steadied the bag tightened with every step, but Flint hardly noticed. Ever since he'd topped the dip in the mountains from which he could look to the next ridge in the direction of Maima village, his joy knew no bounds. His home was only one day's journey away. He had added nine knots to his string since leaving Turtle Village, nearly three ten knots since leaving home.

He dismissed the little worm of anxiety that arose when he saw the blue skies smudged by dark clouds from what looked like a huge forest fire. He hoped the fire was much farther away than it seemed. He didn't want to vary his route. Nothing must slow him down. Not with the journey's end in sight.

The burden he had carried, uphill and down, was feeling as light as his spirits. He, Flint, had fulfilled his task without a hitch and in record time too. Although he was not proud by nature, he knew that his accomplishment would make everyone in the village view him with different eyes. Perhaps the *kacike* and his nobles would deign to take notice of their humble *naboría*, though he'd left them at war with his patroness Matron Greenstone. Yet what other boy of less than fourteen summers had gone alone on such a journey?

The successful conclusion of this feat would enable him to take a new name, to begin the accumulation of names that—like his tattoos—would mark each significant accomplishment on the path of life. He already planned to use the generous gift he believed Matron Greenstone would present to him to order a beautiful *cemí* for the family shrine from the finest workshop in the village. Perhaps an image created by the owner's young niece Night Orchid.

And then there was the other, secret triumph to be savored, to be shared with no one but his mother Crab Claw. He thought of how he would take her outside the village to a place where no one could overhear, to tell her the story of how he had managed to obtain the precious seeds of the tree that heals all pain. And perhaps—he kept stumbling on what he would do when the time came—perhaps he would withhold from her the only really frightening part of the whole trip, where he nearly lost not just that treasure, but his life.

Every time Flint thought of the miracle seeds, of holding them, of how they made his hand tingle, he was also forced to think of the dream in which the object that caused his hand to burn with fire was not a miracle seed at all but a stone.

The dream had come after Flint left Turtle Village for home. It haunted his waking thoughts, flashing into his mind at awkward moments, so he knew it was one of utmost importance. But what was it saying? It featured the sea, so was it simply a story of his journey to the coast? It featured a woman, so was it foretelling his transition to manhood? The most chilling aspect was that the dream had not occurred during the night but in the daytime, early one morning as he stood on a plateau, waiting to greet the sunrise.

He had chanted the morning blessing, letting the sacred herb trickle through his fingers. Up to that moment, the morning had been alive with the familiar sounds of the forest. As he'd let fall the last shred of *tabako*, he became conscious of a hush, a stillness that kept him rooted to the spot and he held his breath, how long he did not know, for he lost track of time. Out of the stillness had come the lone voice of a bird, a bird that had no right to be in that place at that time; not in the high mountains; it was a bird of the sea and coastline, such as he had seen at Turtle Village.

Its cries had so shattered the silence that it almost unhinged him, for in that moment he was just surfacing from a dive he had made to the bottom of the sea where a woman of great beauty, her hair unbound, had smiled and beckoned him with her eyes. He swam toward her and took the stone she held out as if this was the most natural thing in the world. It was as if she had been waiting for him, for this precise moment, just as the first medicine man Guahayona had found White Shell Woman waiting beneath the sea with the emblems of his craft, the sacred stones for his rattle.

Flint knew he had been dreaming, and shook his head in bewilderment at having dozed off so soon after a good night's sleep; it was the squawking bird that had awakened him.

But as he watched the bird disappearing, Flint had been stunned to find himself sitting on the ground, holding in his hand some shiny thing, a rock crystal refracting light. Where had it come from? He must have taken it from his pack without thinking, as he had collected a few of the most beautiful pebbles and shells from Turtle Village to take home as gifts— though he had no memory of one like this.

He had felt drained and sat for a long time, trying to collect his thoughts and his strength, surprised that so much time had passed. For Sun was now high in the sky, when his last waking memory had been of greeting its birth that morning.

Flint was trembling in all his limbs as he took up his pack and got ready to continue his journey. Without thinking, he had dropped the crystal into his medicine pouch. He'd stumbled a bit as he set off. But as his strength came back, his thoughts of homecoming helped push the strange dream aside. It was nothing more, he told himself, than a reminder of his trip to the sea.

Chapter 35

Sunlight filtering through the trees marked Flint's emergence from the gloomy canopy of the dense forest into more open country dotted with towering royal palms. The path, though overgrown, was easier to make out. Without realizing it, he slowed his pace, so involved was he in the fantasy of his first meal back home after a diet of trail rations, his mouth watering at the thought . . . *A nice pepperpot stew with* agouti *perhaps or fish with some fresh* kasabe *to dip in it, smoked mussels hopefully, baked squash, and a nice long drink of* mabí *to wash it down. Then sweet corn cakes smothered in wild honey and almonds . . .*

So deeply was he savoring the meal that he didn't notice when he moved from the sun-dappled path into a dark tunnel formed by huge trees and wild creepers overhanging the trail. He was forced to brake so suddenly he almost toppled. He instinctively raised his *koa* as the hair on his scalp lifted and he felt his head growing while his feet stayed rooted to the ground. His senses were on full alert. He remained perfectly still, eyes searching, ears listening for the smallest sound. But no leaves stirred, no birds or insects murmured. The whole world seemed to hold its breath.

He cautiously raised his left hand and used it to loosen the carrying strap from his forehead, and without further movement allowed the pack to fall to the ground, using the back of his heel to break the fall. Even so, the stillness magnified the sound as it hit the ground.

Moving his head slightly, out of the corner of his eyes he studied the bushes on the high banks on either side but saw nothing amiss. He had been stopped at a critical point in the path, just where it bent to avoid thick roots and curved back on itself, so he could see nothing ahead and nothing behind. He was hemmed in by an invisible force. Whatever spirit had planned this had selected the ambush carefully. But why? And he of all people? He had done nothing to offend anyone. He wanted to shout this aloud but fear sealed his lips.

Flint peered down at the path and studied it carefully for footprints even though he knew a spirit would leave no tracks, unless it happened to be the dread bush spirit that walked with its feet turned backward in order to deceive. Then he saw it, looking for all the world like a bunch of dried sticks windblown from a tree—a contrivance, deliberately set in his path.

Flint's hands were shaking so much he knew his weapons would be useless in a confrontation. He was dying to call out even though the sound of his voice could be captured and used against him by a clever enemy. But his throat was so dry no sound came. Flint hoped his adversary would show himself soon or he was sure his knees would give way. He tried to slow his breathing, to impose stillness and patience on his mind as he did when he waited for game. To focus, focus on a still point in front of his eyes.

"Flint!"

Flint jumped. Blessed! Had he heard his name called? Not his everyday name but his traveling name that was known to no one but his parents and the holy man who had bestowed it on him when he left home, another way of protecting him on his journey.

Flint's heart was racing wildly as he looked toward the high bank from where the sound came. For a spirit to know his secret name meant it already had him in its power.

"Flint!"

The call came louder this time, and although the voice was hoarse like a spirit, it did seem human. Flint spun around as he heard the breaking of sticks behind him and the bushes parted to reveal the *behike*. Candlewood.

Flint slumped as the tension drained from his body, though the *behike* up close was almost as frightening as a real bush spirit. He let his *koa* drop and fell to his knees. Clasping his hands in front of himself in submission, he began the recital of all nine of Candlewood's ceremonial names.

"O stop, boy," Candlewood commanded, coming to stand in front of Flint, who dared not raise his eyes.

"Greetings, Elder," the boy murmured, sitting back on his heels but with his hands still clasped and his head bowed. Candlewood stood there saying nothing for an inordinately long span of time.

When Flint finally lifted his eyes he was shocked at the *behike*'s appearance. Candlewood was very old, and looked more than ever like a broken-down tree loaded with moss. He was quite tall with skinny legs and his head was crowned by gray locks that he left long and loose, parting only enough to reveal shining earspools of mother-of-pearl. His sunken cheeks made his beaky nose appear larger and his powerful eyebrows were like black caterpillars above his deepset eyes. His body paint was smudged, but beneath his breastplate were tattoos of his powerful protective spirits.

The *behike* began to sway on his feet and tottered over to a fallen log to sit down. Forgetting his fear, Flint rose and offered him water, but the old man indicated his own container and lifted it to his mouth and drank deeply. His woeful appearance took the edge off Flint's fear, for he looked on the verge of collapse. Flint wet his lips several times before he mustered the courage to speak.

"Elder, I have no food to offer you, but I could go and find something for you . . . with respect, that is . . . Berries or . . . parrot . . . I could trap one easily . . . if you are hungry, that is . . ."

Candlewood shook his head, but said nothing and stared at Flint as if weighing him up.

Flint kneeled again and sat back on his heels, afraid to even breathe under the *behike*'s scrutiny. Everyone knew Candlewood's ways were old and not always understandable. But attracting his eye was something most people tried to avoid. Flint was trapped.

When Candlewood finally spoke, he wheezed as if every breath was painful. "Young Flint, you have been on a journey. You bring important items for Matron Greenstone. You have fulfilled your mother's heart's desires. You are due home before sunset."

Flint was not surprised at Candlewood knowing this. But his heart leaped at the next statement: "Young Flint, this day another path has been chosen for you." The boy waited for more, knowing he had no say in the matter, whatever it was. The last thing he expected was Candlewood saying, "From now on you will follow me."

Flint opened his mouth then shut it quickly. He'd been trained from birth to obey his elders and Candlewood was of the highest rank, next to the *kacike* the most important personage in their village. Besides, he was rumored to be the most powerful man in the world.

"Yes, Elder," he said, and bowed his head, trying to hide his dismay. Normally a *behike*'s follower would be a boy destined to be like him, one who had been touched by the spirits or showed some sign of being called to the vocation from early childhood. It was unheard of for an ordinary boy, as Flint considered himself, to be chosen. It was true that he had a remarkable knowledge of the bush and its pathways for someone his age; he knew all the plants used for healing and ceremonies and the proper way to collect them so as not to offend the Lord of the Forest—but that was all.

"Young Flint, the world has been turned upside down." Candlewood had to pause to catch his breath before each sentence. "Consider this day like no other. The beginning of a new age. In time, all will be made known to you. Come. We must hurry."

Flint bent down to collect his pack, giving himself time to wipe any expression from his face. He was devastated. Not to reach Maima before day's end and see his family again after such a long journey? Not to stand proudly in front of Matron Greenstone and hand over her treasures? Not to accept the congratulations and new respect in people's eyes?

Candlewood used his stick to rise slowly to his feet. He pointed at Flint's pack. "You will not need these where you are going. Carry only what you must and leave the rest behind."

"But my lady . . ." Flint bit off the protest at a look from Candlewood. "Yes, Elder."

The old man's instructions made no sense. Flint could not imagine what would happen to him if he returned home without Matron Greenstone's precious goods. Acquired on a journey no boy his age had ever undertaken. Leaving him with a sore back, aching limbs, and calluses on his feet, but a triumphant heart and a head full of the most amazing sights and sounds. He couldn't wait to get home to sit in front of the fire surrounded by family and kin and tell all. And now the elder was about to ruin everything. Perhaps the *behike* was what his enemies said he was, after all: a spoiler.

Flint suppressed the hot tears that threatened to spill out along with his angry thoughts, and guiltily glanced sideways at the fearsome old man who was said to read people's minds. His stomach knotted at the thought of leaving the precious trade goods behind. Not just Matron Greenstone, but what would his mother say, his uncle, at such a failure? It would be a blot on the family's reputation for having produced such a useless son. They would be disgraced forever. The Matron would see to that. No, there was no way he could return home without the—

"Don't get ahead of yourself, young Flint." Candlewood's tone was mild but the boy lurched, unsure of what he meant. Had the elder been reading his thoughts? "The *cemíes* have their ways of rearranging our affairs. We are but pawns in their hands."

Under Candlewood's unwavering stare, Flint did as he was told and opened his pack; he removed his blanket and *hamaka* and wrapped them together, hanging them from his back in place of the heavier pack. Everything else he carried on his person as he always did: his ration bag, his water calabash and cooking calabash and spoon, his medicine pouch with what was left of his *tabako*, his reed tube in which he carried his *bixa* and other paints and his vomiting spatula, his tinderbox and flint, and, hanging from his belt, his small and light axe. His throwing spear and *atlatl* he wore crosswise hanging across his back.

Before closing his pack, he pulled out a package wrapped in wilted papaya leaves and tied with string. A gift of jerked shark steaks sent by the leading matron of Turtle Village to Matron Greenstone. He stuffed it into his ration bag before carefully noting markers so he could find his other possessions later. He set off behind Candlewood, who had plunged into the bush. Flint winced as brambles and coarse ferns scratched at his face and body and insects colonized him. Blessed! Where was the elder taking him?

Chapter 36

It was dawn when Night Orchid awoke. She had no idea where she was nor how she came to be outdoors. Scratching at insect bites, she whimpered as the full horror of the night came back. "Blessed Mother, help me," she gasped, her hand automatically clutching the *cemí* which hung around her neck, not even thinking how it got there. She crept out from the bushes but felt faint when she stood, and fell back to the ground. She retched and vomited and in between lay full length and clawed at the ground and howled until she lay silent from exhaustion.

She must have fallen asleep again, for when she came to, she could feel the heat on her body from Sun, who was already two fingers in the sky. She was cheered by the thought that Sun could still rise, for it meant that there were still some of her people to pull it from the embrace of night. All she had to do now was find them. Even though she was late, she closed her eyes and whispered the morning blessing before taking stock of her surroundings.

She was far from home, that is all she knew, on the edge of a high ridge from which she could see the surrounding countryside, though she had no consciousness of climbing in the night. She looked carefully around in all directions but recognized nothing. There was no sign of her own or any other village. No indication that other human beings even existed, nothing but the tree-clad slopes and mountains blue in the distance. Nothing but the dark primeval forest at her back.

How she'd arrived at this place and what happened the night before seemed as remote and unbelievable as a dream. Was Maima really destroyed? In her heart she knew it to be so. Her parents were among those who had continued to believe and trust in the *behike* Candlewood, and she trusted him too. Candlewood had rescued her from the hut. He was not given to idle gestures and cruel jokes, no matter what his enemies said. Besides, wasn't Candlewood the one who had cured her as a child, casting out the bad spirits that had caused her to fall unconscious and foam at the mouth whenever they took hold of her body? Didn't she owe her life to him?

She was standing right on the edge where the ridge was bare of all but shrubs and the thick underbrush where she had hidden. Immediately behind the bushes and confining her to this little edge of clearing, the thick forest began, a forest that should be avoided by all except the hunters who only went into it fully protected against the monsters that lurked.

Night Orchid was without protection of any kind, for so she had entered the *guanara*, waiting to be fully clothed once her period of seclusion ended. She had none of the artifacts of daily living: not even the body covering of sacred red *bixa* paste to keep insects and bad spirits away. She had no medicine pouch or any weapon, nor the tools of her trade—her axe and chisel and gouge that were never far from her. She was naked except for the raffia belt holding her menstrual pad in place and the cotton wrap she had tied around her body.

Holding up the string around her neck to look properly at the pendant Candlewood had given her, she was shocked to see that it was *guanín*. She could tell from the smell, the mixture of gold, copper, and silver which Our Lady preferred. She had heard visitors say that while gold meant nothing to her people who gave it freely to the *paranaghiri*, not understanding its value to them, the *paranaghiri* did not understand the real value of *guanín*, the holy metal modeled to reflect the colors of the bird of transcendence, Kolibri, the hummingbird.

The pendant was an object of great wealth and power that a girl like her could never aspire to own. Yet this is what Candlewood had given her as her guide. For there was not the slightest sign of the path she must have taken in her flight the night before. No turning back. Facing the rising sun, she saw a faint trail, a clear sign that she had to carry on. East, as Candlewood had instructed.

As she put one foot in front of the other, she felt a blow from behind as if someone had slapped her. She spun around, her heart hammering. There was no one there. But in that instant she remembered the package Candlewood had given her. *Guard it with your life,* he had said, and she'd left it in the bushes where she was now groveling on hands and knees to find it.

When she picked up the package, and looked at it closely for the first time, her souls almost left her for she saw what it was. The missing Bundle. It had to be. "Why me?" is all Night Orchid could wail, feeling like the child she was. "Why me?"

From all around her came the reassuring cry, *Jiu, jiu, jiu.*

There was no mistaking the Bundle, for every year during solstice, it was taken out of the temple and hung from the ceremonial pole in the longhouse for all to see. Every Taíno child had the opportunity to gaze on this object as it was unwrapped from its most sacred covering, the dried bladder of *hicotea*, the land turtle, mother of the race, that was killed ceremoniously for just this purpose. After the ceremonies to invoke its blessing for the coming year, the Bundle was re-wrapped in several protective layers before it was returned to its hiding place. The object that Night Orchid held was in its outer covering, a small, ordinary-looking bag of tanned sealskin.

Night Orchid's whole body was trembling so much that she almost dropped the holy relic. Then she looked at it again and couldn't believe what she was experiencing. That she, the child of Pebble and Mockingbird of the Mud Fish family, low-ranking members of the Owl Clan, could be entrusted with something so precious.

She was tempted to open it to check if it was real, but fear held her back. Whatever it was, she had been ordered to guard it with her life. But why her? And how had the *behike* Candlewood got hold of it? Was he the one who had stolen it? Had he taken it back from the thief? What was he doing back in Maima village? How come Bright Star or Cedar Wax had not mentioned him? Or had he been walking about invisible the whole time, as some claimed he did?

Night Orchid was stunned at this new burden thrust upon her, yet pleased in a way, for it meant the precious object had not fallen into the hands of their enemies. It still belonged to them, the believers. The ones who would never forsake the holy ones for the foreign idols. Now here it was in her hands. How was she supposed to take care of it?

"Night Orchid has turned into such a sensible girl," she once heard her mother confiding to a friend.

"Who would have thought it, after such a miserable start?"

"Exactly. But she's the kind of girl you'd want beside you if you were ever in trouble. She'd know exactly what to do."

"Candlewood knew how to right her souls."

"That's why I no longer worry about her. As if she was born old and knowing things."

And though she had overheard this just after her mother and the other women had been praising the beauty of her sister, and the stamina of her brother Cloud who was on his way to becoming a fine ballplayer, Night Orchid felt uplifted by her mother's remarks, as if she had been singled out for something special. She was keenly aware from an early age that she was the least endowed and the least favored of the children. Plus, she was constantly reminded in so many ways of the difficulties of her childhood. But after her mother's remarks, she had made a vow to be sensible and brave if she couldn't be beautiful, to make her mother proud of her.

Thinking of her mother now only made her cry afresh. What use was it to be anything at all if her world no longer existed? Who would care if she was sensible or not? But then, feeling the Bundle that was still tightly clutched in her hand, she thought that someone did care. Candlewood had cared enough to save the Bundle, and as long as it existed, her world still existed, a world that went all the way back to First Time.

She didn't know where that world was located now or what form it would take. She only knew that she was the Keeper of the Bundle, and she had to fulfill the task that had been entrusted to her, to be, if nothing else, worthy of her mother's evaluation and Candlewood's trust.

She untied the cotton wrap, not noticing that the object for which her parents had given so much trade was now dirty and covered in burrs, ripped in places with some of the precious beads hanging by threads. She wrapped the Bundle into a corner and folded the cloth several times around her waist and then tied it and adjusted the folds so that the Bundle lay flat against her body and hidden from view. She didn't know why she felt the need to hide it since she seemed to be totally alone, but her spirits lifted from just this one decisive gesture.

The wrap felt strange against her body, yet she pretended it was the skirt she would have been given at her Coming Out, the sign that she had joined the ranks of women. She set off on the trail, with every stride feeling the soft Bundle against her belly. Somehow it felt reassuring, as if it too was alive and breathing, as if she was not alone in the world after all, but in fortunate company.

Chapter 37

Despite his age and frail condition, Candlewood made good progress at the start, but eventually began to slow and lean more heavily on his stick as they traveled silently in single file. At times, it seemed as if they were hardly moving. Flint itched with impatience at the pace.

Candlewood stopped frequently, his body racked by coughs and constant wheezing. They were traveling now through pine forest, the undergrowth thick with spiky ferns and the path slick with pine needles. No bright splash of blossoms relieved the green haze. Flint longed to ask questions but dared not. Where was the *behike* taking him and why? He estimated that they were less than a hand away from darkness.

He stopped as the *behike* paused and did something he had not done before. Candlewood turned and faced the direction from which they'd come and gazed for a long time. He held up his head and sniffed the air and Flint followed his eyes and listened with his hunter's mind too, but there was nothing to see or hear.

Candlewood nodded as if in satisfaction and turned back without looking at Flint. The boy had no idea what that was about. Had he been expecting pursuit of some sort? But who and why? This caused Flint's insides to churn with a nameless fear to the point where he kept glancing back. He was barely putting one foot in front of the other, too tired and full of despair to care anymore. He felt hot tears pricking his eyes and blinked hard so as not to break down.

"You can cry if you want, young Flint. No one is watching."

Flint nearly leaped out of his skin. The man had eyes in his back! And was that a cough or a chuckle he heard rumbling from that deep throat? Flint tried to still his beating heart.

You must act like a warrior, Flint. Warriors never give up. He could hear his uncle's voice when as a small boy his spear had fallen short of a target or his trap had unraveled just as a bird perched on it. His uncle had been saying this since he was five summers. Being a warrior, he knew, meant acquiring the virtues of The People, no matter one's station in life: fortitude, endurance, bravery, honesty, generosity, unwavering dedication to duty, absolute loyalty to the leader, respect for ancestral laws, and unremitting vigilance and offerings to the *cemíes*.

Without warning, the landscape changed again and they plunged into a mist forest where the gnarled, stunted trees and ferns covered with hanging moss emerged from the fog like ghosts. The old man kept appearing and disappearing in front of Flint.

Suddenly the mist came down so thick Flint stopped in his tracks. When it lifted, he found himself in a small clearing, but the *behike* and the path had disappeared. Flint stood there as the mist swirled around him, as if playing, lifting to touch the towering trees some distance away, then clearing to give him a glimpse of the deep valleys and glittering peaks as far as the eye could see, before descending to ground level again. He had a rough idea of where he was now. But where was Candlewood?

"Elder," Flint began calling softly at first, then louder when there was no reply. "*Guama?* My Lord?"

His words seemed unnaturally loud, for there was no other sound but the dripping of water off the leaves, the murmur of the tree frogs, and the mournful cadence of a solitaire.

Flint moved from one end of the clearing to another to find the path, yet there was no break in the ferns. He saw his own footprints going in circles on the damp ground, but no other. Candlewood had flown! Flint's heart pounded in his chest. *The* behike *has flown away and left me stranded. Is this another of his jokes?*

Flint felt his resentment building again. Why was the *behike* doing this to him? What had he, Flint, ever done to invite such punishment? Why had the elder chosen him to torment?

Then his hunter self took over and he stood perfectly still, not moving a muscle, using his ears. He stood for a long time, emptying his mind, processing each distinct sound. Finally, he heard it: a sound out of place.

He thought it was a faint voice and started up in that direction, but then it was calling him from another place, a tree on the opposite side of the clearing. "Flint," faintly and with what sounded like an evil laugh. The boy felt stupid when he rushed to the tree only to hear the voice again from a different direction. The *behike* was surely playing tricks on him.

The anxieties of the day finally took their toll. Flint threw himself on the ground and burst into tears. He didn't care. He knew it wasn't manly but he had had all he could take. He didn't want to be considered a man. He didn't care if the *behike* killed him now. What did it matter? Nothing mattered. He sobbed himself to exhaustion.

Completely drained, he continued to lie there on his side, eyes closed, one ear to the ground, letting the sounds of the forest gradually fill his consciousness. Soon he began to sense a presence by smell. A human smell. He opened his eyes and saw two dirty feet, the old man's horny toenails, and heard his cackle followed by a coughing fit. Flint sat up, ashamed and fearful of the punishment, but Candlewood merely smiled.

"Come, we'll have a good rest for tomorrow."

Tomorrow? Flint shook his head as he stood. He wished it was already tomorrow. He never wanted to go through another day like this one.

He scrambled up and followed Candlewood. The *behike* soon halted and pointed to a sheer cliff in the side of a hill above them. "There," he said.

O Blessed, Flint thought, *we are not going to climb that.* But when he looked more closely, he saw a dark hole at the base of the cliff. A cave. Shelter for the night.

As Flint trailed the *behike* up the slope, his mind was already traveling to the fire he would light, the tea he would brew, the hope that the elder might have food stashed away. With a destination in sight, his dark mood began to lift.

Chapter 38

The cave was a single chamber, not very deep, the roof sloping upward at the back to three times the height of a man. There was a small opening to the sky through which the dying light filtered. Bats twittered and flew about then settled back on the ceiling.

The cave was dry and smelled strongly of *tabako* and guano. It seemed a comfortable little nest with calabashes and three firestones set just under the hole where smoke escaped. While Flint undid his packs and looked around, Candlewood slumped to the ground with his back against the cave wall, coughing.

Flint was pleased to see a stack of wood and full water jars so he wouldn't have to go outside and risk being seized by an *opía* prowling the darkness looking for human prey.

He arranged wood in the fireplace while casting worried glances at Candlewood. With a fire blazing and water boiling, he unrolled his *hamaka* and his blanket and took them over to the *behike,* since there was no sign that he had brought his own. He spread out the blanket near the fire and helped Candlewood ease himself onto it; the old man seemed to have gotten so weak he could hardly move himself. He lay on his side, feet drawn up and his face to the wall. *Guay!* Suppose Candlewood died on him, what would he do?

Flint kneeled beside Candlewood and whispered, draping

the blanket across his shoulders, "Elder, I am making tea. It will make you feel better." The old man barely twitched in response.

As the scent of mint filled the cave, Flint took a calabash over to Candlewood and helped him sit up and take a deep draft before he dropped back down again. But the tea seemed to revive him, for in a few minutes he sat up and drained the cup. Flint poured more tea and they drank in silence. He was pleased to see that Candlewood seemed livelier. But he worried that his own food pack was empty and it was too late to go scavenging outside.

He couldn't help thinking that if he had gotten home as planned, he would now be eating some of his mother's pepperpot stew.

"It might not be as good as your mother's, but you just might find a little *ajiako* in the pot."

Candlewood was reading his mind again. Was there really stew to be had or was this another of his jokes? Flint picked up the blackened cooking pot and when he took the lid off, it was stew all right. He immediately placed it by the fire to heat.

"And here!" Candlewood reached into his pack and with a flourish pulled out *kasabe*. Flint couldn't help smiling as he piled more wood on the fire.

When they finished eating, Candlewood had another surprise. He indicated Flint's ration bag and held out his hand. "Now I will have a nice slice, thank you, of Matron Greenstone's barbecued meat."

Flint was glad he was sitting down or he would have fainted. The man knew everything. Matron Greenstone's jerked shark steaks! Flint might have yielded on the point of stashing her other treasures, but no way was anyone going to touch Matron Greenstone's smoked meat. She had expressly given the most careful instructions regarding its packing and carriage.

Flint did not move. He sat there looking open-mouthed at Candlewood while the old man smiled faintly at him. It wasn't a sinister smile, but fatherly, as if he knew that Flint would not deny him. Flint in years to come would have no memory of getting up and reaching into his pack and bringing out the food. But he must have, for Candlewood hadn't moved yet the package was in his hand and he was already cutting the string with his knife.

"Mmmmmm," he said as he bent down to smell the rich aroma of spices used to cure it. Candlewood sliced off a bit and popped it into his mouth. He said "Mmm" again, while Flint watched in horror. This, he knew, meant certain death. If Candlewood didn't end up killing him, Matron Greenstone would.

Candlewood sliced off a piece and held it out on the knife toward Flint, but the boy almost gagged on his fear and shook his head. It was one thing for someone else to consume the meat, but for him it would be sacrilege, compounding the error. It would be theft.

Candlewood merely smiled at Flint's refusal and popped the meat into his own mouth. With each bite, he seemed to regain his strength and a kind of impish humor—he kept darting smiles at Flint as he ate. Finally, when he had had enough, he wiped his knife and rewrapped the package which was now considerably smaller. He put it into his own pack, where the *kasabe* had been stowed.

"Flint, I assure you Matron Greenstone will not miss it. Were she in a position to know, she would welcome our consuming it. Since you don't want any, there will be more for me in the morning." And he had the nerve to pat his stomach and belch loudly. Then he fished around in his pouch, stuck a big wad of chewing *tabako* in his cheek, and lay back down with every sign of contentment.

Flint shook his head at the trouble the *behike* was causing and the unfairness of it all. The elder soon snored loudly, wrapped in Flint's blanket. The boy pulled his shivering body closer to the fire. It was going to be a long night.

Flint was jerked awake by the sound of Candlewood's voice.

"Tomorrow, Flint, I will tell you all. You will become a new person. And soon, you will take *kohoba* with me. Sleep now, my spirit warrior."

Candlewood began to snore again, having said the very words that would keep Flint awake. What did he mean by *telling all*? Flint would become a new person? Was something wrong with the old one? Why did he call Flint a warrior when he hadn't yet come of age? And, most thrilling and horrifying of all, how could Flint take *kohoba* when he hadn't yet undergone the initiation into manhood?

Kohoba was the means by which the gods spoke to men and men could ask questions of the gods. The sacred powder could only be consumed by those who had experienced the rituals and were tough enough to withstand the power engendered by that communion. *Kacikes* and nobles, priests and medicine men, the initiated and bravest warriors.

For a boy to take *kohoba* would not only be the ultimate sacrilege but the power would surely be too much for his frail being. Flint began to wonder if Candlewood's souls had shifted as some feared, so that he was no longer responsible for his actions. Well, that might be so, but the old man could not force him to commit that transgression, and that was that.

Flint folded his arms across his chest and sat back on his haunches. He searched for answers in the dancing flames but none came. He wondered why the elder would want to destroy his sleep that night, knowing the effect his words would have. Why couldn't he have waited till morning to say whatever he wanted and so spare him the agony of speculating on top of freezing to death?

Chapter 39

Slick with sweat and itching from insect bites, Night Orchid was barely conscious of moving. Sun had already sailed far west and the shadows were lengthening. She was dying of thirst. Food was to be had in the forest, fruit and berries and nuts and even vines that yielded water when cut, but she was too scared to enter that dark canopy. And not a single animal scurried across her path.

The trail itself offered little shade for it was cut into the escarpment that fell away to one side, and though she had to watch her footing on the slippery shale, it did give her a sweeping panoramic view of the surrounding country. Yet the very openness contributed to her loneliness, as the mountains and valleys seemed untouched by human footprint, alien and uncaring. The only thing that kept her going was the sight in the far distance of a clump of trees that seemed to follow a vertical line down a slope, giving her hope of a spring or stream.

As she walked, so many thoughts flitted around her head. The bleeding had ceased so technically it was the first day of her womanhood, but she wasn't sure if she was a woman or not, for the ceremony had not been completed. What had happened in the village last night? Had she caused a catastrophe by her careless opening to Sun? Yet the *behike* Candlewood had saved her. He had given her protection. What did it all mean? Why had she been left in the world with nothing? How would she live? Night Orchid didn't think she was talking aloud but she might have been for the voice came out of nowhere: "You have been chosen. Only obey."

She nearly jumped out of her skin. She turned around and around, but there was no one in sight. It was a spirit. She was so frightened she fell to her knees as the bad feeling of the morning came back and threatened to overwhelm her. "I am only a child!" she shouted. "I can't bear this anymore! What do you want of me?"

She howled and threw herself on the ground, but hopped up as the hot stones touched her skin. Her hand brushed the pendant and she held it, feeling instantly comforted. She stood like that for a while, breathing deeply. She slowly scanned the landscape, trying to decide where Maima might be. As she moved her eyes down the slope, she saw movement below. Her souls leaped as she watched the speck become larger until she could make out that it was a person, climbing up. Friend or foe? Should she show herself? Call out? She felt faint again but gathered up her courage to lay flat on the ground and stay perfectly still as she fixed her eyes on the figure.

She stifled a cry as the person came nearer. Taíno! He had a pack and over his shoulder a colorful cape that glinted in the sun. Bird feathers! A noble. Someone from Maima?

Her fingers dug into the earth as she tried to make herself as small as possible. Much as she was dying for company, prudence warned her to watch and wait. She unconsciously touched the Bundle and adjusted the wrap to make sure it was hidden.

Suddenly, she stood up straight and gave a whoop of joy, waving frantically and calling out. It was Heart of Palm, her brother's age mate.

He looked up in shock, and drew his *atlatl* and nocked a spear so swiftly the movement was like an elegant dance as he pivoted, searching for the source of the sound.

She called again, louder this time: "Heart of Palm, up here! Look above!"

Only when she threw pebbles did he peer in her direction and cautiously call out the standard greeting to strangers: "I see you?"

She had moved to the very edge of the cliff but could feel the shale giving way, so she lay down full length and waved both hands as she continued shouting.

Heart of Palm relaxed his throwing hand and moved closer to her, shielding his eyes to see better.

"I see you, friend," she called out, "Night Orchid, sister of Cloud!"

"Night Orchid! Blessed! Are you alone?"

"Yes."

She watched as he sheathed his spear and glanced around, trying to figure out how to get to her.

"I think our paths come together there," she pointed.

He looked and nodded.

Night Orchid scrambled to her feet, tiredness forgotten. She ran until she saw Heart of Palm waiting and flew into his arms. He lifted her off the ground and held on to her tightly, staggering around with her as they both burst into tears. When he put her down, they stared into each other's eyes and sat down and put their heads on their knees and rocked and started weeping again. It was a long time before either one could speak.

Chapter 40

F lint awoke to a pinpoint of light. The blanket that he'd given to Candlewood the night before was empty. Outside, he found the *behike* facing the rising sun and intoning the morning blessing. Flint joined in, frustrations forgotten in the age-old ritual. As soon as he was done, Candlewood turned, smiled, and pointed downhill to the spring. Flint washed and floated for a while wondering what the day would bring.

Back at the cave he found Candlewood combing his thin strands of hair with his fingers. Flint bowed and reached into his pack for the red *bixa* paint, but Candlewood stopped him.

"Not today," he said. "Today we paint ourselves with *jagua*, you and I."

"With black, Elder?"

Candlewood nodded.

Here was another surprise for Flint, another instruction that made no sense. Red was the color of everyday wear, the one daubed on casually for protection from insects and spiritual dangers or painted on ceremonially by the warriors going to battle.

Jagua was the sacred black dye, the color of birth and mourning. When someone died, the closest relative of the deceased would be painted in black from head to toe, relatives once removed would paint half their bodies, and kin that were not as close their faces, hands, and feet; non-kin would paint only their faces. *Jagua* would not be renewed, and with daily washing the color would fade to nothing by the ninth day. Only the widows would continue to renew it for a time.

Jagua was the special gift offered to the Taíno on the morning of First Day when they emerged from the cave—Cacibajagua—already stained with the sacred juice. Which is why the holy color was reserved for the most sacred rituals, including death.

The last death in the village had been some moons before Flint left on his journey. Was there another death? Why couldn't the old man just tell him? Why would they use *jagua* now? Was this another of the elder's whims? But Flint realized it wasn't, for Candlewood was looking as grave as he had ever seen him.

"First we will have our tea. Then we will paint each other, you and I."

Flint felt the old uncertainties flooding back. Not least because for the first time Candlewood's voice was gentle. Which was even more frightening than his usual bark. But nothing more was said while they drank their tea.

"Good," said Candlewood when the pot was empty. "We will sit and I'll tell you a story."

Once outside, Candlewood did as he had done the previous day—he stood for several minutes staring into the distance and sniffing the air. He did the same in all directions before nodding in satisfaction. Flint was amazed at how sprightly he looked, how firm his walk was as they set off for the spring.

Candlewood used his vomiting stick to cleanse his body of all impurities before the holy act of handling *jagua*, and Flint did the same. Then the old man sat on a rock and handed his paint calabash to Flint, who pulled out the small brush attached to the stopper.

Flint took up the brush, unsure of the relationship of Candlewood to the dead person and where to start painting. "Where, Elder?" he asked.

"Everywhere!"

Flint startled at Candlewood's spurt of anger and booming voice.

"Use it all up until there is no more. There are many demons to fight."

Flint fearfully approached the *behike* and worked his way around his body, applying the sacred paint.

Candlewood began to talk, in the soft, gentle voice he had used before. "Some things are too terrible to be told directly, young Flint. I wanted to have one day with you to gauge your strength. To see how you handle difficult and bewildering situations. You have done well."

"Thank you, Elder."

"It is my duty to prepare your souls for what is to come. This I have dreamed. Mine are old souls, but not even I am capable of comprehending the evil power that has been let loose."

Flint's breath caught in his throat.

"Power, as you know, young Flint, comes in different forms, and we humans are subject to its whims. Power unleashed is nothing more than the gods fighting each other for control and using us humans as their playthings. They will favor us as we intercede with our offerings and our prayers. But no matter how careful we are, one little slip might be enough to anger the *cemíes*, and we are done for."

Candlewood was saying nothing Flint did not already know. It was part of the teachings given to all the young, from the *ni-taíno* elite to the humblest *naboría*. In this, every child of the nation was equal. For only by understanding the ways of power and how they could harness blessings and ward off evil could each individual hope to survive.

Flint had finished applying *jagua* to the *behike*'s back and was moving on. "Excuse me, Elder," he said, lifting one stringy arm, surprised at how light it was, as if all the flesh inside had shriveled away, leaving nothing but skin and bones. This was going to be difficult. He had to be extra careful to ensure that the paint did not get too thick in the creases and leave unpleasant marks that would be displeasing to the *cemíes*.

Candlewood held up his arm automatically, as if Flint wasn't there. The boy was flooded with the amazing thought that he, Flint, had reached the stage where he could get close enough to the *behike* to be actually touching his body, without fear, when Candlewood struck him a sharp backward blow.

"Pay attention, boy. This is no time for your souls to wander. What I am telling you is of the utmost importance, not just for you but for the entire Taíno nation."

Flint was so frightened he almost spilled the precious liquid.

"Good. Now listen, Flint. You have been chosen. Why you, I do not yet know, except that you are some sort of tunnel through time, the one that goes forward and the one that goes back and unites us in the present—not even I can fully understand the ways of power. But I did not come across you by chance. You intruded into my dream and I was instructed to find you. A survivor."

"S-survivor?" Flint's hand holding the brush stopped in midair and his mouth flew open, but he couldn't get another word out.

"Flint, yesterday you saw smoke."

"Yes, Elder, and I wondered . . ."

"You were right. It was Maima burning. Burning from the night before. A fire let loose as far as the *konukos*, even."

"Ma—?" Flint could only croak.

"Power was unleased in our village two days ago, a power that proved stronger than ours." Candlewood leaned closer to the boy as if afraid of being overheard. "The power of the *paranaghiri*."

"*Paranaghiri* . . . ?"

"Yes. In person. They came. They destroyed. Everything."

"Everything?"

"All is lost, Flint. They killed everyone down to the smallest child. With their huge knives. So sharp one even sliced through one of the great poles holding up the *kaney*."

Flint was distracted by the thought of a blade so sharp that it could slice through a pole.

"The fire was just the finishing touch," Candlewood continued his slow, sad recitation, "to ensure that those who did not die from their wounds would go up in smoke."

Flint was trying hard to assimilate what Candlewood was saying. That Maima village was no more. That everyone was dead? His parents? The *kacike* and the nobles? The servants? Matron Greenstone? No, it was impossible. Over ten times two hands of people lived in Maima. How could they be killed all at once? Didn't they fight? Hide? Run away?

Flint must have spoken aloud for Candlewood said, "All, Flint. Except for the women attending to them that they fled with. And, well, with one or two important exceptions . . . and that is something we have to be concerned about."

"My mother, Marou . . . ?"

"Everyone."

Flint bowed his head and said nothing while Candlewood reached inside his medicine pouch for a pinch of *tabako*.

"I saw them all, Flint. Blessed! I witnessed all the bodies

there. You will be happy to know I was able to sing their souls."

"Thank you," Flint whispered. He knew that an honorable death by violence was the best kind of death, for there was nothing to prevent the souls from immediately flying on the wings of Kolibri to Koaibay. The abode of the noble ones: brave warriors, women who died in childbirth, and those whose blood was spilled by others.

The souls of those who died of illness could not secure such immediate departure without an inquest. And such deaths belonged to a different abode, that of Mother Earth. Knowing of his parents' fate, Flint could only hope for a death that would enable him to join them as Star People in the sky.

"The Cloud People witnessed the slaughter and wept," said Candlewood. "A gentle rain was falling when I left."

Candlewood reached back with the hand that was half-painted and, taking Flint's palm in his, guided the boy to stand before him. Flint kneeled in front of the *behike*, before sitting back on his heels. His souls were flying around inside of him and he feared that he would fall on the ground in a fit, the way that girl Night Orchid was said to do before Candlewood cured her. *Please help me,* he wanted to say now, *my souls are leaving me too.* He forced himself to be still until the drumming in his head faded and he could hear Candlewood's voice again.

"They were gathered in the plaza to greet the *paranaghiri*."

Flint's heart leaped. How could all this have happened in the time he was away?

"Everyone was ordered to come. As if anyone would stay away—well, Matron Greenstone and her supporters did, they remained in the communal longhouse, but of course she is a law onto herself. Everyone was in the plaza, painted and dressed. They were scared, but excited too. To finally see the *paranaghiri* they had heard so much about . . ."

Candlewood sighed. "I was there, young Flint. I was there all the time though no one could see me. I couldn't say anything yet I knew our fate. And there was nothing I could do."

Candlewood paused so long that Flint opened his eyes. The elder's body was shaking, and when the boy looked closer, he was surprised to see tears streaming down his face. Flint closed his eyes again; he felt too filled up for any more words.

He heard Candlewood loudly blowing his nose and then felt his hand on his shoulder. "I will paint you and then you can take a break. Go for a walk, Flint. Be as free as the birds. So little time is left."

Chapter 41

"Night Orchid, you are alive! How did you get away? It's only by a miracle that I . . . I . . ." Heart of Palm stopped speaking, shaking his head from side to side.

Night Orchid wondered if she looked as haunted and bedraggled as her companion. His face, his whole body was scratched and bleeding and dirt hid some of the bruising. His topknot was awry with strands of his long hair loose, two feathers still in place but torn and broken.

He wore an intricately carved nose ring of *guanín*, one earring in his right ear with freshwater pearls, a harpy eagle feather hanging down to his shoulder—all rare items of trade—a large spool in the other ear, and many strands of *sibas* around his neck. But the jewelry and the soiled finery just added to his broken appearance. In place of the usual arrogant stare, Night Orchid was seeing the face of a troubled boy, tear-streaked and bewildered.

Heart of Palm might have been reading her mind, for silently, almost absent-mindedly, he started to take off the jewelry, leaving the nose ring and earring and a small necklace. Into the sealskin pouch he wore across his chest he solemnly placed the rest.

When he untied the string around his neck that held up the soiled and damaged feather cloak and folded it carefully,

Night Orchid was alarmed to see blood oozing from a piece of moss crudely tied around his upper arm.

"You are wounded," she said, and reached out to examine it, but he swiftly turned so she wouldn't see.

"It's nothing."

She sat down on the ground and he did the same, an uncomfortable silence between them. He turned the feather cape inside out, rolled it up, and tied it tightly with the string, leaving a long loop for carrying.

"Blessed," he finally said, his voice a croak. He turned to her and managed a weak smile. "I could do with water. I don't suppose . . . ?"

She shook her head.

"You were in the *guanara*." He shook his head in wonderment. "Today would be your Coming Out day?"

Somehow, he seemed awed by the fact. Or perhaps it was with seeing her here, a young girl alone in the wilderness. Or he was simply in a state of shock, for he fell silent for a long time, staring into space, while Night Orchid bit her tongue, wondering what to do.

"How did you manage—?" he finally asked.

"I heard all the noise and screaming and the crackling of fire getting closer and the smoke . . . I . . . just panicked and ran."

She didn't know why she held back mentioning Candlewood, except that she knew that Heart of Palm was part of the opposition to the old *behike*.

"I knew I shouldn't leave the hut, but . . . the smoke . . . I couldn't breathe . . . I was so scared . . . I will be punished, I know."

"Night Orchid, you don't understand. There is no one to punish you. Or maybe we are all being punished. Maima is no more."

The girl said nothing. She knew that a disaster had occurred. Candlewood had said so. Perhaps some people had
died. But *everyone?*

Heart of Palm started to tell her about the night. In a
measured way, as if he had collected himself, but with only
broad brush strokes of the events.

"Maima was still smoldering this morning. See the
smoke—" He pointed to the southwest, continuing in a
strangled voice, as if in a dream, "The lances . . . the snorting
of the horses . . . the cries . . ."

"No, please, I can't." Night Orchid retched as she rose
and staggered some distance and sat down again as her feet
gave way. Her head swirled, as if her souls were leaving her,
and the whole world fell into darkness.

Night Orchid came awake with her head pillowed on something soft and Sister Wind whispering over her body. She felt
so peaceful she kept her eyes closed, for she knew she had
died and gone to Koaibay. But the aroma of food wafted
from nearby and her mouth started to water. Meat was being grilled! They said in Koaibay the dead enjoyed life there
as much as they did on earth. But grilled meat? No. They
feasted on *guayaba.* She slowly opened her eyes.

She was lying in a little shelter formed by huge boulders
under a feathery guango tree that filtered out the sun that
was now descending on the far side of the sky. The day gone.
What had happened and where was she?

She sat up and looked around. The tree was on a grassy
slope beyond which she could hear running water. There was
no sign of Heart of Palm, but her head was resting on his
beautiful folded cape and the pouch with his jewelry was
nearby.

She drank greedily from a water calabash sitting beside

her, amazed that she was still alive. When she stood, she felt her legs trembling and her body rocked with fatigue. She dragged herself down to the water, a small bubbling stream. She was floating on her back when she suddenly remembered the Bundle. She felt beneath the cotton wrap to ensure it was still there, protected in its layers. She glanced around as she did so, praying that Heart of Palm would stay away for a while longer, yet feeling guilty for he had already been so kind. Imagine allowing her to use his feather cape as a pillow. What a thing to tell her sister, was the next thought, one that she instantly regretted.

As she entered the pool again, she remembered her menstrual cloth. She untied it from her waistband and gave a sigh of relief to see there was no blood. She washed the cloth and laid it on the stone to dry before lowering her body again, floating there with her long hair streaming out behind her.

Chapter 42

During her time in the *guanara,* Night Orchid had been given damp moss to wipe her body, but water was otherwise taboo. Had everything gone according to plan, once the bleeding stopped she would have sent a message to her mother who would have come to ascertain that it was so. To her ululations, all the married women would have come running, ready to take the girl to the pool for her ceremonial washing. The men would have known better than to hang around. Most would have set out to scour the forest for beads and feathers with which to adorn themselves and create noisemakers for her Coming Out. Any male who would have caught sight of the girl, even accidentally, would have submitted to being ritually chased and beaten by the matrons with the sticks they carried.

The women would have been freed of their regular duties to enjoy this special day. Children and babies would have been looked after by others. It did not happen often, perhaps two or three times a year; in a large village with many girls as age mates, they would have a Coming Out for several girls at a time.

The women in a body would take the girl back to the women's lodge on the edge of their *yuka* plantation where, after purging themselves, they would eat soft mushy boiled *yuka* pudding made only for these occasions and drink *mabí.*

They'd sing the secret women's songs, tell bawdy stories, and, with many salacious comments and gestures, introduce the girl to all the rituals of marriage.

Then came the most important part of the proceedings, as Night Orchid's mother had explained it. She would be given an infusion to relax her, then she would be made to lie on a mat, inside a circle of seated and chanting women, while the eldest woman in her family used a sharp stone in the shape of woodpecker's beak to penetrate her and break her hymen.

Just as Inriri Kahubabayael had done to the woman created from *jobo*, the sweet plum tree, but with no sexual opening, when the world after its second destruction had been created with men and no women. Woman's blood had flowed for the very first time (and turned the woodpecker's head feathers red). And just so, once and ever after, every woman had to be prepared for her first penetration by the human male. "Better to suffer now," the women cautioned, with many a nudge and sly wink, "so you can enjoy it later."

The girl undergoing the ritual would never cry out or show the slightest discomfort, focusing instead on the up-coming grand fiesta in her honor and the presents she would receive. Afterward, she would lie quietly while her grand-mother or another elder wiped her down with bast dipped in rosemary-flavored water, from time to time feeding her wild honey from a long spoon. Later, she would be ceremoniously painted and dressed in her finery, and the torch-bearing women would escort her to the longhouse where the whole village waited, just as Sun in its full glory sank in a ball of fire in the western sky.

Night Orchid felt the tears coming and fought to sup-press all thoughts of what might have been. She tried to focus entirely on the moment, giving thanks again to the *cemíes* for providing her with the luxury of a bath and food to come. How did she deserve such bounty? She lay back in the cool water, emptying her mind, cleansing her souls, willing her guardian spirit to enter and heal her. She lay there listening for its call. *Jiu, jiu, jiu.*

Night Orchid smiled. The whole world was filled with the little pygmy owls called *siju*, but the tiny creatures were good at blending into the forest. Hers she would never see, but she knew it was always there. It had come to her in a dream when she had seen four summers and it would never leave until her dying breath. Now she heard its cry, increasing in volume and intensity, ending in a crescendo. It came to a stop but it left her feeling unreasonably safe and happy.

She moved out of the water and wrung out the wrapper and retied it around her waist. She liked the soft caress of the fabric around her legs and calves. It did feel like a substitute for the short skirt she would have been entitled to wear once she was inducted into womanhood. Now what was she?

The question brought back all the loneliness and misery of the last few days and she begged her spirit guide to help her fight against it.

Back at the camp, Heart of Palm looked up from the tree root where he sat and smiled, surprised to see her looking so buoyant. Her smile was even broader when he handed her a leaf with potatoes roasted in their skins and iguana steaks, grilled to perfection.

As she chewed she was pleased to note that Heart of Palm also looked like a new person, clean with shining hair neatly tied back into his topknot.

Chapter 43

Painted and dismissed by Candlewood, Flint lost track of time. He sat and saw nothing, his mind a total blank, as if his souls had been swept up into the air and obscured by Sister Cloud.

A drilling woodpecker startled him into consciousness and he rose hurriedly.

Candlewood seemed not to have moved at all. As if he had been simply waiting on Flint's return, the *behike* started talking as soon as he spied him.

"Blood was spilled that day in the plaza when I wrung the neck of the blasted bird. Not that it wasn't the right thing to do, by the Blessed . . . But I did it in anger. That is not our way. And there was never a proper cleansing afterward." He paused. "Don't think I have not been punished for it. But I also know that avenging power on Maima was not mine. It was sanctioned by the *cemíes* and I was but their instrument."

Flint was shocked by the old man's tone. He had no idea one could speak of the holy ones in so casual a fashion.

"It wasn't my action that caused the blood, for I was careful in twisting the neck," Candlewood continued. "And I have been bothered by that fact ever since. The fact that the bird bled at all was pure witchcraft."

Flint knew that he was right, for the blood had faded as soon as it had run, and disappeared as if it had never been.

So those who were not present had a hard time believing it had ever happened since there was no mark to show, and even those present had begun to doubt the truth of their eyes.

"I knew then that Maima was doomed; our enemies were far more powerful than I imagined. I alone did not have the power to fight it. I could only place it in the hands of the *cemíes* and wait for guidance." He sighed and Flint could sense his mood shifting again. "I never knew the dream would come too late to save our people."

Flint wondered what the dream revealed, but all Candlewood said was, "We need the *paranaghiris'* weapon to fight the *paranaghiris'* magic. Nothing else will do."

Candlewood paused a long time before he resumed talking, and now had a positive lilt in his voice. "The circle has turned again, Flint. The weapon is almost in our hands. The chosen ones are on the way. So long as we reach Cauta in time."

Cauta, the sacred mountain! Where the Taíno emerged from the cave on First Day and received the laws. Flint wondered what this had to do with where they were now, perhaps several moons away. But Candlewood was back to the story of his departure from Maima.

"When the blood of that foreign bird was spilled, it opened a door into another zone. One in which power became unhinged. The door through which the *paranaghiri* were able to look and so choose us for their act of vengeance."

Candlewood was silent for so long Flint thought he had fallen asleep. He himself was feeling so wasted he was starting to nod off.

"Look how isolated our village is, how difficult to find, how poor we are compared to other places for we have no demon gold. Why us? Why was Maima chosen? And who guided them? Was a spy planted in our midst?"

Flint lifted his head but quickly glanced away for the old

man's gaze was frightening. Who indeed? As far as Flint was concerned, there was only one candidate—Shark Tooth.

"You saw the cross he wore, Flint?"

The boy nodded.

"The insignia of the *paranaghiri*. What do you think it signifies?"

Flint shook his head. He had never thought about it. Just knowing it was there was frightening enough.

"It signifies a man on a dead tree." Candlewood took up a stick and started to draw a cross on the bare earth. "Do you notice anything strange about it?"

Flint shook his head again.

"This is a cross with four roads like any other. But notice how one road is so much longer?"

"Yes, Elder."

"The road of travails, Flint." Candlewood was tapping the long arm of the cross. "The *paranaghiri* road. The one on which they plan to march and conquer us. This is the insignia of a world unbalanced and at war with itself. What happens when there is overwhelming and hungry power unleashed on one side. That fully intends to crush the other."

Beside the *paranaghiri*'s cross, Candlewood swiftly drew the familiar representation of the Winds of the Four Quarters, the twin brothers who balanced the world. Each arm of the cross turned in a different direction, but all were perfectly balanced at the center.

Candlewood looked at Flint and said nothing, and Flint looked at the two crosses and understood. Candlewood sighed. "The world is already out of balance. Perhaps the cross of the other has pulled power out of joint. Perhaps it can never be put right again. What do we do then? Do we fight it or acquiesce, allow the total obliteration of our people, our culture, who we are?"

Flint sat there pondering, his head in a muddle. The last thing about the cross made sense, but it was scary too, this unbalanced future. He still did not understand how all of this fit together or what it had to do with him. Or the destruction of his home.

He was so beyond surprise he did not immediately take in what Candlewood said next: "You are part of the solution, Flint. One of the chosen. The spirit of the brave medicine man Guayahona who dared to challenge the ordinary lives in you. You have the song. You have received the stone to make the holy *maraka*. I am your humble teacher."

A *maraka*! Instrument of a *behike*! Candlewood had truly meant it when he said Flint would be his apprentice. Flint didn't know whether to laugh or cry.

As they rested, Flint found himself thinking not of the destruction of his world but of the destroyers: tall men like ghosts with hairy faces and covered bodies who had come out of the east in *kanoas* like floating houses. Men he had still to set eyes on.

At first, many people had taken them to be gods, but now even the smallest child knew this was not so. For the story of how the men of the *kacike* Agueybaná on Quisqueya had proven they were mortal had traveled from island to island and mouth to mouth until it passed into history, though it had happened less than twelve moons ago.

How a soldier came alone to the river Guaruravo and the Indians offered to carry him across on their backs, though he was armored like a turtle in heavy metal. And how in the middle of the river they let him fall and held him down. Then they took out the body and laid it on the riverbank and waited, and waited, and waited. Three days they waited to see if he would rise again. But he didn't. The flies came.

The worms came. The vultures came. His flesh stank and rotted away like any Indian's. And so everyone knew. The *paranaghiri* were not immortals.

What were they though? Everyone had an opinion. Shark Tooth had insisted that, despite the evidence, they were the immortals of a new age whose coming had been prophesied in the *areitos* of long ago, sent to bring The People new ways of living and new gifts from the skies. Only Shark Tooth's followers in the village believed him, but they had been growing in numbers since Candlewood's desertion.

Flint had once heard Candlewood say the *paranaghiri* were possessed by a demon called Gold who ordered them to kill and maim and torture and enslave in its name. In Turtle Village he had heard how the great warrior Hatuéy who escaped from Ayití and gathered his followers in the eastern mountains of Cuba had held up a basket of gold and told them, "Here is the god of the Christians."

When Hatuéy had been captured three moons later, the Christians tied him to a stake and asked before setting him on fire if he would be baptized and worship the Christian god so he could go to Heaven. "Are there Christians in Heaven?" Hatuéy had asked. When they said yes, he said he would rather die.

Flint wished with all his heart that the world he knew—a world of security and plenty, a known world—was not changing so swiftly. Then came the realization that that world no longer existed. A reality he still couldn't comprehend. That there was no Maima, no Crab Claw or Marou or other relations, no *kacike* Runs Swiftly, no Matron Greenstone. Not even his tormentor Heart of Palm. All forever lost. Nothing left in his life but one tired old man who had just told him that it was his job to get him safely to the other side of the mountains, to the holy cave at Cauta.

But first, they would fast in preparation for his initiation that would enable him to receive the communication of the gods.

Chapter 44

"So how did you escape?"

The questions came naturally after they had eaten their fill.

"I had just left the plaza." Heart of Palm spoke quietly, with long pauses between each sentence. "Answering the call of nature. When the noise and commotion began, I started to run back but the *paranaghiri* were everywhere. I climbed the nearest tree. I saw everything. When the first building started to blaze, I got down and ran since there was nothing I could do. I just kept running. Till I ended up here. I don't think they will pursue us this far. But one never knows—on their horses they can cover huge distances. They are animals, Night Orchid. Evil animals. To think that I . . . to think that we . . . believed . . ."

He fell silent and gritted his teeth and Night Orchid understood the savage wounds on his arms. The cuts had been made by his own hand, to obliterate the tattoo, the mark of the Rooster Society. She had heard her brother and other boys whispering about it, about the group that was opposed to the old ways. *Adapt to the new or die* had been their motto.

"At least no one can track us here."

Night Orchid picked up the uncertainty in Heart of Palm's voice. "You mean they might be following us, the *paranaghiri*?"

"I doubt it, but they do have Taíno trackers with them."

"Blessed! But if I was in the hut and you were in a tree, they wouldn't know about us, would they?"

"They're not the only ones."

"What do you mean?"

Heart of Palm didn't answer. He angrily threw a chip of wood into the fire which briefly flared up, lighting his hawkish face.

She cast her mind back to what had been happening at Maima over the last few months, but to tell the truth, she had been totally wrapped up in herself. She had known she was nearing the age of womanhood and looked forward to it. She and her two age mates had been separated from the younger girls and their play and given more and more womanly tasks as part of their training. Last year, for the first time, she'd accompanied the women to the *yuka* plantation, though she would not be allowed in their lodge until she came of age, for that is where the women went for the three or four days each month when Sister Moon bled them. She and her age mates had dressed up, played house, and dreamed of husbands.

Heart of Palm's voice brought her back to reality. "I've been thinking. I have done nothing but think. It was all a plot. To kill the Taíno nation from within. To subvert us from the true ways. They brought Taíno with them, you know. From Xamayca, but still our kin. I talked to them and discovered that one had a cousin that was married to my sister's son. We planned to get together the next day . . . They said they were slaves to the *paranaghiri*. They call them *encomiendos*, the ones commanded to go with them by their chief who is himself like their prisoner. And this is how it is on all the islands now. All have been conquered, their people enslaved. Night Orchid, our land of Cuba is the last to be taken."

They sat for a long time in silence.

"I don't know if any others escaped. The girls were not there at the plaza. They were assigned to the lodge where they housed the *paranaghiri* and the Black Robe. They . . . O Blessed! Night Orchid, your sister Bright Star was among them."

Hope leaped in her breast. The house for visitors was erected on the southwest side of the village, far from the main plaza. Perhaps the girls had been spared, or ran away.

She must have said it aloud, for Heart of Palm added, "The *paranaghiri* were taking to the paths and killing the survivors. Butchering everyone they came across."

She breathed deeply and tried not to think. "So what happened after they set the village on fire?"

"I—I don't really know. They were still mounted on their horses. It all happened so quickly. When anyone least expected . . ."

Night Orchid tried hard to imagine the scene but couldn't. She saw only darkness and dark shapes moving and heard the screams, inhaled the smoke.

"They might have taken the girls with them, you know," Heart of Palm said.

"What?"

"That's what's been happening elsewhere. They take the women and . . . even the married ones."

"You mean—?"

"Yes, as their slaves or—whatever."

Night Orchid prayed for the safety of her sister. She didn't know what was worse, to be captured by foreigners or to be alone in the world, as she was.

Without discussing it, they began spontaneously listing everyone in the village—not by their real names, for that would bring down the ghosts, but by the names they were called—family by family, and the count was both a roll call of the dead and a reminder of those they had shared their lives with.

Heart of Palm could tell her which families had defied the *kacike* and taken their children to the temple so they wouldn't be baptized by the foreign priest, only to be torched there. And which families had joined Matron Greenstone in the longhouse. They tried to remember the people who were away from the village at the time, for whatever reason. When Heart of Palm included the *behike* Candlewood among the absent ones, Night Orchid didn't correct him.

Heart of Palm failed to mention one person—the man called Shark Tooth. The man whom he had followed blindly. The one who many believed would be the new savior of Maima. The man whose fate he was now unsure of. Had he survived the massacre? The thought made him uneasy and fearful, for if the man had all the power he claimed, who knows where he could be. Or what shape he had taken. Heart of Palm had last seen him stealthily following the priest and the black man to the visitors' lodge. Had he escaped the slaughter?

"The boy Flint." Night Orchid's voice jerked Heart of Palm out of his mental nightmare when she remembered one missing from the list of absentees. "Unless he came back early."

"No, Flint hadn't returned yet. Matron Greenstone was in such a stew waiting for him and whatever he was bringing her." He smiled at the vision of the formidable lady, and then had to forcibly suppress the image of Matron Greenstone inside the burning longhouse.

Night Orchid thought it would be nice to have Flint there to lead them out of the wilderness. Heart of Palm wanted them to follow the river valley downstream where they could be sure of coming to a village. At least it would take them closer to the coast where they had relatives; her kin would take her in. But what use would she be if she was not marriageable? Now that she had time to think, she did not know if she was a woman or not, since the ceremony hadn't been completed. What would be the fate of an unmarriageable girl?

Night Orchid tried to put that thought out of her mind. There was no question of which direction to go. Candlewood had instructed her to go east, and east she was bound, no matter how much Heart of Palm tried to dissuade her. Even if it meant she traveled alone.

Chapter 45

Heart of Palm lay back in the water and tried to cleanse his mind. Unable to sleep, his arm throbbing, he had left the camp at dawn and gone upstream to bathe, welcoming the punishment of the cold water. The state his souls were in, he would welcome any opportunity for penance, any means by which he could justify his suffering, anything to dull that other, deeper pain that gnawed at his insides and threatened to rip him apart. The voices that cried, *Coward!*

Only the presence of Night Orchid kept the voices at bay, and he was glad that she had finally given up her foolish idea of heading east. He needed her company. Last night she'd agreed that the most sensible thing was to head for the coast. They'd planned to leave that morning.

And now she was gone. It took awhile after his return to the camp to realize it. She had taken her things. They had foraged enough to make rough traveling packs, gear for crude fishing or trapping, and water bailers. She had come with nothing, and he had shared his *bixa* paint and the last of his *tabako*.

He picked up a stick and slammed it hard on the ground. Again and again. *How dare she!* He silently cursed her and stomped around the campsite for a while, slashing at everything, until he cooled down; there was nothing he could do.

For several turns of the sun they had shared meals and slept under a lean-to palm shelter, hidden from human intruders and protected from the wind by large boulders.

He had not revealed to Night Orchid his fear of being tracked, not by humans as much as by the evil spirits that had overtaken Maima, that had invaded his souls since that fateful night and which he believed were out there in the night, searching.

He went on full alert, weapons in hand, trying to read the threat in every unusual sound or action. Unlike Night Orchid, he could no longer pray to his *cemíes*, for he had abandoned them. Or they had abandoned him. He was lost. He knew he should do penance, have his souls cleansed, beg forgiveness, and start all over again. Be the person he once was, before all the changes started to happen. But there was no going back and no one to help him now.

Like the others, he had hitched himself to the promise of Shark Tooth. Now he did not know what to believe and he was tormented by speculation. Was it Shark Tooth's betrayal that led to the destruction? What had he to gain from such action? Was he an evil sorcerer as his enemies claimed, able to shift his shape at will and feed on human souls? Or was he just an ordinary man with the ability to convince people with his stories? Were the souls of the people of Maima the price he paid for some pact with the gods of the underworld that would give him power? Or was his pact with the *paranaghiri*? Was he even now tracking down the last survivor, his evil spirit cast in the guise of that lizard sitting on the branch, the screech of the nighthawk?

Heart of Palm found himself shivering, but it was not from the cold.

Even after Night Orchid had agreed to move south with him, he couldn't help feeling fearful of where they were headed and what they might encounter, of what evil might be following them. Most of all, he had been fearful both for and of the girl, and he didn't know why since she was nothing but a child. Yet here in the wilderness, although he could not explain it, she had seemed more substantial, as if she had acquired power. And most troubling of all was what she was hiding. Some secret knowledge that she was unwilling to share.

It made him wonder about her account of that night. How come she had ended up taking the same route as he had even though he hadn't known where he was going? How had she managed to cover so much ground in that space of time? What was she hiding with her cotton wrap?

And the question that puzzled him most of all: where had her amulet come from?

The little frog shone on her chest as if it were made of the holy metal *guanín*. But it couldn't be. Yes it was, he was sure of it. How could a girl of Night Orchid's status acquire such a treasure? He had wanted to ask but dared not, for each time he looked at the little *cemí* and framed his tongue around the question, the frog's eyes seemed to blink and he'd found himself struck dumb.

He knew that when a girl entered the menstrual hut she was stripped of all jewelry and sacred emblems except for what her mother painted on her face. So if she had simply fled the hut, as she said, how and where had she acquired the *cemí* image she now wore? And, finally, why was she so insistent that they should head east?

"Why east?" he had asked more than once. "There's nothing there but the holy mountain Cauta."

"That's why," she had replied.

"But it's many mountains away. Far. Why would you want to go there?" They both knew it was a place of pilgrimage, though not at this time of year. When she didn't respond, he added, "There is nothing and no one there."

They had been seated on a rock by the stream, enjoying the sunshine. She didn't answer but she had a strange little smile on her face.

"How will you find your way?" he had asked.

"I'll follow Sun and Star."

She'd said this with such confidence he was almost persuaded she knew what she was doing. But he was sure she didn't, she was just a stubborn little girl with a foolish idea in her head.

He was relieved when he had finally persuaded her that the only sensible direction was south, toward the coast and people.

Now in the camp he had just trashed, Heart of Palm sat down on a rock to take stock. He noticed the leftover meat from the night before, wrapped in leaves and tied with string and hanging from a tree limb out of reach of animals. It looked as if the girl had taken none of it, and Heart of Palm sat down and consumed it all. *Serves her right, let her starve,* he told himself with each bite. He couldn't help feeling insulted by her action.

Then he remembered how joyful she too had been when they met and thought that whatever had impelled her to set off alone again must be a powerful force indeed. Perhaps he should have trusted her more.

But now, his breakfast finished, he told himself he had tried his best with her and would simply head south as planned. He hoisted his bags and weapons onto his back. Then he paused: he had to make sure he knew what direction she was headed.

It didn't take long to pick up her tracks—she was definitely on her way east.

He stood for a long time without moving, remembering how good it felt to be with another human being. How awful it was to be alone. Besides, she was carrying a mystery with her, and if they parted now, he would never find out what it was. What had he to lose if he followed her for another day or two? He could go south at any time. Besides, it was against his warrior spirit to leave the girl alone and unprotected, perhaps the last survivor from his village.

He tried to suppress the thought that he also needed to redeem himself for not acting on the night Maima died. For not plunging in with his weapons and dying a warrior's death. Why had he been spared?

He decided that for the time being, he would follow Night Orchid but not catch up with her, not until he was sure which way the wind was blowing and who she might be meeting. He would not be made a fool of again.

For days Heart of Palm tracked Night Orchid on her lonely pilgrimage until one morning, to his horror, he watched her disappear in a thunderous roar and a cloud of dust, as the hillside where she stood crumbled away and fell into the valley below.

This time he did not hesitate. He was far enough behind to be unaffected by the landslide, but it took him awhile to penetrate the dust and he was forced to stand still as the ripping sounds tore at his heartstrings.

He began to work his way down the valley. It was slow going as he slashed through the bush. He didn't believe the girl could survive such a fall, for even now, trees and rocks were still tumbling down the precipitous slope. He stifled a sob. This time, he vowed, he would prove himself a warrior. No matter how long it took, he would find her. Even if it was only to sing her souls to Koaibay.

PART III

THE CHOSEN

Chapter 46

Sekou's flight into the unknown the night of the massacre ended weeks later when he found an abandoned hut in the hills and stopped running. But even with shelter, food, and water, his spirit was not at ease. He did not want to think of his future and what could happen to him. He had a sudden urge to pray.

"Hail Mary . . ." he began, and reached for the crucifix his mother had placed around his neck as she hugged him one last time in Sevilla. His hand dropped when he remembered how he had ripped off the silver cross and thrown it into the burning village as he fled. Thoughts of Maima, the massacre, his flight, his mother, his lost father, his *guatiao* Tamayo in Xamayca whom he would never see again—it was all too much. For the first time since he'd fled Maima, he sat down and wept.

When his sobs ceased, he found himself sitting on the floor in front of a little shrine of *cemí* images on a shelf, now covered in grime and cobwebs. For something to do, some action to take his mind off his predicament, he set to and removed everything. He carefully cleaned the shrine itself and then every single item before replacing them. Tomorrow, he thought, he would bring the *cemíes* new offerings. Not for himself, but for the spirits of the people who had passed through and who, he felt in his bones, would never pass this way again.

He could recognize most of the Taíno images and the spirits they represented, but felt no special reverence for them. They did remind him, though, of the carved wooden images his mother had kept hidden in their own small shrine at home, in a room off the back courtyard of the casa. Images, she always whispered, that were very, very old and had been passed down to her father, son of the griot Baba Sec, images of the gods of her homeland. Which was not Spain, she said, but the kingdom of the Jolof in the great land they called Africa from which she'd been taken as a child.

She had taught Sekou who these gods were and their names, and their relationships to the humans who served them, and she had instructed him how to serve them too. "For one day, God willing, you will return to the land of your ancestors." But she had also taken him to the grand Church of Santa Ana where she accompanied her mistress to Mass twice a day. And she had cried and given him the crucifix when at the age of six his master sold him to Captain Lorenzo de Burgos of the caravel *Niña II*. Home port: Palos.

Sekou had traveled so much in the eleven years since then, seen and done so much, that he now found he had completely forgotten everything about the African gods. Nor could he even call up his mother's face. He felt distraught about this, and although night had not yet fallen, he flung himself into the frayed *hamaka* and slept the sleep of exhaustion.

That night he dreamed of date palms and how the growers in Mesopotamia said that palm trees fell in love with each other and that if one died, the other would wither away or the female would cease to bear fruit. He did not know what that kind of love was like and wondered if he would ever find it. Growing up among sailors and soldiers, he knew very well what men and women did to each other, a kind of rutting like animals that he couldn't bring himself to take part in despite his companions' urgings. Apart from his mother's, the only other kind of love he knew existed as a word sent by letter from men far from home to their wives, their feelings as dry as the parchment which bore the words. Perhaps it was the wives at home who did the withering.

These thoughts came to him on waking, but he knew what the dream was urging him to do: go back down the trail into the valley. The palm trees there weren't date palms but would still yield nuts which he could use to make oil. It wasn't the olive oil of Spain he was used to, but it would do for cooking and burning in the little lamp he planned to make, and for mixing with *bixa* to protect his skin as the Taíno did.

When Sekou set out for the valley that morning, he was dressed like a Taíno man in waistband and breechclout, and like a Spaniard in sandals and leather hat. He wore in a loop over one shoulder, rancher fashion, a crude but strong carryall he had woven from hastily stripped *bejuco*. His sharp steel knife rested in a sheath he wore crosswise, along with his leather water bottle. In his right hand he hefted a *koa*.

He felt slightly self-conscious, as he did whenever he embarked on a new life, afraid of being trapped between worlds. Like the first time he went aboard ship with Captain de Burgos and became a sailor. Like the time the captain, in debt, sold him in Xamayca to the widow Lares to help her on her *hato* and he became a rancher. Like the time the widow's new husband sold him to the trader and the trader sold him to Comandante Pánfilo de Narváez, who took him to the barracks at Villa de la Vega to live the life of a soldier.

This time he was setting out into the unknown, on his own, and he found it just as frightening.

Chapter 47

Traveling back down the path, Sekou had eyes for all the things he had ignored on his flight. He inhaled deeply the freshness of the morning air, the smell of the pine trees, and was awestruck by the spectacular mountain views. He was feeling relaxed for the first time in weeks and was not even conscious of whistling a hornpipe tune and jigging along with it as he gathered oil palm nuts in the peaceful horseshoe-shaped valley. A mighty cliff towered over it on one side, casting shade, and the grassy clearing was enclosed by woodland so dense it seemed as if no human had ever penetrated, though he himself had hacked his way through, the scratches on his face and body testifying to his struggle.

He was standing with his back to the cliff, face lifted to capture warmth from a sickly sun, when a thousand screeching monsters came roaring down the hillside on trumpeting horses and screaming winds, tossing clouds of dust and grit as the world exploded. With his eyes closed tightly against the dust cloud that enveloped him, feet rooted to the spot, it took Sekou several heart-pounding minutes to realize what was happening: the cliff above the valley was breaking away. The landslide gained momentum as it hurtled toward him with an ear-splitting shower of earth and rocks and trees pulled up by the root, giving him just enough time to come to his senses and scramble to safety.

The sounds of the tearing hillside echoed and reverberated in the wilderness as startled birds squawked and twittered and flew in widening circles into the skies and quivering small animals scurried to watch from a safe distance as the avalanche seemed to go on and on. Finally, with one last shudder, it came to rest as smaller stones and debris continued to trickle down and the earth settled again into what now seemed an unnatural silence.

From a distance, Sekou stood stock-still, eyes tightly closed, hands covering his nose and mouth against the dust that blotted out the sun. He shook his head to get his hearing back and tried to slow the beating of his heart and still his trembling body. He finally opened his eyes into a dirt fog filling the entire valley.

When the dust settled enough for him to penetrate the gloom, he saw that he was cut off from the path where he had left his pack and the nuts he had gathered. The only way back was across the pile of rocks and uprooted trees that filled half the valley floor.

He began to crawl slowly and carefully, one foot and handhold at a time, his only thought now to hurry and gather his possessions and head away from this cursed place, back to the abandoned *bohío* that he now called home.

Sekou was balancing gingerly on some rocks when the sound came from below, near the edge of the pile of rubble, a sound like an animal cry. He froze. He waited, and when no sound came, he moved slowly forward, listening, until it came again. It sounded almost human now, but he couldn't believe anyone, man or beast, could have survived such a tumble.

Then he saw a pile of earth and small stones moving as something tried to burrow its way out. He carefully crawled toward it, thrusting aside a massive tree trunk and upended root. His breath caught when he reached the spot, for he saw it was not an animal but indeed a small person there, who by this time had pulled their head and shoulders out of the rubble and was straining and groaning with the effort to free their arms and the rest of their body.

It was hard to make out any features, for the body that emerged was completely covered in white marl, even the long hair down their back and shoulders. As their hands came free and they wiped the dirt and blood from their face, Sekou could see brown skin emerging. It was a girl. She was still moaning as she renewed the effort to pull the rest of her body from the debris.

"Wait!" Sekou called out in Spanish. "Don't move!" For he could see her movements were threatening to bring down the rubble resting precariously above.

Her head whipped around at the sound. She let out a small "*Guay!*" and clapped her hand to her mouth, her eyes wide with terror.

He greeted her in Taíno: "I see you, friend."

She didn't answer but stayed rigid with fear, half-buried, unable to run, clutching her *cemí* amulet which hung around her neck and moving her lips in intercession to her guardian spirit. He continued to crawl cautiously toward her, carefully moving rocks and rubble out of the way.

"If you move, more rocks will fall." He spoke in a soft voice and smiled at her, signing with his hands that she should keep still.

She kept praying and grasping her *cemí*, but she seemed to understand him for she stopped struggling to free herself.

"*Datiao*," he said as he moved closer and tapped his chest. "Friend." She didn't answer his smile. "*Daca* Sekou." He crawled a few more inches. "What are you called?"

He was speaking softly, as to a child, for he could see she was very young and he wondered what she was doing alone in the wilderness. Or had her companions been buried in the rubble?

She made an effort to speak but had to wet her lips several times before the words came out in a whisper. "You speak our language?"

He realized that her shock was not only at encountering someone else in the wilderness but at seeing, for the first time he was sure, a Black man.

"Yes," he said, "a little. *Yamoca*." Still smiling, he held up two fingers to indicate how little that was.

Instead of consoling her, this seemed to frighten her more. She pulled away from him as if she could escape and squirmed to unearth the rest of her body, as she whispered, "Where are they?"

"Who?"

"The others. Panol." She was looking around wildly. "Kill me now," she whispered. "Please."

"What? There are no others. I am alone."

Her fear was so real he wondered if she had heard of the massacre at Maima.

"Not Panol," he said, pointing to himself. When she didn't seem to understand, he added, "*Naboría*," using the Taíno term for commoner or servant. She looked at him blankly so he tried again: "Lost? Outcast?" Still, she didn't respond. "I ran away from the Panol." He tapped his chest and mimed running.

He wasn't sure how much she grasped his mixture of Taíno and Spanish but she seemed less frightened now. She looked away as if trying to weigh him up, deciding whether or not to trust him. She glanced around wildly again, and then for a long time she simply peered down at the rubble covering her, remaining perfectly still, as if she had given up all hope of life. He could feel some great sadness emanating from her that matched his own, and he held his breath and stayed unmoving on the mound of rock where he was perched.

Finally, as if she had come to a decision, she sighed, turned her head, gave him the glimmer of a smile, and tapped her chest: "*Daca* Night Orchid."

Chapter 48

Sekou helped Night Orchid to extricate herself from the rubble.

"Alone?"

She nodded, then winced with pain when she tried to stand up. She grabbed onto him so he lifted her up and carried her to safety, amazed at how little she weighed. She sat on a big rock while he examined her foot. Her ankle was already swollen. He manipulated it to make sure it wasn't broken, but she had at least a very bad sprain. He looked up at her to try to explain this but she had her eyes closed and he was dismayed at how beaten and battered she looked, with blood from bruises and cuts seeping through the dirt that clung to her skin.

He could see she was close to puberty but had not yet come of age as her hair was not cut and she wore no signifying tattoos or ligatures on her arms and legs. Nor had she been put into a *nagua* with the appropriate skirt length for her age group, though she wore a cotton wrap, now filthy and torn, tied around her waist.

Most surprising to Sekou, for he had never before seen such a thing on the islands, she was without adornment of any kind, not even family or clan insignia, except for the superb little carving of a frog, representing the mother goddess Attabey, that she wore around her neck. This only added to her mystery, for it seemed to be of solid gold and excellent workmanship, something that a greedy Spaniard would kill for. Yet it was not strung on a circlet of precious stones as one would expect, it hung from dirty strands of sisal twisted together and knotted.

Sekou opened his mouth to speak but realized this was no time for questions. He unslung his *botella* and offered it to her and she drained it. She was no doubt dying from hunger too. The skin on her face was dry and pinched like an old woman's and she was wincing with pain.

The most important thing was to get her to the hut and shelter, he knew, but how was he going to manage that if she couldn't walk? She didn't weigh very much so he could carry her, yet the trail was still overgrown; he had hacked his way through the bush and thorny shrubs but it would be hard going uphill with the girl. Still, they needed to get moving. The sun was like a sodden eye behind a haze of dust, and a dull sheen to the air heralded rain.

He stood in front of her and looked down at the top of her head. "Night Orchid . . ."

She lifted her head and stared at him with her big eyes.

"*Bohío*. Up there," he indicated with his head, "we go."

She looked where he pointed but shook her head and closed her eyes as if the effort was beyond her.

"I will carry you. It's not far. There's food and water. And a *hamaka*." He smiled encouragingly but she lowered her head and shook it from side to side.

He made his way over to where he had left the string bag with the nuts he had gathered. He had planned to husk the nuts before leaving, but even so, they would be a considerable weight. If the rough carryall he had knotted together from *bejuco* was strong enough to carry a load of nuts, it could surely stand the weight of the girl.

He was testing the bag for sturdiness when Night Orchid cried out. Grabbing his knife from its sheath, he spun around to find a man standing behind the girl some twenty paces away with his *atlatl* nocked and a spear pointing straight at him.

"No!" She gestured at the man to put his spear down.

"*Akani*," he said. "Enemy." His throwing arm did not relax and he had a crazy look in his eyes. He had wiped his face but the rest of his body was covered in marl and dirt and blood from cuts and scratches.

"Heart of Palm. No. *Datiao*."

Sekou relaxed slightly as the girl clearly knew the stranger. But who was he and where had he come from? She obviously had the same thought.

"What are you doing here, *guama*? I thought you went south."

Sekou was surprised at her tone, which was sharp for such a little girl.

"I was following you." The stranger said this without relaxing his stance or his gaze, but there was something in his voice. Was it shame?

Now this was even more of a mystery, Sekou thought. He had not relaxed his own posture either, though he no longer felt that initial rush of danger that had galvanized his movement.

"Following me? And you left me to—to—" Night Orchid choked on the words as the man cut her off.

"He was there, Night Orchid. I saw him. He's one of them."

She was silent for a moment. "You mean he was at Maima?"

"Yes."

"I know, *guama*. His name is Sekou. I never saw him,

I was in the *guanara*, remember? But Cedar Wax told me about him."

Sekou didn't have time to process the startling information that they were from Maima and the girl had been hidden in the menstrual hut. For the stranger had paused only slightly as if assimilating what Night Orchid had said, then, without warning, launched his spear with all his strength. Sekou threw himself flat as it ripped into the woods behind him.

Holy Toledo! His heart was beating wildly as he leaped up and rushed to put a stout tree between himself and the madman. He peeked out to see if he could get into position to throw his knife without hurting the girl, but the stranger had nocked another spear and was ducking around now as if to circle him.

This is madness, Sekou thought. "I am not your enemy!" he shouted. "I am on your side!"

The girl started to shriek loudly, "Stop it, stop it, stop it!"

Perhaps her hysteria conveyed something to the man, for Sekou could see him stop, lower his weapon, and stand still for a while before putting the spear back in its sheath.

The man walked over to the girl and started to murmur to her in soothing tones, as if to a child. He reached out to touch her and then drew back, unsure what to do, as she buried her head in her hands and wailed loudly, rocking back and forth. He stood there for a while with a rueful expression, then looked around and stared angrily at Sekou, his eyes murderous still, though he had relaxed his posture somewhat, as if deflated by the girl's actions. As if a crying girl was something he couldn't cope with. That was one thing they had in common, Sekou thought; nor could he.

Now that Sekou could study him more closely, he saw

that the man wore the topknot and insignias of a warrior and, despite dirt and grime, was more refined and powerful than he had first appeared. As he sheathed his knife and walked toward the man she called Heart of Palm, he couldn't help wondering what kind of hold the girl had over him, for he showed her a kind of deference that was unusual for a man of the upper classes toward to a girl who was clearly *naboría*.

"I see you, friend," he said, stopping halfway. "I am called Sekou."

Heart of Palm said nothing but raised his eyes. Sekou held his gaze and the two young men glared at each other to see who would break first. The angry newcomer did, as he dropped his hand on Night Orchid's shoulder and straightened his back as if to indicate that she belonged to him.

"She needs help," Sekou said. "I have shelter, food, water. I am alone." He lifted both hands to show them his open palms and pointed up the trail.

Heart of Palm still said nothing, though Night Orchid had stopped crying and she too seemed to be waiting on his answer.

Finally, the man spoke: "How do we know you don't have an army of murderers and your horses hidden somewhere?"

Sekou laughed. "Look at me, I have been running ever since that night in Maima. You too, right?"

Heart of Palm stared at him without expression.

"You didn't see me kill anyone. I wouldn't be a part of it. That is why I ran away. If they find me, they will kill me."

Sekou could see Heart of Palm studying him from under his hooded eyes, as if mentally comparing the jaunty young man dressed like a Spaniard who rode into his village to this scarecrow looking as scratched and battered and worn out as himself.

He didn't soften his gaze, but he looked down at Night Orchid and then kneeled and examined her swollen ankle. Then he retrieved his pack and placed the straps across his shoulders and lengthened them until the bag fell down to the small of his back. He kneeled again and indicated that the girl should climb on his broad back, and she did so, her arms tightly locked around his neck, the pack providing a seat for her and the straps keeping her firmly anchored in. He stood up straight as if Night Orchid was no more than a tiny doll and indicated with his chin that Sekou should lead the way.

Sekou grabbed his string bag and shoveled in as many nuts as he could before hoisting it on his back and looping the cords around his shoulders. With his stout stick to beat the path before them, they set off up the trail.

There was no sound from the birds that had gone silent, except for one that seemed to be following them, its persistent cry of *Jiu, jiu, jiu* increasing in volume, then ceasing, then starting up again. No matter how hard he looked, Sekou could not spot the noisemaker which he thought might be the little pygmy owl that hunted both night and day. But suppose it was a spirit bird? The thought made him shiver.

The more he walked, the more the blood rush from the morning's frenetic activity drained away and Sekou found himself filled once more with the fear and horror that had driven his headlong flight from the burning village. The precipitous and unplanned escape had kept him going heedlessly, without coherent thought.

But once he'd found shelter, he couldn't keep the awful images from crowding in, as they did now. The shrieks of the dying. The smell of burning. Blood spurting from pieces of flesh torn and ruptured by swords, skulls crushed by maddened horses.

He tried to banish the images and focus on the immediate

task, clearing a path for Heart of Palm and the girl. Yet the idea nagged at him: how was it that two people from that very same village had intersected his path? In the twelve days since he fled Maima, he'd had no plan, no aim, no idea even of where he was on this strange island as he zigzagged up-river to hide his footprints.

Where had they suddenly come from? How had they escaped the slaughter? Were they together or not? Where were they headed? Was it coincidence that their paths had crossed?

Sekou had lived in the islands long enough to know the Taíno did not believe there was such a thing as coincidence. Every action was orchestrated by the *cemíes*, the spirits that ordered their lives down to the smallest gesture. This meeting must have been ordained. But to what purpose? What on earth could the *cemíes* want with him, a poor Black runaway?

Chapter 49

Sekou hastened his pace, worried that he hadn't stocked up enough on kindling or food. Whenever the bushes parted to reveal the hills and valleys beyond, they could see the dark sheet of water headed in their direction. They made it to the shelter with a mere finger of time left before the rain thundered down.

He dropped his bundle and indicated the *hamaka* where Heart of Palm gently deposited Night Orchid. She opened her eyes briefly, then closed them as she eased her body down.

The hut wasn't much, a travelers' stop, but it was sturdily built in the pattern of all Taíno *bohíos*, though now little more than a skeleton of beams and uprights enclosing a circular space some ten paces across.

The thatch roof had rotted and fallen and spiders and vermin had taken up residence. Sekou had cut new posts to replace the uprights and collected broad thatch and vines to fix the roof. It was a difficult task to undertake alone, but by midafternoon of the second day he had managed to cover enough to provide shelter, working with the urgency he had known of sailors furling sails before a storm. By evening he could proudly stand outside and view his handiwork.

His tying was not in the style of the Taíno thatchers he had watched so many times; he used seamen's knots. He had mastered them a long time ago, in another life it seemed to him now, when the captain had bought him off his mother's owner in Sevilla to serve as cabin boy.

Table, table, Sir Captain and Master and good company, the table is set; the meat laid out; water as usual for Sir Captain and Master and good company. Long live Their Majesties by land and sea.

Sekou shook his head at the memory of the dutiful small boy he once was.

He was brought back to reality by a groan from Night Orchid as she shifted her body in the *hamaka* and the *Jiu, jiu, jiu* of the blasted bird that seemed to be annoyingly close, almost as if it was inside the hut.

Heart of Palm, who didn't even seem to be breathing heavily, was looking around the hut as if taking stock of everything—the fireplace with three stones and a blackened grill placed against the open-sided mud and plaster wall, the ledge above it that held clay cooking pots, water jars, and a grinding stone, the oversized gourds that hung from the ceiling on fraying cords, and the detritus of the previous occupants pushed to one corner and covered in dust and cobwebs.

His survey completed, Heart of Palm placed his bag in a corner along with his weapons, then hefted his axe and stepped purposefully out the door.

Sekou filled a gourd with water and handed it to the girl, who held it with both hands and drank greedily. He knew she needed attention but they had to get supplies in fast. He took the water calabashes down to the stream to fill them and was overjoyed to find several large mountain mullet caught in the trap he had set before leaving that morning. They were still thrashing about when he threw them into his basket that was lined with the river coco leaves he would roast them in. In the distance, he could hear the sound of Heart of Palm chopping wood.

When Sekou returned to the *bohío* with his basket laden with fish and some ripe fruit he had grabbed in passing, he was surprised to see the *hamaka* empty while a huge bundle of dry wood and sticks leaned against the hearth, along with a fat iguana.

He soon had a fire going and a boiling pot of water giving off the scent of mint. He cleaned the fish and wrapped them in the leaves, ready to throw them on the barbecue as soon as the others returned. All in all, Sekou was pleased. He decided there was just enough time to collect more wood and ten minutes later dashed back in with a bundle as the rain came pounding down.

The Taíno were back, both looking clean and refreshed, their long hair still wet and dripping from the bath they had obviously taken. The Taíno were the cleanest people Sekou had ever met, if possible bathing several times a day, and the return of those two made Sekou conscious of how dirty he was. He rushed out again, running through the rain to the stream where he scrubbed himself with sand and splashed about happily.

Night Orchid was back in the *hamaka*. Now that her body was clean, the bruises and cuts were more apparent, some swollen, many oozing blood, and Heart of Palm was dabbing at them with a wad of lace bark he was tearing off from a freshly cut block beside him, pressing fleshy *toona* sap on each wound to stop the bleeding.

From the way he splinted her injured ankle and tied it up with *bejuco*, Sekou could tell Heart of Palm was used to dealing with such injuries; he guessed from the young man's muscular build that he was a ballplayer.

Sekou had watched *batéy* played many times and marveled at how tough the game was and how calmly the players accepted their injuries. For the heavy rubber ball could not be touched with hands or feet but was kept in the air and bounced back to opponents with hips, buttocks, shoulders, and other parts of the body. Even with the knee and elbow pads the serious players wore, hardly a game ended without injury, and even death was not unknown. Yet so seriously did each village take *batéy* and the competitions it spawned that even women and girls played.

As Heart of Palm silently worked, Sekou sliced up a ripe papaya and handed it around and made tea. Soon, huddled near the fireplace in the section of the *bohío* that didn't leak too badly, they ate and drank while the rain pounded on the thatch, water gurgled in rivulets outside, and the tantalizing smell of steamed river fish and grilling iguana pervaded the hut. None of them felt the need to speak. The elements had imposed a truce.

Chapter 50

Without blankets, they shivered that night even though they kept the fire going. Sekou and Heart of Palm curled up on either side of the *hamaka* on tattered rush mats. But the rain never let up, the floor was wet, the north wind was bringing exceptionally cold air, and the smoke from the fire was blowing into the room rather than going up the smoke hole; in short, they were cold, damp, and miserable.

Sekou could stand it no longer. Since arriving at the *bohío*, he had washed and put away in his backpack the clothes he had worn almost to shreds, clothes he had once been so proud of: the linen shirts, the wool long johns and undershirt, the leather trousers and jerkin he had been wearing the day of his flight. His metal armor he'd abandoned in the village.

He took his leather pack down from where he had hung it and put on his long johns and shirt, feeling Heart of Palm's eyes on him. Although he was reluctant to part with anything, he took one of his extra two shirts over to Night Orchid and covered her with it. The other he offered to Heart of Palm, who had also risen and was putting more wood on the fire.

The youth shook his head, then went over to his own pack and unrolled a beautiful feather cape and put it around his shoulders and sat down by the fire. The cape made him look larger and more menacing in the dancing firelight and Sekou recognized it as similar to those worn by the young warriors of Maima who had formed an honor guard around their *kacike*. He wondered if his guest has been one of them. He was too tired to care. As soon as the warmth from the clothing crept through his body, he slept.

Sekou awoke to a dull, gray morning. It was raining a steady drizzle, the kind of rain that would last for days. There was no sign of Heart of Palm, though the air was fragrant with the scent of tea.

Night Orchid was sitting in the *hamaka*, her face puffed up and her eyes almost swollen shut, but she was holding up the linen shirt. She had probably never seen a sewn garment before, nor any fabric but woven cotton, and she was examining the shape of the garment, especially the sleeves. Then she turned to the metal fasteners, and gave the seams and stitching the most minute attention, running her hand over everything as if she couldn't believe the feel of it.

Sekou tried not to burst out laughing at her seriousness. When she glanced his way and caught him looking, she dropped the shirt and put her hand to her mouth in embarrassment.

Sekou smiled and stood up and held out his arms so she could see how the shirt he was wearing fit, and he couldn't help twirling around and around so she could get a good look. Her eyes sparkled and she stifled a giggle. For a moment, she was a child again.

"*Camisa*," he said in Spanish, pointing to his shirt and the one she held.

"*Camisa*," she repeated, and giggled again, pointing to his long johns.

"*Pantalones*," he said.

"*Pantalones*," she repeated, laughing as if a clothed man was the silliest sight she had ever seen. Sekou started laughing too.

At that moment Heart of Palm walked in and they instantly stopped, like guilty children. He did not even look at them as he came in dripping water and threw down an equally wet bundle of leaves. The other two watched silently as he undid the bundle and took out a beautiful palm heart and laid it on the fireplace. Sekou instantly started salivating at the thought of the upcoming treat and Night Orchid clapped her hands.

The rest of the bundle contained more fruit and fat *toona* leaves. These Heart of Palm took over to the *hamaka*, then sliced one and started pressing the healing salve on Night Orchid's wounds while she obliged by turning her body this way and that.

Sekou went to stand where he could look outside but saw only dripping leaves and a gray blanket of sky. He wondered what he would do with himself for the entire day, already feeling uncomfortable in Heart of Palm's presence. Although the youth showed no further signs of hostility, he exhibited no friendliness either, having said very few words since they arrived.

Sekou was a chatterbox himself, always glad to be in the company of other talkers, so the presence of people who did not speak much always made him uncomfortable, not to mention a huge silent man who had actually tried to kill him. Had he actually meant to hit him with the spear? It seemed so unbelievable now. Here he was dying for company after the misery of so many days on his own—did this man have to be one so surly and threatening?

Now that he had a chance to properly study Heart of Palm, Sekou was surprised to see he was quite young, close to him in age, not the much older person he had first taken him to be. It was his expression, Sekou decided, that made his handsome face look hawkish and angry. The crease across his broad forehead looked as if it was a recent acquisition.

He tried to envisage Heart of Palm as the handsome youth he really was, at a ball game, attired in the stone elbow and knee protectors, with his painted insignias and warrior tattoos, laughing and in control of the game, of life itself.

Sekou paused to give a moment's thought to Heart of Palm's sudden loss of everything—his home, his family, his friends, his place in the world. Then he smiled to himself, surprised that he had so easily forgotten that this was exactly his own situation.

Chapter 51

It was Sekou's sword that was to elicit the first glimmer of interest from Heart of Palm. The sword that would make him bitterly curse his own foolishness and lead to some of the most fearful moments of his life.

The sword and its sheath of embossed leather was Sekou's proudest possession. It had been a gift from Comandante Narváez, whose wife had sent him a much finer one from Spain along with a letter bewailing his absence. Sekou knew this because his master had asked him to compose a suitable reply.

Sekou's beautiful penmanship, his ability to read and write, to do complicated sums and keep the books, to navigate by the stars and calculate by compass, to ride and groom a horse, to compose verses that could be sent to one's wife as one's own, were a few of the skills the boy had acquired in his short life and for which Narváez had paid such a high price.

Sekou's master was the envy of many, including Velázquez who after a week of watching the boy at work at his captain's side, writing down his orders and conveying them to others or carrying them out himself in nimble fashion, had offered to buy him off his friend for double the price Narváez had paid. Triple, he said, when Narváez didn't budge.

Sekou knew this, for Velázquez made the offer in his presence. Sekou had at first felt immense pride at the judgment of such a fine caballero, for before coming to take charge of Cuba, Velázquez was known to be the richest man on Española, a favorite of the king, a fine horseman, and a dashing figure, much admired by everyone.

But Sekou's pride soon turned to shame as the men went from enumerating his accomplishments to a raw assessment of his physical qualities, commenting on the sturdiness of his bones, the soundness of his teeth, his height, and his potential as a breeder as soon as he was found a suitable mate. Then they had turned without pause to discuss a horse in like manner.

"You are a good boy, Sekou," Narváez had said when, a few days later, he presented him with the sword. "May you remain as sharp as this blade. Use it to fight for the honor of our blessed Majesty, for the glory of Spain, and for our blessed Queen of Heaven." Narváez had kissed the crucifix which hung around his neck and crossed himself.

Sekou had not had the opportunity to use his sword in defense of the earthly king or the Queen of Heaven. Nor to murder defenseless Indians. Instead, he had used it to hack his way through the wilderness in which he had taken flight. He could never get out of his head the image of Comandante Narváez, so cold, sitting on his horse with that smile on his face as death flowed around him. What manner of man was that? The priest, Narváez's friend, had been shattered too, Sekou could tell, by the way he carried himself from that moment on and his silent invocations to the Heavens. He wondered again—but only for a moment—what had happened to the man he had been assigned to take care of. The priest whose name was Bartolomé de las Casas.

As soon as he settled himself in the *bohío,* Sekou had cleaned the sword carefully and put it away in its sheath. He had tied the loop of the sheath to his cordovan leather back-pack that he'd grabbed as he fled Maima and which he hung from the rafters. On top of the clothes in the pack he rested his quill and parchment and his second most treasured possession, a book belonging to the widow Lares's first husband, which she had given him, for she could not read. The edges were already tarnished from Sekou's handling.

It was this book that opened the door to friendliness and threw him off guard. What Sekou later cursed as his foolishness began late on the fourth day in the *bohío* when he had let Heart of Palm handle his sword. He had gone to his pack to take out the book, for he thought reading would relieve the boredom that was setting in. But the sword was attached to the pack and when he placed it all on the floor, he had seen the other young man's eyes widen with interest. He even leaned over for a better look. Then, to Sekou's great surprise, he had walked over and bent down and traced with his fingers the intricate scrollwork of the leather sheath. Sekou read this as a sign of friendship, and had drawn the sword out and made a few passes with it, before holding it out for Heart of Palm's inspection. His eyes glittered in excitement and Sekou allowed him to hold it in his hands and examine it before he gently took it and put it away.

"I will show you how to use it. Outside. When the sun comes out again."

Heart of Palm nodded and the idea seemed to somehow rearrange his features. From then on the scowl disappeared, to be replaced with a pleasant nod. Sekou felt a lifting of his spirits. This was the breakthrough he'd been waiting for.

He extracted the book from the bag and prepared to sit in the best light to read. What he hadn't counted on was the effect this new object would have on his companions. He had hardly opened up the brass latch and turned to the first page when there came a gasp from Night Orchid, who was looking over his shoulder.

"Talking leaves?" Her mouth was wide open in amazement.

Clearly, Night Orchid had heard of this marvel even if she had never seen one.

Sekou turned and smiled at her and held up the volume. "*El libro*," he said.

"*Elibro*," she repeated, and leaned over to gently touch it, then quickly pulled away as if it burned. Heart of Palm, who was squatting over by the fire, said nothing, but Sekou could tell the book held his interest too. This was another piece of powerful magic the Spaniards had brought.

"Is it true that it speaks to you," Night Orchid asked, "from great distances?"

Sekou nodded.

"How?"

"I look into it with my eyes and I read it."

"Read?"

Sekou realized how difficult it was to explain, with no corresponding words in their language. But he was inspired. "This," he said, tapping the book, "is like an *areito*. Or rather, it could contain all the *areitos* that your *kacike* would have known."

"All?" Night Orchid looked doubtfully at the object.

Sekou was referring to the oral histories that were memorized and sung on special occasions, a record of the tribe and the nation's history. Just as his great-grandfather the griot had memorized the history of the kings of Jolof in far-off Africa and sung them over and over, his mother had often told him.

Night Orchid considered what he said. "But how would it know our sacred *areitos*?"

Sekou could see that he had an uphill battle. "Not your

areitos," he said, "my *areitos*. Stories. We call them stories. This one is many stories of the adventures of a man named Marco Polo."

"He speaks?"

"Yes. No." Sekou himself was getting confused. "Here, let me show you. I will look in this book and I will use my voice to tell you what the story says."

"Okay." But her voice held doubt.

Sekou settled himself in a comfortable position on the mat. He opened the book at Chapter One, page one, and began to read, in Spanish.

Here the Book Begins; and First it Speaks of the Lesser Hermenia

There are two Hermenias, the Greater and the Less. The Lesser Hermenia is governed by a certain King, who maintains a just rule in his dominions, but is himself subject to the Tartar. The country contains numerous towns and villages and has everything in plenty; moreover, it is a great country for sport in the chase of all manner of beasts and birds.

He stopped after the first paragraph and closed the book, thinking he had demonstrated enough. To his surprise, Night Orchid said, "Go on," and when he looked at Heart of Palm, he nodded. Sekou resumed reading aloud, then stopped again and made to close the book. But they kept on urging him to continue.

So swept up did he become in the adventures of the Polo brothers, which he was familiar with from reading them over and over, that he forgot his listeners.

They relate that in old times three kings of that country went away to worship a Prophet that was born, and they carried with them three manner of offerings, Gold, and Frankincense, and Myrrh; in order to ascertain whether that Prophet were God, or an earthly King, or a Physician. For, said they, if he take the Gold, then he is an earthly King; if he take the Incense he is God; if he take the Myrrh he is a Physician.

So it came to pass when they had come to the place where the Child was born, the youngest of the Three Kings went in first, and found the Child apparently just of his own age; so he went forth again marveling greatly. The middle one entered next, and like the first he found the Child seemingly of his own age; so he also went forth again and marveled greatly. Lastly, the eldest went in, and as it had befallen the other two, so it befell him. And he went forth very pensive. And when the three had rejoined one another, each told what he had seen; and then they all marveled the more. So they agreed to go in all three together, and on doing so they beheld the Child with the appearance of its actual age, to wit, some thirteen days. Then they adored, and presented their Gold and Incense and Myrrh. And the Child took all the three offerings, and then gave them a small closed box; whereupon the Kings departed to return into their own land.

Sekou stopped only when it became too dark for him to see. He closed the book, a little embarrassed that his listeners would not have understood a word. But Night Orchid was smiling at Heart of Palm as if something joyful had taken place.

He remembered how at the *areitos* he'd attended with Tamayo in Xamayca, the recitations would go on all night while everyone listened entranced to the stories they'd been hearing since childhood. They would fall asleep and wake up and start listening again. Each telling of the deeds of their ancestors made their actions seem fresh and exciting. New heroes and their accomplishments were added as characters, while scenes and events were woven seamlessly into the historical record. All would sit silently on their haunches for hours on end, drinking it in, while the *kacike* recited and tapped the sacred slit drum, the *mayohuakan*, and the holy men blew *tabako* smoke from their long cigars that summoned the *cemíes* to partake in the communion.

Sekou rose, stiff from sitting. "*Pantalones*," Night Orchid said, hopping around the *bohío* and trying out her ankle. "*La camisa. Elibro.*" She recited the words with a breathless air, as if a whole new world was opening up before her.

Two days later when Sekou awoke, there was no sign of Heart of Palm. He thought nothing of it, for he was used to Heart of Palm rising early and today for the first time the rain had ceased and there was a faint glimmer of gold from the east. It was only later, when he returned to the *bohío* and noticed that all the young man's possessions were gone, that he realized Heart of Palm would not be returning. Night Orchid lay in the *hamaka* and did not move or say a word for the rest of the morning. Later she would tell Sekou she felt an ache in her heart that her last connection with her old life had been severed without even a goodbye. She was distraught about Heart of Palm's desertion, after he had taken the trouble to follow her when they'd parted the first time.

* * *

They passed the next few days in a daze. They had had no plan before this, only taking the time they needed for Night Orchid to heal. But Heart of Palm's departure had created a new kind of anxiety that wasn't there before. What should they do now?

Chapter 52

A fter the miserable rainy spell, they were spending most of their time outdoors. Not even the mosquitoes could dampen their lifting spirits. Night Orchid was gradually testing her injured leg walking with a stick, and Sekou helped her gather thatch to make a bag. Her scratches and bruises were healing and her face and body had plumped out. She dug around the hut and its environs salvaging whatever she could to fashion the day-to-day items that she needed. Now she was sitting on a tree trunk trying to attach a makeshift handle to a broken chisel.

"*¡Maldita sea!*"

The shout was so loud that every bird in the vicinity took flight. Night Orchid dropped her chisel as Sekou came streaking out of the *bohío*. He was shouting and stomping his feet, making fists at the sky, throwing himself on the ground and groaning before jumping up again. He had just discovered that Heart of Palm had taken his sword.

He had gone inside to get the book, for listening to him read had become Night Orchid's favorite pastime. When he pulled down his pack from the rafters to get the volume, he realized his sword was gone.

"I will catch him if he flies to the ends of the earth! I'll kill him and take back my sword!" He was shouting in Spanish so Night Orchid didn't understand a word, yet his gestures were clear enough. His first impulse was to set off then and there after Heart of Palm, but the girl calmed him down sufficiently for him to realize how foolish that was. They had no idea where he was headed or even when he had slipped away.

As darkness fell, they retired to the *bohío*. Sekou threw a huge log on the fire and they sat before the crackling blaze, neither showing any interest in cooking or eating. Sekou hoped he wasn't conveying to the girl what he really felt, a sickening fear in his gut that Heart of Palm would return with the sword to kill him. Kill the girl too, if she refused to give up whatever it was she had that he so desperately wanted.

He hadn't told Night Orchid of an incident that happened earlier, shortly after their arrival. He still had no idea why the girl had decided to trust him, a stranger, with something that was obviously precious to her but which she wanted hidden from her fellow Taíno.

The second morning after settling into the *bohío*, as Heart of Palm stepped outside, Night Orchid had taken a package from the folds of her wrap and thrust it at Sekou. "Please, hide this for me. Say nothing—"

In that instant, Heart of Palm returned. Sekou whipped the package behind him, and the youth did not glance in his direction. Dripping wet, he went over to the fire and started to wring the water out of his long hair and fix his topknot with his back turned to the other two. Sekou shoved the package into the thatch beside the nearest big gourd hanging above his head.

What he hadn't told Night Orchid was what happened next. She had left her shirt lying in the *hamaka* and had gone out and washed the wrap in the rain and hung it up to dry. She soon returned and kneeled by the little shrine, talking to the *cemíes* and presenting offerings, flowers and shells she had gathered outside. Heart of Palm picked up her shirt as though to admire it, while his eyes raked the bottom of the *hamaka*. He even bent down and looked beneath it before setting the shirt back down. He glanced at Sekou, who studiously turned away.

What was in the package? Sekou gave up trying to speculate. He had felt a sharp jolt when he handled it. He had touched power. So what did that make Night Orchid then?

Later that night, still sitting by the fire, she said, "He wanted to go south. I told him I had to go east. I left him and set off on my own. I didn't know he was following me."

"Why was he following you, Night Orchid? What's in the package?"

She didn't answer at first and he could see in the firelight she was fingering the little *cemí* around her neck and her lips were moving. When she finally spoke, her voice was so low he could barely hear her: "I—I can't tell you. It is the most precious thing in the world. I have to take it east. To our *behike* Candlewood. I am chosen."

After that, silence again fell between them. Sekou was still wrestling with his confusion when her voice came out of the darkness, full of confidence now.

"I know how you can get your sword back, Sekou. Come east with me. Our *behike* Candlewood can find anything. He will fly and locate it. Candlewood is the most powerful medicine man in the world."

Sekou only grunted. He had no intention of going east to find some medicine man. Every village claimed their *behike* was the greatest. How did she even know Maima's *behike* had survived? In fact, how had she herself escaped? Heart of Palm? Were there others?

Sekou mulled these thoughts for a several minutes, then decided: South is where his sword had gone and south is where he was going. First thing in the morning.

Night Orchid went to lie in the *hamaka*. "Tomorrow," she said, "we will collect what we need. We'll leave the day after. Rest now."

Sekou couldn't believe what he was hearing. Not even a woman yet and already so bossy? Who did she think she was? Her soft snoring just annoyed him further. How could she sleep at a time like this?

Then a new thought struck him. Heart of Palm wouldn't have gone far, or south, because he also wanted what Night Orchid had in her possession. Perhaps the package was protected by the spirits after all. Night Orchid too.

He, Sekou, was the one without protection of any kind. He had thrown away the holy cross and fallen outside the grace of the Christian god. He was as much a heathen barbarian now as the Spaniards said the Indians were. He was more certain than ever that Heart of Palm would slay him.

The huge shadows thrown by the blazing fire added to his nervousness. He kept his *koa* by his side, seeing the stout hardwood stick as the only means by which he could parry a blow from the sword, and his hand never strayed far from his knife. He felt like jumping out of his skin each time an owl hooted or a rat squeaked or a bat flew low over their heads. Even the familiar flashing glow of the fireflies disturbed him.

His heart was pumping the way it had the first days of his flight from Maima, when he heard or saw a Spanish soldier or an Indian tracker in every animal scurrying in the undergrowth. His greatest fear was dogs—fierce bloodhounds brought from Spain to subdue the islanders. He had finally grasped what it felt like to be a native on these islands.

Up to the moment of his flight, Sekou had been the good servant: obedient, faithful, and attentive, anxious to please yet proud of his accomplishments and the status they brought him.

For such an inquisitive and quick-witted child, even his life on shipboard had proven an adventure, despite the long hours, the rotten food, the endless tedium of the flat ocean, the fear brought on by life-threatening storms, and the occasional beatings and coarseness of his companions. The captain between bouts of drunkenness and foul-mouthed cursing had been pious and kind to him and had taught him to read, write, and acquire many skills that few others, Black or white, had.

Sekou had simply accepted as natural the existence into which he was born where he was owned by another.

His sudden plunge into the life of a runaway triggered new thoughts about those very masters that were now so explosive he was trying his best to contain them. The shock of Heart of Palm's treachery and his own stupidity was threatening to let loose all the anger and bitterness that had laid inside him all these years, unacknowledged, and were now set to tear him apart. He wondered, *Is this what it means to be free?*

Chapter 53

The sound brought him sitting bolt upright, knife in hand, heart racing. He listened for a few seconds then lay down again, feeling foolish. It was only Night Orchid, singing softly to herself. It was the song to Anacaona, the *kacika* who was brutally murdered at Xaragua on the island of Española on orders of the Spanish captains, of which the same Velázquez who now ruled Cuba was one.

> *Golden Flower*
> *You live in us still.*
> *In the shining mirrors of the sky*
> *And the glitter of morning*
> *You live in us still . . .*

Sekou knew the chorus and the words by heart for he had been hearing the song ever since he came to the Indies. Every night, Night Orchid sang it as she lay in the *hamaka*, joined sometimes—much to Sekou's surprise—by the powerful baritone of Heart of Palm. It seemed the only time he used his vocal cords. Hearing it now brought back an unwanted memory of another night. The night of the Maima massacre when the people trapped inside the longhouse defiantly sang it in the face of certain death. Somehow, the life-affirming purity of Night Orchid's voice tonight made him want to weep.

Sekou didn't sing because music made him sad. For the first time in years, he thought of his father who had left their home in Sevilla when Sekou was three years old, among a group of adventurers rushing to seek their fortunes in the newly discovered lands across the seas. Sekou's father had eagerly followed the son of his aristocratic but poverty-stricken master who had promised to free him and his entire family when they returned home covered in riches. It was all everyone dreamed of, since the return from the Indies of Colón and his men, after each voyage triumphantly bearing in procession to Their Majesties chests overflowing with gold and pearls, exotic plants and spices, rare birds perched on the shoulders of the wild-looking but handsome red people they called Indians who they brought back as trophies.

Though his mother dragged him down to the port every time the cathedral bells rang to signal another returning caravel, Sekou's father and his master had never been among the group that trickled back, enriched or broken by their dreams. When Sekou himself was taken by Captain de Burgos, it was the thought of meeting his father again that had given him the heart to bear the first difficult months on board the *Niña II* that sailed for the Canaries, then to the Indies and back to the Canaries again, but never to his home port where his mother lived.

In his wanderings, his heart had lurched at the sight of every Black man, until he would discover up close that it was not the man he sought. Sekou no longer had a precise image of his father's face, but he knew he would recognize him instantly from the length of his limbs, his quick laughter, his smell of aniseed which he constantly chewed, and the melody of his voice as he sang and played the *djembe*, the musical instrument of his African homeland that his father and grandfather and all the generations that came before them had played.

Sekou's father had planned to teach the boy to play, but up to when he left home, the child had been too small to carry and play the instrument at the same time, so he could do no more than beat the drum while his father held it and laughed his melodious laugh and his mother clapped her hands at her clever child who was making such music and moving his little feet in a dance. *Five is the proper age to start learning any instrument,* his father had said before he left. *I'll be back to teach you.* He told his son that until his return, he should practice every day on the little toy drum he'd made for him and hung around his neck with a pretty red and white cord.

Sekou had cried bitterly when he was taken from his home and not allowed to go back for his toy. After that, he had lost all interest in music. So why was he hearing now from far away what sounded like the sacred *balafon* and a soft voice singing in the tones of the *Cante jondo* of Andalucia?

Sekou forced his mind back to his immediate problem: he needed a plan. From the time Comandante Narváez had taken him to the barracks at Villa de la Vega, he had known that he was not cut out to be a soldier. He was a good swordsman, fast on his feet and nifty with knife or lance or with his fists, if need be, and he had cracked a few heads in his time in seaport brawls. But he knew he could not kill, certainly not slaughter the Indians in cold blood as he had witnessed from his time in the so-called *Nuevo Mundo.*

His flight from Maima had convinced Sekou that his only hope now lay in joining the Indians in their struggle to free the islands. He had desperately wanted Heart of Palm to see that. He had hoped that his overtures of friendship, like teaching the youth the rudiments of swordsmanship, would have done it in ways more potent than words.

But Heart of Palm's action had taken him right back to

his darkest moments. He had to accept that he was what he was, a fugitive, alone in a strange country, and, on top of everything else, at the mercy of a crazed Indian warrior armed with flint knife and axe, *atlatl* and spears, and, thanks to Sekou's stupidity, Toledo steel.

Chapter 54

The next morning, Sekou stepped out of the *bohío* to gather what they needed for traveling. He wondered how on earth he was setting out to do exactly what Night Orchid wanted, when she called him back. She wanted him to retrieve her package.

He was seized by a sudden frisson of fear as he stepped back inside, remembering how on her first morning in the *bohío*, Night Orchid had gazed for a long time at the three large gourds that hung from the ceiling, ones Sekou avoided. She had touched her *cemí* pendant and bowed. "Greetings, Grandfather Ahiacabo, Guarokael," she had whispered, adding, "good spirits here."

Sekou tried to control his trembling as he pushed his hand inside the thatch to retrieve Night Orchid's package. He touched one of the gourds and it crashed to the floor, pieces flying in all directions.

Sekou was horrified to see a skull grinning up at him amid long bleached bones.

He wasn't aware of letting out a sound but he must have, for Night Orchid put her finger to her lips to hush him. She kneeled and lifted the skull, cradled it tenderly. Sitting on her haunches, she began to rock back and forth and croon to it, as if comforting a child. She hummed a melody without words that went on and on, in a voice that got deeper and deeper and seemed to come from some part of herself that existed outside of time.

Sekou stood there, unable to move, swaying from side to side despite himself, and his head grew light as if he were being transported to another world. He had no idea how long they stayed like that until Night Orchid broke the spell. She abruptly stopped chanting and began to speak to the skull in her ordinary voice as she stood and bore it with both hands over to the shrine.

"Grandfather," she murmured, "forgive us for disturbing your sleep. You might have grown tired and wish simply to depart now. Mama Attabey, Baibrama . . . are here . . ."

She touched the little *cemí* figures as she named each one and placed the skull and then the bones and all the detritus from the broken gourd on the shrine and carefully rearranged the offerings to them all, the *cemíes* and the ancestor who had been so rudely disturbed. Then she bowed deeply and stepped backward before turning away and resuming her chores as if nothing had happened.

Sekou was left shaken. He knew the Taíno buried loved ones in the ground and reinterred the special ones after a year, cleaned the bones and the skull and after another elaborate ceremony buried them inside urns or in gourds that they hung up inside their homes, where they became honored ancestors and protectors. After all, it was from just such an accidentally broken gourd that the bones of Yayael, son of the One Who Cannot be Named had spilled out, giving mankind fish and the waters of the sea. That was an *areito* from First Time that he had heard many times.

He had known what the gourds in the rafters were and avoided touching them. But their presence made it seem as if the shelter had been more than a place for transient visitors.

Now that Night Orchid had added the broken gourd

and its contents to the shrine, it was overcrowded. Sekou could have sworn he heard voices coming from the pile, like the fragmentary voices he thought he heard from the thatch from time to time. He shook his head to clear it and felt an urge to get away. There were too many things that passed his understanding.

He took up the string bag and set off to do a task he could manage: combing the woods for food in a land of plenty.

When Sekou returned, he found Night Orchid smoking river shrimp and mullet to take on their journey. He had left her bemoaning as she had done every day that they had no *yuka*. *Yuka* was to her and every other Taíno their staff of life, their daily bread, and their means of communion with the supreme being through his representative Yukahú; the planting and harvesting of *yuka* regulated their calendar and their spiritual life.

Kasabe was eaten at every meal—and in between taken on journeys for food and offering to the spirits and stored against hard times; a good stock of dried *kasabe* bread was the signal to every village—the *yukayeke*—that Yukahú watched over them.

But here at the crossroads there was no *yuka*, though the travelers had left signs of their presence flourishing in the fruit trees from seeds or cuttings they had planted before passing on: *guanábana, caimito, anana, guayaba, jobo, mamí, aguate*. The fugitives had every day enjoyed these bounties, as well as the sacred medicines like *toona* used in healing Night Orchid's wounds and the holy *bixa*.

Sekou didn't bother to point out to Night Orchid that he had none of his own bread either. He did understand from the time spent with the Taíno in Xamayca how *yuka* was the foundation of their world. But, he told himself, Night

Orchid also needed to understand that that world no longer existed. They had all entered the unknown territory of *el Nuevo Mundo* where men with names like Velázquez and Narváez were destined to cut a swath of terror, enslavement, and death.

Chapter 55

By the time Sekou awoke the next morning, Night Orchid was ready for travel. She had bathed and washed her hair and inserted a flower into the plait. Two circular images painted on her cheeks represented Attabey, and her *bixa*-anointed body reflected the red of the rising sun. She had woven a small genital covering and wore protective sisal bands that tightly encircled the flesh at her ankles, knees, and elbows. She was armored for the journey. She seemed a totally different person from the battered and bloodied girl they had carried into the hut, the only reminders the purple bruises and the healing scabs of her wounds.

Outside, the fresh air swept away some of Sekou's mental darkness. Rain was a worry though, for while the sky was clear, the weather gods were waking again, flashes of lightning followed by thunder rolling in over the hills. But he no longer relished the idea of staying in the *bohío*, not with the thought of skulls and bones lying around. He knew the Taíno liked to live close to their ancestors, but he much preferred his in a consecrated churchyard some distance away. Sekou told himself he did not believe in ghosts, yet the idea of the dead so close made him shiver. Or perhaps it was the idea he hadn't abandoned of Heart of Palm lurking, ready to strike.

As he headed back to the hut, he was surprised to find Night Orchid hobbling to meet him and shouting, "Sekou, hurry, we have to leave! Now!" She grabbed his hand and started pulling him toward the *bohío*. "Hurry, hurry. There is no time!"

Sekou's stomach churned with fear. "He is here?"

"No, no. Spirits are loose. They want us to leave."

"*They?*" He barely noticed their possessions strewn on the ground outside the *bohío*.

Without answering, Night Orchid hoisted her string bag on her back and adjusted the tumpline across her forehead. Then she took up her stick and set off, limping slightly. Sekou watched her for a moment, open-mouthed, then sprang into action. He collected his possessions and ran.

The *bohío* was located at a crossroads where two trails met. The trail Night Orchid took was the one she had been traveling on that followed the contours of the hills. The path just skirted the edge, wide enough for one but rough going in places where thorn trees and brambles had to be slashed and thrust aside.

As he hurried along, Sekou wondered about Night Orchid's behavior. She had talked confidently of finding the *behike* Candlewood, but when he had asked how long it would take, she had simply smiled and said, "I don't know." At the time, Sekou hadn't taken her seriously. But as he hastened to catch up, he wondered if she had spoken the truth. *¡Dios mío!* he thought. *Where will it end? How did I ever get myself into this?*

He tried to seem manly and purposeful but his courage wavered as the dark clouds headed their way. The lightning flashes grew more frequent and the thunder claps closer together. He doubted there was shelter ahead. He called out, intending to tell Night Orchid they should turn back and wait out the storm in the hut, just as a crack of thunder exploded in his ear. Lightning sheared through his body and drained it of life, spinning him around. A small part of his mind recorded the image of the large *ceiba* tree that hovered over the *bohío* splitting in two and exploding into flames. It fell on the thatch roof in slow motion.

Night Orchid spoke softly in his ear: "Grandfather wanted to go."

Sekou had no strength left to inquire what she meant. His *koa* clattered to the ground as his hand went limp and his bags fell.

Chapter 56

Sekou found himself lying in the shade of a tree near the trail with no memory of how he got there. He cautiously opened his eyes and looked around.

The sun was almost at the western edge, so a whole day had passed. The packs and baskets were on the ground to one side, and on the other was Night Orchid, her hands busily stripping a *henequén* leaf for thread. She ceased humming when she realized he was awake and smiled at him, but said nothing. He tried to marshal his thoughts but the images crowded in—the exploding tree, the flaming hut, their narrow escape. How had Night Orchid known? Who was she? And why was she sitting there so tranquil now, as if nothing had happened?

He sat up, suddenly angry. He wanted to take her by the shoulders and shake the truth out of her. What was going on? How had she escaped from the burning Maima village? Why were she and Heart of Palm conspiring to make a fool out of him? What other tests of his sanity could they devise? For they were devils in disguise, he knew now. Working in concert. Shape-shifters. Out to trap him.

He knew of such monsters, his mind flashing to all the tales he had heard. Of dead sailors reincarnated as Hai Ho Shang, a large fish with shaved head that would seize boats and drag them down to the depths. Of the Harpies or Birds of Hell. Of the beast with a head at either end so when one slept the other kept watch. Of the animal with a mirror on its head like a glowing coal. Of Ceberus the watchdog at the gates of Hell who has three heads, six eyes, three mouths, and a triple bark. The fire-spitting Chimera. Huge dragons with their scaly bodies and broad wings. Gigantic jinns that can disappear through solid walls. Ku the dog-man, or the Lamias, beautiful women from the waist upward, writhing serpents below who whistled to lure men to their deaths. A world full of wonders and monsters and dangerous beasts. How did this seemingly innocent young girl beside him fit in? When would she transform herself into the monster that she was?

He realized his heart was beating too fast, and his breathing was quick and shallow. He was about to faint again. But he needed to be calm so he could fight this enemy. He closed his eyes and tried to control his breathing as the ship's doctor had taught him, focusing his mind on a pinpoint of light until he began to float in a timeless world. How long this lasted, he did not know, but when he finally opened his eyes there were no evil monsters; instead, he was flooded with calm and marveled at the beauty of the world around him. How had he not noticed?

He looked at Night Orchid out of the corner of his eye and saw that she had not moved. She was still combing the *henequén* leaf for thread, winding it around a makeshift wooden shuttle, and humming her aimless little tune. She was a girl whose hands were never idle.

He remembered how, despite the wounds and lacerations on her body and her obvious stiffness from the fall, she had spent time in the *bohío* digging in the dusty debris heaped up to one side, or searching the grounds outside for discarded objects that could be useful.

She had roped Heart of Palm into helping her cut *hen-equén* and beat and macerate the leaves to extract the fiber which they hung up to dry and which she wove into a carrying bag. She had pulled apart pieces of an old *hamaka* and used a handmade hook to fashion a medicine bag from the cotton threads.

One day Sekou had entered the *bohío* to find her poking around, picking up bits and pieces, examining them, throwing some down and putting others aside.

"What are you doing?"

"I need tools."

"What for?"

She had looked at Sekou strangely, as if she couldn't believe his ignorance. "My work."

"What work?"

"My carving. I'm a carver in my uncle's workshop."

Sekou thought it unlikely, given her age, but said nothing.

"Here," she had said, lifting a stone axe without a handle and setting it to one side. "This will do. I need to sharpen it and find a handle. Sekou, you can help me. Look—" and she held up two of the pieces she had rescued—"a whole chisel. And a shell gouge." She kept on turning things over and releasing new clouds of dust. "If only I can find something to make a drill. A sturdy manatee bone. That would be so nice."

She had been silent for a while as she continued her search, then turned to him and asked, "Why did the Panols have to leave their land to come and take ours?"

"I—I don't know."

"But you are one of them."

"I am not."

"You speak their language. And you have a sword. And . . . talking leaves. And . . . *pantalones, camisas* . . ."

"They stole my family too, you know." He was getting angry.

She looked surprised. "Really?"

"The Panols came to our land, which they named Africa, and stole my family and took them to Spain. Lots of people like me. Spain is where I was born. But I am not a Spaniard." He had been surprised at his own vehemence in asserting this, something he had never even thought about before.

"So what are you then?"

"What do you mean?"

"What is the name of your clan, your family?"

"We don't have clans. We took our Spanish master's name, I suppose . . ." His voice faded in embarrassment.

"But you must have a lineage. How else can people know you?"

In that moment he had forgotten about Baba Sec and his Jolof bloodlines. "Well, I do have a blood brother Tamayo in Xamayca. I was adopted into his clan."

"And your *guatiao*'s clan?"

"Owl."

"Owl! That's my clan too. Imagine! We are family, Sekou. That means we cannot marry."

She said it lightly, though it had startled him; he still thought of her as a child. But all Taína had to marry, and in another year or two she would be ready. In truth, he had liked it when she said, *We are family,* and he thought of it now.

He told himself with a feeling of surprise: *Night Orchid is the only living, breathing human being I know in this world. I have to trust her. Maybe she is a witch. Maybe she has superpowers. Who knows?* No matter what happened between them, he had to admire her resilience, her industry, her optimism, and her still untarnished belief in goodness in the world.

He wondered about her and her people and what they had done to bring such harsh retribution, the total destruction of their world. The Taíno were being attacked everywhere he knew, on all the islands. Killed for sport or brutalized by dogs or turned into slaves. But usually the large-scale killings or roundups happened according to a plan. He knew this from his time with Narváez. *Kill the* kacikes *to destroy the leadership. Kill the* behikes *to destroy their religion. Kill the warriors and young men to strike at insurgency, or chain them to dig for gold and work them to death. Rape the women and keep them as breeders and servants.*

But the killings he had witnessed in Maima had been unplanned and unprovoked, born of bloodlust. Swords sharpened on flint. One man's thirst for blood had set it off.

Sekou knew he had to speak. He wet his lips and forced the words out through a voice that sounded like a croak: "Night Orchid, it's time for you to open your book."

She looked at him curiously.

"Tell me everything in it about your people and your village. About Maima. What made the *cemíes* desert you?"

Her hands stilled and she looked up at the orange and purple painting the evening sky as if to gather her thoughts. Her small mouth worked in silent communication with her *cemí* spirit, then she abruptly stood and gathered her things. "We must find shelter before night."

He found himself standing too, with no argument left in him as he hoisted his bag on his back. His legs were still shaky and he staggered a bit, but he hurried to get ahead to chop at the overhanging bush in their path. As they walked, he felt his strength returning, though he couldn't shake off a feeling that another kind of darkness was following them, and he kept turning around to look back the way they had come.

After the third time, Night Orchid said, "Don't worry, Sekou, I have eyes in the back of my head." She said it lightly, but with everything that had occurred, he was half-inclined to believe her.

He was pleased when the path started to turn away from the cliff and take them into the pine forest. It was deeply shadowed from the towering trees that grew closer together, but the going was much easier as the trail was clearly marked and the low canopy was pierced by the last of the sunlight.

When they came to a large tree with dry branches creating a cozy shelter, they dropped their bags and slumped to the ground. Too tired to light a fire, they ate roasted fish from Night Orchid's pack and lay on their backs and looked through the leaves above them where the Star People glittered and the Milky Way streamed.

"It will soon be time for solstice," Night Orchid said, then stopped speaking as she realized this year there would be no celebration. She sighed, and Sekou reached out to hold her hand.

Sekou was almost asleep when her voice came out of the darkness: "It started with the bird—I don't know if it is so, but that's what people said. The Bird of Evil Omen that Trader brought to our village."

Chapter 57

Not far from where Sekou and Night Orchid rested, Heart of Palm dug himself a hollow nest of branches and dried leaves. He was close enough to keep an eye on them but too far away to hear what they said. He wished with all his heart he could join them. He had never left off shadowing them from the fateful day he had taken Sekou's sword.

Shame had kept him close to the *bohío*, shame that prevented him from revealing himself, from developing any kind of plan. He had been brought up *ni-taíno*, a son of nobles, trained from birth in honor and respect. How could he have fallen so low?

He'd had no intention of stealing Sekou's sword. In a moment of rage, he had taken it to hurt him, thinking he would hide it and watch his frustration as he searched for it, his most treasured possession. All of his bottled emotions had become centered on the young man. His smile, his good nature, his learning, his possessions, his knowledge of the world. The way he and Night Orchid had bonded, sharing laughter and—he was sure—secrets. Secrets that the girl should have shared with him.

How dare he come and take from Heart of Palm all that was rightfully his, his entire world?

Heart of Palm knew this was unreasoning. But he needed

someone to blame. For everything. In his past life, he would have challenged his antagonist to a wrestling match, or a stick fight, or organized a team to trounce him at a ball game. Failing which, if it was a really serious dispute, the *kacike* would have settled it. But nothing of that world was left. Nothing.

He had planned to return the sword to the *bohío* after a few hours. But one day and a night passed while he skulked out of sight, and then it was too late. The sword would not let go of him. Like the monster Skull Woman, a head that rolled about and searched for a body to cling to, the sword became a thing that clung and whispered and spoke in the language of the *paranaghiri*. An evil object that both repelled and seduced him.

Like the man Shark Tooth, he now thought, who had also repelled and seduced them. Shark Tooth, who invaded his waking thoughts and compounded his nightmares like a dark shadow, one that manifested itself in every reptile that crawled and sat and watched. Or was he that bird? For Shark Tooth had whispered that he too could amass enough power to soar like a bird, master of all realms.

Heart of Palm had witnessed the lightning strike the *bohío*, the anger of the *cemíes*, the roll of thunder that had dropped him to his knees with his hands over his ears and his head to the ground. Guataúba had spoken. Why hadn't he been killed? He had watched from safety as the flames devoured the hut and the last charred pole fell, then he ran to follow in the trail of the other two because he could not bear to be alone.

His souls were in disarray—the clinging sword had taken him over. He would have given it up at any moment, if only *it* would let go.

Chapter 58

Shark Tooth trudged wearily up the path that followed the river, furiously batting at the sand flies and mosquitoes, cursing the screaming parrots, the monkeys jumping in his path and chattering, the zigzag scurrying of iguanas, the susurration of the leaves, the sound of the water gushing over rocks. He hated everything about mountains, about the countryside, wondering how a life that seemed so sweet could so swiftly turn bitter. How could it all go so wrong? Again.

Still, he was lucky to be alive, lucky to have followed the priest to the visitors' lodge and be away from the main plaza when the killings started. Lucky that the arrogant Indian who had come with the Spaniards had elbowed him out of the way when he tried to translate for the *kacike*. Which was a good thing, really, since he knew nothing about the *paranaghiri*'s language. Nothing but the few words the Old Man had shared with him.

Shark Tooth thought now of how the Old Man had boasted about the *paranaghiri*, as if they were superior beings. Why hadn't the Old Man spoken about their arrogance, their cruelty, their violence?

Their voices, their gestures, remained loud and threatening even after they had ridden far away from Maima. They had stopped at a broad sandy beach on the river to rest the horses and demand food from the now surly Xamaycan Taíno servants who were scrambling about, lighting fires and unpacking bags.

Drinking and laughing loudly, they had stood around in little groups making gestures that relived their favorite moments of the slaughter they had just taken part in, twisting their swords to show this disembowelment, or that one showing the way he had swiped a head clean off. That is, the ones who were not standing in a little cluster surrounding each of the girls they had taken with them, forcing them from the priest's house where they had cowered, terrified, not knowing what was happening outside, not realizing they could have run away.

Too late, each had been grabbed by a stinking soldier and swept up on his horse. When they stopped at the river, her deliverer became the first to have his way before he thrust her aside to become fodder for the men standing around in a circle, watching and laughing, waiting their turn to straddle her.

The only one angry was the man in charge who had stayed on his horse and calmly watched the slaughter and destruction of Maima with an expressionless face. He was furious now, striding up and down and shouting. He wasn't angry about the girls. The word "Sekou," which he yelled frequently, was the only one Shark Tooth understood, for the priest had been shouting in vain for the Black man as Maima burned.

Hidden in the visitors' lodge, Shark Tooth had witnessed the priest in tears, having tried in vain to stop the slaughter. It was a useless gesture as the horsemen arrived and dragged the screaming girls out. The priest was still standing there with his hands pressed together, looking into the sky, his lips moving, when the Indians who had accompanied him brought his horse and helped him up, running behind him with his baggage on their heads as they had done when they arrived.

Shark Tooth had attached himself to the end of the little cavalcade as it moved off to follow the main body of the Spaniards, deciding that this was the safest place to be.

He remained hidden when they stopped by the river, and behind the boulder sheltering him, he had heard enough from two Taíno talking as they led a string of horses to the water to know that the comandante was furious because he had lost his most expensive possession—the Black boy Sekou.

For the first time since fleeing Maima, Shark Tooth smiled. He had no doubt he would be well rewarded if he could find and return him.

PART IV
THE CAVE

Chapter 59

Seated on his *duho* outside the cave at Cauta, bent over in contemplation, elbows on knees, skinny ribs exposed, looking as frail as a dried almond leaf blown hither and yon, Candlewood finally lifted his head, his long white hair feathering out like wings, and sniffed the air through his beaky nose. He gave a nod of satisfaction.

"Our visitors are gathering."

Flint knew better than to ask questions. His duty, he had learned the painful way, was to serve the holy man, to learn, to obey, and be silent. "Speech gets in the way of the voices," Candlewood had told him, "those inside and those of the spirits outside, those in Dream and in our waking. Only by learning to hear all the voices will we learn what we need to know."

All their talking had been done while they prepared for the journey after the *behike* had intercepted him. Their time since then had been passed mainly in silence, except when Candlewood gave instructions or asked questions of his apprentice. Silence was in keeping with Flint's own nature, so he did not find it a hardship. Except at times like this, when he had no idea who the expected visitors might be.

Candlewood had never said what the purpose of their journey was. Flint had put a knot on a string to mark each day. Three moons had passed since the destruction of Maima.

Despite his seeming frailty, the elder had vigorously taken the lead along the route the pilgrims would have taken from Maima to the holy mountain to refresh the Sacred Bundle, as if he too was refreshed by the holiness of his task. Even though, Flint knew, this time there was no Sacred Bundle, for Candlewood had told him of its loss.

Usually Flint would not have been shown the pilgrims' path until he reached manhood and made his first pilgrimage at the end of his initiation. "But in these times," Candlewood had said, "as fast as the arrow flies, boys are suddenly men and young girls find themselves women with responsibilities. So we are rushed into the Fifth Age that is already upon us. Who is there to deflect it?"

The route they followed was overgrown, but as they chopped at the vegetation, the path emerged faintly like a smoky ribbon unwinding before them, leading them on, the earth pounded hard as rock from the generations that had trod it. Flint took note of the subtle markers deliberately left on the way, and the fruit trees, roots, and medicinal plants that flourished on either side, the discards from travelers that would grow and thrive and provide sustenance for those who came after.

Now Flint wondered if anyone of their world would be left to keep the path open, or if it would begin to fall back to nature as the ball court and longhouse were already doing. Or would the *paranaghiri* find their way up to the very mountaintops to destroy it all?

Flint had not realized when journey's end was reached. The cliffs of pitted limestone rocks seemed to get ever higher as they climbed. As they neared the summit and a seemingly impenetrable wall of rock, Candlewood had stopped, dropped his pack, and kneeled. Opening his flint box, he lit his cigar, his fingers trembling as he puffed to get it lit. As he walked forward, he had blown *tabako* in all four directions, calling out loudly each time in a language Flint did not yet understand.

Flint had come to an abrupt halt as Candlewood interspersed speaking and blowing smoke with listening, then speaking again, conversing with the holy spirits. Flint could feel power flowing all around them, gaining in strength as a mighty wind swirled through the trees and the leaves fluttered and whispered.

Only when Candlewood had taken the next few steps did Flint's eyes open enough to see the black hole in the wall of rock. They had reached the cave.

Emerging from the bushes and lianas smothering everything else, but standing clear of all vegetation, moss, and dirt, as if its own power kept it pristine, stood the massive carving of Mácocael, the guardian sentinel, the one who had been turned into stone by Sun for his failure to carry out his duty as watchman on the day of Emergence. His likeness stood at every village entrance as a warning against the peril of inattention.

Flint's heart had been pounding so hard it felt like the *mayohuakan* was beating inside him. To have reached the cave. To be standing outside of it. To enter the holy of holies. But as soon as they'd saluted Mácocael, the *behike* put out his hand to stop him.

"Not yet," he had said. "You are not strong enough. I must prepare."

Flint had swallowed his disappointment and laid down the food bag he was carrying.

"I will meet you at the ball court to greet Sun every morning," Candlewood said. He had pointed out a faint path. "That will lead you to the longhouse where you will stay." Indicating the food bag, he instructed, "Take that with you."

This meant, Flint knew, that Candlewood was embarking on another fast, leaving his body completely empty for the spirits to enter his *kohoba* visions.

Now, here they were, three days later, Candlewood with his body looking more wasted than ever, yet confident of the events he had seen in his vision, for he was giving Flint precise instructions.

"The two we expect will arrive soon. Go to the head of the path to greet them in my name. Let them rest for they have had a hard journey. Tomorrow morning, we will gather at the ball court to greet Sun." Candlewood paused for a long time and again lifted his head and sniffed the air like a dog and eventually said in a sarcastic voice, "Perhaps others will be joining us." He gazed at Flint without speaking, as if taking his measure, and ended on an enigmatic note: "Now is not the time for fear. Be prepared, Flint, for anything."

As if that was not enough, as soon as Flint took off, Candlewood called him back with the kind of chuckle that to the boy meant that the elder was making a joke at his expense. "You will be pleased, Flint, to see a familiar face from Maima."

From Maima? Flint's heart began to flutter inside his chest as he frantically ran through his mind all the people this could possibly be, starting of course with his mother and father. In his heart, he knew that Candlewood would not be cruel enough to hide the fact that Flint's nearest and dearest were alive. No, Candlewood had witnessed their dying. He had told Flint so, how on that awful day he had witnessed Crab Claw fleeing to her husband's side; Matron Greenstone's brother Maura running to clasp her in his arms and their sinking to the ground together as the flames consumed the longhouse where—to everyone's surprise—Maura had joined them that morning. Candlewood had spoken of the maddened horses, the ashes, the smoke.

So lost was Flint in these images, feeling the acrid scent of burning in his nostrils, hearing the screams, that he only half heard what else Candlewood said: "Do not be afraid of the other, Flint. Though he comes from a people you have never seen before, he is now our brother."

Chapter 60

Flint sat on the hill overlooking the spot where the main paths met—one going east-west across the ridge, the other the pilgrims' path they had taken. Candlewood had not told him from which direction the visitors would come.

He waited and watched all day, turning his head this way and that until his vision blurred. He had long drained his water calabash and was very thirsty, but he made no move. He was practicing to be as still as Candlewood on his *duho*.

Finally, his vigil was rewarded by the flight of some white egrets from the trees overhanging the path to the west. The birds flew high into the sky, then wheeled and slowly headed back to their feeding trees, the only movement breaking the stillness.

Flint jumped down from his perch and set off to meet the strangers he now saw heading his way. There were two of them, a tall man and a small woman, walking unsteadily. Flint was mortified that the girl recognized him first.

"I see you, Flint!" she called out. "O Flint, is that you?"

Only when she was a few paces away did he recognize her as Night Orchid.

She clasped his hands and looked into his eyes in wonderment. And then she glanced around. "Candlewood? Is he here? Where is he?"

"Greetings, Night Orchid. I too rejoice to see you. Candlewood is not far away. He is expecting you."

She grasped his hands tighter. "O please, take me to him."

"I am sorry, but not today. He will meet with you tomorrow."

To Flint's suprise, she burst into tears. "No, no no. I have come so far. I must see him. I can't bear it anymore. It is too much for me." And she sank to the ground and threw her hands over her face and wailed.

"Night Orchid . . ." Flint was so focused on her that he had forgotten her companion, who kneeled down and placed a hand on the girl's shoulder. A black hand, and a face under a leather hat equally black, as if completely stained by *jagua*. But no, *jagua* was never so dark, and the face was not Taíno. What kind of devilry was this?

Flint took a step back, his face mirroring his horror. The strange man looked at him and smiled. "I see you, friend. I am Sekou."

The man's use of Taíno only added to the strangeness, and Flint tried to speak but couldn't. After an awkward silence, the man added, "So you are Flint. I have heard Night Orchid speak of you."

Night Orchid gave one last sob and lifted her head, as if remembering her manners. "Flint, Sekou is a friend. He rescued me and saw me safely here. His people come from a land far away. The other side of the world. Many planting seasons away." She smiled and her voice grew animated. "He has talking leaves. Flint, you must ask him to let *elibro* speak. It is the most amazing thing in the world."

Bewildered by the stranger, the shock of seeing Night Orchid, her odd outburst, wondering what *elibro* was, Flint took her lifting spirits as a sign to move on. He bowed to Sekou while murmuring a welcome, then reached down and took the girl's heavy pack as the Black man helped her to her feet.

"It is not far," Flint said, as he led them to the path. "Everything is prepared for you."

"So Candlewood knew I was coming? He was expecting me?" Night Orchid asked.

Flint turned and smiled. "Yes, he knew you were coming."

That seemed to satisfy her, for she said to Sekou, "See, I told you. Candlewood knows everything. He is the greatest *behike* in the world."

Flint chuckled to himself; although Night Orchid seemed to have grown in the many moons since he had last seen her, at heart she was still a child. And yet he couldn't help wondering how she had escaped Maima and how Candlewood knew to expect her. And where did the stranger come from? Although he was hungry for answers, he knew that his first duty was to get them comfortable and fed.

As it turned out, there was little talking over the next hand of time. The travel-stained newcomers dropped their packs in the longhouse and went to wash in the stream nearby while Flint heated up tea and pepperpot stew. They fell on the food with deep murmurs of satisfaction. But they were both yawning before they even finished the meal and dropped into *hamakas*, quickly falling fast asleep.

Flint cleaned up and banked the fire. There was still some daylight left, and he went and sat at the entrance to the longhouse. Since his arrival, he had weeded the verges and made the ball court presentable after its seeming neglect; he had done the same for the longhouse. Flint tried but couldn't empty his mind, couldn't keep out the questions and the thoughts racing around in his head. And he couldn't help wondering why, instead of making him happy, this meeting with Night Orchid was bringing on tears.

Chapter 61

Flint didn't even realize he was humming the song to Anacaona until another voice joined in and Night Orchid sat down beside him at the entrance to the longhouse. She had combed and plaited her hair and seemed the same but different, then he noticed that she had small breasts and was on the way to becoming a woman, although her hair had not been cut and she wore no insignias. In the time he had been away from Maima, he now understood, he had lost not just his people but several moons of what had been happening in the daily life of the village before its destruction.

They sat and hummed companionably for a while, but Flint's face grew hot when Night Orchid turned to him and said with a smile, "I am so glad to see you, Flint," for he was not used to talking to girls or even sitting so close to one that was not his kin.

"And I you, Night Orchid."

He paused, afraid to ask the question on the tip of his tongue. "Are we—and the *behike*—the only three left of our village?"

"No," she said to his great surprise. "There is one other that I know of. Heart of Palm."

"*Guay*!" Flint was stunned to hear this. His old antagonist, of all people. And yet he was pleased. "What . . . How do you know?"

"Because he met me on the trail from Maima and he stayed with us—Sekou and me—for a while. Then he left . . ."

"Where did he go?"

"I don't know. He didn't tell us."

She said nothing more and Flint was struck by the frown on her face. She played with the string of her medicine bag and finally spoke: "He wanted to go south, to the coast, to find some of his people." She was again silent for a long moment, and then it burst out of her. "Flint, he did something unforgivable. Heart of Palm stole Sekou's sword. Then he ran away."

"What?" Flint would never have associated the proud, arrogant *ni-taíno* with something as cowardly as theft.

"We've been worried ever since. All the way here. We feared he would come back and try to kill us."

"No, that's impossible." Despite Flint's wariness of the young man who used to tease him unmercifully, he couldn't imagine him committing murder.

"He's changed, Flint. Everything's changed. The world has been turned upside down. I think Heart of Palm's souls turned and have come loose."

Flint thought about the peril one faced if a soul came loose and there was no *behike* strong enough to fly off to go find it. This was a perilous journey and only the strongest—such as Candlewood—would be willing to undertake it.

Flint was lost in contemplation of what Night Orchid was saying, until she broke the silence again, and told him everything that had happened since her first meeting with Heart of Palm on the trail, and how he had changed from seemingly being her protector into a figure that menaced her dreams.

"I don't know, Flint, there is evil on the loose. All the way here, I could feel dark wings beating and a shadow over us, even when there were no clouds. But when I looked, there was nothing there. Have you felt it, Flint? The darkness?"

When Flint didn't answer, she remained silent for a while, then she surprised him. "Sometimes I saw him in the darkness—the witch, Shark Tooth. In our *yukayeke*, I hid whenever I saw him coming. There was something in his eyes when he looked at me . . . . I'm terrified, Flint—do you think he can find us here?"

Shark Tooth! Flint had almost forgotten about the man. "It's all right, Night Orchid, you are safe now. We are under Candlewood's protection in this sacred place. Nothing can harm us."

He said this boldly, but in his deepest soul he could not forget how often on the trail Candlewood himself had stopped and sniffed the air, as if something evil were indeed pursuing them. That there were dangers out there other than the *paranaghiri*. Had Shark Tooth managed to escape from the burning village? Candlewood had not mentioned him at all. If he had the powers some people said he had, could he have flown?

But Night Orchid was smiling at his words of reassurance and stood up. "I would like to go and look at the ball court."

"I'll take you there."

"Thank you, but I'd like to go by myself." Touching her amulet, Night Orchid added, "I'd like to pay my respects to Mother Attabey and thank her for bringing me safely here."

Flint watched her walk away. He was still troubled, for nothing she said had told him how she came to be here and what the connection to Candlewood was. Her story only began when she was already on the trail, alone and by herself. But what was she doing there in the first place? And how did the strange Black youth fit into any of this?

As if these thoughts had conjured him, Sekou came out

of the longhouse and sat down on the step that Night Orchid had vacated. He held his face up to the sun as if drinking it in and stretched lazily. He was quite tall, much taller than Flint, his limbs were elongated, unlike the compact Taíno bodies, and all his movements were fluid, as if listening to some inner music.

Flint watched him out of the corner of his eye, suprisingly comfortable in his presence. The more he saw of Sekou, the more he realized that his ebony color and his hair were really the only strange things about him. His face was quite beautiful, and his broad lips turned up at the edges as if he were constantly smiling. The shape of his head was like Flint's, unbound, so his high forehead more than anything endeared him to the boy.

Flint hadn't yet seen any *paranaghiri*, but he'd heard enough to know they were different from Sekou. Were there other people out there, so different from them, waiting to be discovered?

Chapter 62

Shark Tooth had stayed hidden until Narváez and his men finally set off. He headed in another direction, hoping to find a sheltered spot where he could rest and collect his thoughts and stop the violent trembling of his body. Nothing had gone as expected.

He lost track of time as he wandered from place to place over the next three moons, seeking shelter where he could in the guise of a lost Lucayan refugee, carefully hiding any connection with Maima, since news of the massacre had generated intense fear and suspicion among formerly hospitable people. He kept moving in an eastward direction without any idea of where he was going, though his target at first was the fugitive Sekou, whom he believed would head for the mountains. He eventually gave that up as he hadn't a clue where the Black man could be. Better, he thought, to focus on Candlewood and the Bundle. He knew that Candlewood was the only one who could have taken the sacred object, and he must be alive somewhere. So where would that be? From time to time he had entered dreams and tried to locate him, but the vision was never strong enough and faded into nothingness each time he closed in.

One afternoon high up in the hills, he sat on a big rock and decided it was time to take stock and plan his next move. His medicine bag contained a bit of the holy herb *tabako*, but not enough *kohoba* to enable him to communicate with the Shark God of the underworld sea—Bagua Guamacajayo. And that is what he had to do. His world had come uprooted once again. He needed to see clearly in which direction to turn. He had consulted the deity only twice before, and the encounters still frightened him. But he was now at such a crossroads that only divine guidance could see him through.

From his perch he could see scattered small settlements where he could stock up on food and water. A Lucayan refugee who had lost his way is what he would be. He carefully removed all his jewelry and decorations and placed them in his bag.

A pack of yellow-skinned dogs rushed to greet him as he approached the nearest *bohío*. They didn't bark but made strange growling sounds in their throats to warn their owners of his approach. As did the flocks of parrots screeching from every tree.

He respectfully called out to an old man leaning on a cane and watching him: "Elder, I see you. Greetings!"

"I see you too. Welcome." The old man waved his stick and indicated that he should enter their compound, but scrutinized Shark Tooth carefully as he did so.

"Elder, perhaps you can help me. I am on my way to join my compatriots at Caimito, but I seem to have lost my way."

The old man laughed. "So you have. You must have taken a wrong turning where the road forks way back there. About a half day's journey away. But come in. We will put you on the right path. You come from far?"

"Yes," Shark Tooth said, naming a coastal village several day's journey to the west. "My brother-in-law sent word that he was at Caimito and I had no boat, so I foolishly decided to walk. I had no idea it was so far."

As he followed the elder between the rows of houses, villagers stopped what they were doing to glance at him, but no one spoke or smiled. Everyone seemed quiet and sober and some were covered in black *jagua* for mourning. There was an air of distraction, though Shark Tooth sensed he was not the cause. These were folk packing up to leave, with *kasabe* stuffed into bags, roots for planting standing in large carrying baskets, mounds of fruit lying around, pet birds in cages, *hamakas* and mats piled up on the ground.

The elder said he was taking him to the *kacike*. But the *kacike* had somehow already been informed, for he met them on the way, a squat man with his hair in an untidy bun and a frown on his face, obviously interrupted in the middle of something.

He greeted Shark Tooth politely and they exchanged names and kin information. Shark Tooth was startled to hear himself give the name of his twin brother Mucaro as his own. It had simply popped out of his mouth. A bad omen, this calling up of the dead. But too late to take it back.

The *kacike* listened to his story and said they would send a boy to show him the right path, but invited him to spend the night. He apologized that they could offer so little hospitality because they themselves were moving. It turned out that as news of the massacre spread, many of the smaller villages had decided that it was unsafe to stay where they could also be killed or taken into slavery, so they were abandoning their *bohíos*. Already many of their kin nearer to the coast had been captured, bound, and sent to dig for gold.

The chief was coy about exactly where they were headed, waving his hand in the direction of the highlands.

Shark Tooth didn't care. The next morning he left with what he wanted: water calabashes, food for several days, and what he needed most: *tabako* and the powder and lime for snuff. Now he could talk to Bagua Guamacajayo. Now he could see where the person he sought was headed.

Shark Tooth walked for a while, searching for a place where he could lie low, inhale *kohoba*, and enter into Dream. The limestone cliffs above the path were pitted with caves and he settled himself in a shallow cavern that gave him a good view of the path where he could not be seen.

He purged himself, then laid out the snuff on a flat rock like a table and sniffed deeply through his two-pronged inhaler of manatee bone. Soon, he was walking on the road to the underwater kingdom of the Shark God.

He had only traversed this path twice before, for the journey was perilous and only worthwhile if the reward was extraordinary and beyond his powers—like this one. For the payment required was human blood, shed in a way that would not expose him to any inquiry, which probably entailed using his magic dart for the kill.

The visit was brief. He hoped Bagua Guamacajayo would enable him to find the people he sought and show him the direction to go. He felt imperiled in a way he had never felt on the cays, for the sea always provided an escape route. He was vulnerable here in the hills, without any idea of where he was, oriented only by the small band of blue sea in the far distance. That alone reassured him.

The dream had gone well. His main concern was locating Candlewood and the Bundle—ownership would give him nearly endless power and enable him to vanquish Candlewood once and for all. He was surprised and pleased to receive more than he'd expected. The girl Night Orchid had the Bundle and was headed to the holy mountain where Candlewood awaited her. Better still—and he couldn't believe his eyes—the girl was accompanied by none other than the fugitive Black, Sekou. How was that possible? Was the wheel turning in his favor once more? Would he be strong enough to capture all of them at once?

Bagua Guamacajayo promised that he could ensure Shark Tooth's presence at the handing over of the Bundle. The rest was up to him. Shark Tooth didn't even have to ask what the payment would be for such an extraordinary gift; he knew the price. He was so excited he little heeded the warning: *Beware of what you cannot see lurking in the shadows.*

He awoke from the trance in a darkness that enveloped him both inside and out. The god of the underworld would help him attain what he desired in exchange for fresh blood. Where on earth was he going to find a body in this empty, forsaken place?

Chapter 63

Heart of Palm lay in the thick bushes overlooking the ball court with a grand view of the playing fields, the longhouse, and the trails. He had hidden well out of sight after following Flint and the travelers to the hilltop.

From what Night Orchid said, he had expected Candle-wood to greet them here, but seeing Flint was totally unexpected. What other surprises were in store?

He was glad to overhear Flint say that Candlewood would not appear until the next day, for he was terrified the *behike* would have looked straight through to his hiding place and he wasn't yet prepared for his searing probe. He had already felt the hot beating wings of the thunderbird as it angrily cast the lightning that torched the *bohío*, lightning that was punishment for thieves. Why hadn't it dealt him the fatal blow that would have ended his agony?

That question had nagged at him day and night as he fol-lowed the two travelers on their journey over so many turns of the sun he lost count. Unable to eat or sleep or gain more than a few hours of rest when they took breaks, he felt as wretched as he looked.

Now he watched with longing as Night Orchid slowly paced the ball court with awe on her face, and Flint seemed re-laxed as he sat at the entrance to the longhouse with the Black youth beside him holding his face up to the last rays of the sun.

He wished with all his heart he could join them, but knew that he was exiled, every day he spent on his own taking him farther away from human contact. Yet he could not bring himself to take the noble way out. More than once he had placed the point of the sword to his chest, or traced the edge of his flint knife on his wrist, drawing beads of blood, wanting to end it all. But some small flame of hope that his life was not entirely worthless kept him going.

As they'd neared the mountain, he tried to bring his disordered thoughts to focus on what he would say to Candlewood. That he had brought the sword to him as a symbol of the dreaded *paranaghiri*, to be destroyed. He'd forgotten entirely that it was the sword that had brought *him*. The sword that seemed to have acquired a life of its own.

Coming here to the ball court was bittersweet for Heart of Palm, for it brought back memories of another time, the happiest period of his life. The summer solstice ceremonies when he became a man. After their initiation, he and his age mates from several villages had been brought on their first pilgrimage to the sacred mountain.

The four-day ceremonies had ended with their playing *batéy* on the sacred court as it had been ordained from First Time: the twenty boys who were newly made men versus the older men, the fathers and uncles, the young representing the vital Sun as it soared across the Heavens, the old men its night journey through the underworld. More rested on the outcome of the game than the feverish betting on all sides.

He had been the one to bounce the ball across the line, and an uncle misjudged his aim and missed, allowing it to touch the earth and harmlessly roll away, thus ceding the game and victory to the youth.

The boys had thrown themselves down on the sidelines,

battered and bloody and exhausted, while women chanted and threw water over them and the healers and bonesetters bound up their wounds. They gritted their teeth and smiled against the pain, savoring their victory. Their win had ensured for Sun what it needed most: the sweat and blood of youth to keep it rolling across the sky for another year.

Heart of Palm was so lost in this memory that he came back to reality with a grin on his face, which made reality even harder to bear. He brushed his long and uncombed hair off his face, the greasy strands a sign of how much he had neglected himself. He felt as if he was already halfway to the land of shades.

That night as darkness descended, he dug deeper into the shadows. Tomorrow at Sun's rising, Candlewood would meet them. Here. Right in front of the spot where he was hidden. What then? The sword had only brought him this far.

Chapter 64

S hark Tooth was tired and anxious and angry. Few
people passed by on the trail below and he had been
watching all day. The ones who came were traveling
in groups. He needed a lone traveler so there would be no
witnesses to their falling, no one to look suspiciously at the
cliff above, no search made of the area to find the cause. His
victim would be found with no sign of injury and would be
carried home; any inquest into the mysterious death would
take place long after he had left the area and Bagua Guamacajayo had had his fill of blood.

Finally, he was rewarded. A lone girl came along, burdened with a heavy carrying basket full of *yuka* which kept
slipping, no doubt the cause of her lagging behind a couple
who were some way ahead. She was fairly young, perhaps
fifteen summers.

He was hidden in the bushes at a spot that gave him an
unobstructed view. It was easy to send the magic dart that
would kill her instantly, the last of four that he had swallowed when he sold his soul to the Shark God. He watched
the girl stumble and fall. Her basket toppled and the *yuka*
spilled to form a semicircle around her head like a corolla.
He took this as an auspicious sign. The god would be pleased
with his payment.

* * *

Not long after, Bagua Guamacajayo's promise was fulfilled—for once Shark Tooth entered into the *kohoba* trance at dawn, he found himself flying to the holy mountain at Cauta. As he soared and turned, he marveled at his bird's-eye view of everything: the ball courts, the longhouse and smaller *bohíos*, a waterfall with a pool below, and the huge carving of Mácocael which guarded the entrance to the holy cave. That visit he would save for later.

Day was breaking as he banked and zoomed in on the corner of the ball court where Candlewood, Flint, Night Orchid, and Sekou were assembling. He watched from high in the sky, then flew lower and lower, impatient at the exchange of greetings, anxious for the moment he'd been waiting for.

Just as Night Orchid reached out to hand the Bundle to Candlewood, a shadow fell, and huge black wings swooped down from the skies to grab the sacred object.

Chapter 65

Afterward, no one could give a coherent account of what had actually happened that morning, for it seemed increasingly like a dream. All agreed that a dark presence descended from the sky and seized the Bundle. But none of them could quite agree on what happened next.

For out of nowhere comes another dark figure, wielding a sword, which he swings; there's the nightmarish sound of it connecting with flesh and bone and sinew, and everyone witnesses a man's head rolling down the ball court, splattering blood. The momentum carries the bloodied sword along, for it arcs through the air and lands on the court with a clatter, just as the person behind it crashes to the ground in front of them.

That's when there's a flash of wings shooting upward from the court into the sky, and then the sound of a screaming bird giving chase. They look up to see a not-unfamiliar sight: a *guaraguao* in pursuit of another bird, with the hawk getting the better of the contest until they are both lost in the clouds.

It brings the onlookers back to earth, where Candlewood seems to have vanished. But no one has time to notice, for when they return their gaze to the ball court, which is now flooded with the first rays of the morning sun, they are shocked to see no headless body, no rolling head, no blood.

Yet lying on the ground some distance away is a sword, and at their feet is the person who wielded it, spread-eagled, facedown.

They are too stunned to move or speak. Candlewood, breathing hard, seemingly appearing from nowhere, bends over with hands to his knees trying to catch his breath, but also to scrutinize the figure on the ground. Finally, he regains his composure and begins to blow furiously on his foot-long cigar. Blowing and blowing until he encloses the little group in a protective smoke ring.

"Hurry," his voice a rasp. "To the cave, Flint. Everyone. Power is loose."

Flint takes hold of Night Orchid, who is still too stunned to react, so he practically carries her along. Sekou, following, is shocked to hear Candlewood say to the man on the ground, "You too, Heart of Palm."

No one would have associated the emaciated and disheveled figure on the ground with the young *ni-taíno*. But there is no time to think as Candlewood rushes them to the cave, his protective smoke ring still encircling and following the little group that now includes Heart of Palm bringing up the rear.

At the cave, Flint hesitates, and it is Candlewood who takes the lead and invites them to enter the black hole, one by one. Candlewood goes in last and, still blowing smoke, murmurs words they cannot hear, to seal the cave entrance behind them.

Chapter 66

As Sekou crawled through the narrow, pitch-black space, the smell hit him—a heart-stopping odor that caused him to hold his breath, a compound of bat droppings, *tabako*, and something else that lent an indefinable sweetness. Once inside, they were able to stand up in the dome-like space, though the frenzied swooping of the disturbed bats forced them to stop moving until the regular inhabitants settled back down to their sleep, piled on top of each other like black slugs on the ceiling.

The cave seemed to be in perpetual twilight, with dust motes floating in the only light source, a beam which came through a hole at the far end. It illuminated a large, life-sized statue of Baibrama positioned to capture it, making the spirit of fertility live up to his reputation as fierce, with perpetually bared teeth, mother-of-pearl eyes, erect penis, and clenched arms, a large bowl for offerings on his head.

The small cavern was the entrance to a much larger cave system that enclosed the sacred spaces that would be accessible only to the holy men—that much he knew. The place where the most powerful symbols of the *cemíes* were kept and also where the most powerful *behikes* such as Candlewood were buried, awaiting their travels to their spiritual home.

Sekou had been in caves before in Xamayca, but never in one that seemed so suffocating, so removed from the real world, so filled with power. His head felt as if it was growing, and he staggered as he moved farther into the cavern to make way for the others. The events of the morning had already overloaded his senses. All he wanted to do was lie down.

Candlewood lit a torch and placed it in a niche, revealing a space bigger than it first appeared but also the source of the sweet scent overlaying all else—the resin from the torch made from the incense-like Tabonuco tree.

"We are safe here," Candlewood said, his voice seeming much stronger and his movements more vigorous as he moved to a stack of mats and handed them out. "Come, sit. We must talk."

Sekou and Night Orchid slid to the ground to sit on the mats; across from them was the dark shape of Heart of Palm, his legs pulled up and his head down on his knees. Flint stood beside the *behike*, who was murmuring instructions, and soon he had a fire going in the hearth which Sekou hoped would take off the morning chill for he was shivering. So was Night Orchid beside him, until he realized she was shaking from silent crying. He was about to reach out when Candlewood came and kneeled in front of her and took both her hands in his.

"Night Orchid, why the tears?" The *behike*'s voice was surprisingly gentle.

"O Elder, I have failed," she burst out. "I am sorry. To have come so far . . ." She choked on the words and succumbed to another fit of sobbing, her chest heaving.

Candlewood waited until she had some control and asked, "What have you failed at?"

His question caused another outburst; this time she seemed angry at him. "Elder . . . the Bundle . . . to have come so far and then to lose it . . ."

Sekou couldn't understand why the old man was smiling in the face of such disaster.

"Come," Candlewood said, standing and pulling Night Orchid up with him. "Come." He summoned the rest of them: "Gather round." When he and the girl were in a little circle formed by the other three, Candlewood spoke in a loud, dramatic voice: "Night Orchid, you have not failed. You have carried out your duty to the end. The Bundle is not lost. Behold!"

And like the magicians and conjurers Sekou had witnessed in so many seaside towns in his travels, Candlewood plucked, seemingly out of air, the Bundle, and smilingly held it out to Night Orchid. All that was missing from the performance was the firecracker and the smoke, and that was almost provided by the sudden crackle and pop of wood from the fire, a sound that brought them back to earth, for there had been a collective holding of breath.

There were gasps, exclamations, cheers, and ululations as the group reacted to this amazing feat. It was hard to believe, given the morning's event in which they all saw the seizure of the object at the ball court. But then, what of anything they had witnessed could they believe?

"Come," Candlewood said again, clapping his hands to break the spell. "Perhaps Flint will make us tea and you'll all hear your own part in the story. For each and every one of you was chosen. But first, with your permission, Night Orchid"—and he actually bowed to her—"I will put this in a safe place, the place where it belongs."

Night Orchid lifted both hands up to her mouth to hide her smile, in a gesture reminiscent of her childish self.

They all turned and watched in awe as Candlewood touched the bowl on the statue of Baibrama. The statue seemed to spin half a turn, and when it faced them again, the *behike* had disappeared into the darkness.

Chapter 67

Shark Tooth came awake with no idea how long he had been in Dream but with an agonizing pain in his neck. It felt as if his head had been severed and not put back on properly. He twisted it from side to side to try to ease the pain, yet that only made it worse and he lay back down and closed his eyes, feeling too exhausted to get up and face the day.

He suddenly sat up and grabbed his axe, for an unwelcome face had intruded into his waking thoughts, that of his long-lost brother Mucaro. He relaxed, and the image faded though he knew it was a bad omen; giving his brother's name as his own when he had stopped at the strange village was tantamount to summoning his *opía*. He wondered why he had made such an error, what malign influence had overtaken his life; he seemed to be losing control. What had he done to offend?

Thinking of his twin's appearance made him even angrier, because while the face was a mirror of his own, it was forever youthful and smooth without a line or a blemish, unlike his own, which Mucaro had marked for life when he had forced him to leave his home, a visible blot that he had never been able to erase. He wondered now if this mark had penetrated his soul, like a splinter which grew into a forest of obstacles that always appeared at the critical moments of his life, when power seemed just within his grasp.

Shark Tooth dismissed thoughts of Mucaro and the rest of his family. What had become of them, he neither knew nor cared. Especially not now when his spirit guide had granted such a boon.

As the dream flight came back to him, he regretted that he had only managed one of his tasks, the seizure of the Sacred Bundle. But that was enough. His capture of the slave Sekou and his vanquishing of Candlewood would have to wait until he could harness power for a second try. The journey had been much harder than expected, and making the return against what seemed like evil winds had left him feeling beaten and battered, like a bird with torn wings. Though he had a cure for that.

Shark Tooth reached for his medicine pouch; his hand was already tingling at the thought of touching the sacred object; he had to look, he had to feast his eyes on the power that would secure his path through life.

He fished in his bag and was surprised to not immediately touch the Bundle. He pushed his hand farther down and when that did not yield results, he looked inside, finally emptying the bag on the ground. He could not believe what his eyes were telling him: the Bundle was not among his possessions. There wasn't much to search in his immediate environment, but he did that anyway, scrabbling in the dirt and bushes, his heart beating faster and faster and a roaring in his head like *Urakán* that only intensified the pain. He sat down and lit a cigar from the last of his *tabako* to calm his spirit and think.

What could have happened? He had a distinct recollection of grabbing the sacred object, of holding it in his hand; he remembered its shape, its feel. Then a shadow looming over him . . . pain, darkness, a falling into nothingness . . . No matter how hard he tried, he could remember nothing more until his shadow slid back into the body of his steed, and he flew off. And that was when the fight began, the *guaraguao* that came shrieking after him and dive-bombed him repeatedly until he'd been forced to let go of the object; the hawk had grabbed it as it fell . . . The hawk!

He had completely underestimated the Maima *behike*. He knew he had power, yes, but never in his dreams would he have imagined him capable of such a swift transformation. Why hadn't Bagua Guamacajayo warned him?

All that effort for nothing! Shark Tooth had never felt so bereft in his life. Even among all the other disappointments that trailed him. This had been so close; he'd savored the triumph even before it happened. Had that offended the god? Had he risen too far above himself? But hadn't the god given him the means to soar?

There was one thing he didn't want to think about, and he tried to push it to the back of his mind. The fact that he had used up the four death-dealing darts that had been implanted in him. How could that have happened?

The first one had flown by accident. This was not long after the Old Man had died and he had struck out on his own, moving from island to island. He had been idly wondering if the dart would really work as promised when his mind-thought let it fly and it embedded itself in the body of a small child playing nearby, the son of the woman he lived with. He had been as shocked as everyone else when the child keeled over, lifeless. The family had summoned a medicine man from another island to conduct the inquest, for a death with no visible cause could not go unnoticed.

He'd been skeptical of the *behike* who came, a cadaverous man with very little adornment, his poverty-stricken condition a sure sign of the poverty of his abilities. Or so Shark Tooth thought. Until the night of the inquest with the whole village gathered when the *behike* came out of his trance to point his finger directly at Shark Tooth. He'd been lucky to escape with his life as he took to sea in the first *kanoa* he could grab and zigzagged his way far from the danger zone. He'd been startled at the *behike*'s discernment and wondered if the man had been able to read his heart, for he had indeed found the child a nuisance, demanding his mother's attention and distracting her from Shark Tooth's desires.

After that, he had been much more careful in using his deadly weapons. But even so, they were done. How could he feed Bagua Guamacajayo now?

He thought how the sea had always been his means of escape. So what was he doing here in this godforsaken wilderness? He looked around at the bare limestone rocks with a stunted tree, a handful of coarse ferns growing out of a fissure here and there; at the valley spread out below with no sign of movement, not even smoke from the small settlements.

He shivered, and gazed at the blue line of the sea. It took him but a few minutes to pack up his possessions and hit the trail.

Chapter 68

A*ll that effort for nothing.* Shark Tooth was not even conscious of his steps as he made his way downhill, the distant sea his only guide. He felt as battered and bruised and hopeless as he had as a youth when he'd run away from home. His one thought was to get away from this cursed place.

And cursed it increasingly seemed as the small *bohíos* he passed all turned out to be abandoned, their residents having fled for safety to the mountains or offshore islands. He had followed the path to one of these small settlements in the hope of finding rest and shelter, yet turned up nothing but empty huts and discarded waste. The nearby fields had all been dug up for whatever crops could be carried and the animal pens emptied. Such an air of desolation hung over the little village that he hurriedly returned to the main path, trying to ignore his massive headache and aching limbs.

His spirit brightened only when he began to catch glimpses of sunlit water through the undergrowth to his left. The swift mountain stream the path followed had broadened out into a navigable stretch and he cut through the bushes to reach its bank. Finding a boat or raft would be too good to be true. And there it was, as if awaiting him: a downturned *kanoa*.

He had no hesitation in turning it over and taking to the water, his spirits lifting as he made the first stroke with the paddle. Very little paddling was in fact needed. He leaned back and let the boat drift on the current, his thoughts drifting along with it, avoiding the most crucial question of all: if the inhabitants were fleeing the coast, was he in fact heading straight toward the dreaded *paranaghiri*?

He put the thought out of his head, certain that he would find the means to avoid them. Though another unwelcome thought kept intruding—the final communication from the Shark God Bagua Guamacajayo that had seemed senseless: *Beware of what you cannot see lurking in the shadows.*

Lulled by the movement of the little boat as it drifted downstream, he shut his eyes and was soon fast asleep.

A sudden stop jarred him awake. The *kanoa* had floated from the broad river course of sparkling clear water to the far side, becoming ensnared in a morass formed by towering mangroves, the stilt roots darkening the water and writhing below like snakes.

Shark Tooth grabbed the paddle and tried to free the boat, but his efforts pushed it deeper into the roots. He jumped out and struggled until he partially righted it. But then it tipped on its side and started to fill with water. As he let go and looked around for a bailer, his body sank up to his waist, his movements releasing the rot of ages, mud and silt bubbling up and fouling the air with their stench.

Shark Tooth groaned, cursed, and abandoned the half-drowned boat. Getting out of the stinking mess was all he cared about now. His feet felt like lead and made a revolting sucking sound with every step as he struggled to clear the swamp.

Halfway to the other side was a large rock sticking out of the water, and he headed for it, aiming to rest in its shade and take stock of his position.

Unseen in the shadows, awaiting his arrival, was a smiling mouth of crocodile teeth. Affixed to the animal's huge jaw.

Chapter 69

Sekou felt the mood in the cave shifting after Candlewood's dramatic disclosure. All were silent as they tried to process the morning's events. Instead of weeping and trembling, Night Orchid now couldn't keep the smile off her face, nor could Flint, and even Heart of Palm seemed more alive to his surroundings.

Flint was handing out hot tea. Inhaling the rising aroma, Sekou couldn't help wondering what the *behike* had taken from his medicine pouch and tossed into the pot, an action he had caught reflected in the shadowy silhouettes thrown by the firelight onto the wall. Whatever it was, it was warming and soothing.

He was dressed like a Taíno, which meant wearing very little, but unlike his new friends who seemed to adapt to the changeable climate, at times like this he wished he could go back to his Spanish clothing. Yet by the time Candlewood returned to sit with Flint, completing their circle, Sekou was flooded with a sense of well-being.

Candlewood drained his cup and put it on the floor beside him and cleared his throat, bringing them instantly to attention.

"My children . . ." he began.

Sekou was struck by the fact that there were four of them so addressed. The Taíno sacred number. *Chosen*, he had said.

Was it chance that had brought them here? Or events that were ordained?

"You come from a world that has been turned upside down. A world that may soon no longer exist. You have helped to save what can be saved. To preserve what can be preserved." Candlewood paused for a long moment and stared into the distance.

They held their breath, the only sound the popping of the firesticks.

"I do not know precisely why you four were chosen to play your part in the saving of our sacred relic. Nor why I was the chosen instrument to see it through. But this, the most important assignment of my life—and the last—is one that has given me the greatest joy as I undertake my final journey. I am saddened because the world as I know it will end soon, so it is foretold in Dream.

"As you already know, three worlds were created and destroyed before our own, the Fourth Age. The time of Divinity, the time of Creators, and the time of Heroes preceded ours. Each was swept away, but each age left behind the precious tokens of the divine presence to sustain us frail humans. We celebrate them in our masks and our dances, our songs and our ceremonies: the gifts of fish and the sea, of fire, *kohoba*, *yuka*, and the gourd from the sacred earth, the stones for the sacred *maraka*. Above all, the earth-shapers left their presence in the sacred *cemíes* to be our oracles and guides."

Sekou felt himself nodding off at what he felt was going to be a lengthy history lesson in a room which had grown displeasingly hot, yet he came alert as Candlewood raised his voice.

"Know this: each time in the past that the world was destroyed and remade, it was because of some offense to the divine, an imperfection in its construction that could not be countenanced. But now, children, our age represents the first time that human beings will be the agents of our own destruction. So it is foretold. What this means, I do not know. Where do we go from here?"

They looked expectantly for an answer, though none was forthcoming. The tone of the *behike*'s voice kept changing— he was chanting now, almost as if reciting a sacred *areito*. But what he said had not yet been memorized.

"My children, you will enter the unknown with no other certainty than this: inside this sacred mountain, this place of emergence, the Sacred Bundle we have just restored is nothing less than our nation's beating heart."

Somehow, it felt as if their collective hearts were beating together, but oscillating wildly.

"In the long run, few of our people will survive. Yet the heart will continue to pump our blood into the veins of our conquerors, so that in tens of tens of tens of time, our spirit will rise again in a people who will proudly say, *I am Taíno*. They will be different from us in many ways; the result of a mingling with other blood, other people, for that is the way of the new age.

"But know this: the spirit of our sacred *yuka* will never die, as long as there is one of our people left to lift the *kasabe* sacrament to their lips and hear the voice of the sacred Bringer of *Yuka*, Ruler of the Sea, Without a Male Ancestor, Yucahuguamá Bagua Maorócoti: *This is my body. Keep me alive. Consume me.*"

Chapter 70

The listeners were spellbound, hanging on to Candlewood's every word. Until he broke the spell and picked up his cup. Finding it empty, he handed it to Flint, who went to the pot to pour them all another round.

Everyone shifted around but the only sound came from Candlewood himself, who groaned loudly at the creaking of his old bones as he tried out a new position on the mat. In the semidarkness, his face seemed spectral, like the death spirit Maquetaurie Guayaba, his forehead and cheekbones all that stood out from under his huge feathered headdress that threw grotesque shadows behind him, the movement of his feathered armbands making him seem like one of his bird ancestors, emblems of eternal life.

When Flint rejoined the circle, they all sat at attention, rapt.

Candlewood brought his hands together in front of his mouth in a gesture of thinking. Which he did for a good long while. Finally, he said, "Now we come to the heart of this matter before us: why you four?" He turned to Night Orchid.

"Night Orchid, when chosen you were still a child, but on this journey you proved yourself a woman, refusing to be turned aside from your goal. You might not know that as a child you were given a hummingbird's heart, as a way to still the war that raged inside you. That warrior's heart beats inside you still. Even when our numbers become few and our hearts troubled, you will rally our people to confront evil; your name will be sung in the last of the *areitos*. Night Orchid, I bless you with a new name to signify your new self. From henceforth, you will be known as Aura Surey, the Morning Star, herald of new beginnings."

Night Orchid tried to hide her broad grin as all eyes turned to her. She acknowledged Candlewood's words with a deep bow and palms together in the position of respect, Candlewood answering with his own.

Next, the *behike* turned to Heart of Palm, who sat up straighter but bowed his head when he heard his name, clearly expecting to be condemned. But Candlewood's voice was gentle when he spoke: "Your souls are in shreds like birds leaving the comfortable nest before the storm and battered by *Urakán*. You have to seek redemption for the choices you made before you can be at peace. You will build and enter a *guanara* to purge yourself of all evil, after which I am commanded in Dream to restore your souls."

The others were surprised by this, and Candlewood must have sensed them stirring, for he raised his hand to still them as he continued: "You started with nobility of lineage. I do not know why you of all your lineage were chosen. But you have been tested and now you need to regain nobility of soul. You will become the warrior you are destined to be and bind others to you in the cause—the noble quest to free our nation. What the final result will be, I do not know, but by your mighty deeds to come, your name like Night Orchid's will join the pantheon of our heroes. You will henceforth be known as Guarionex—Brave Noble Lord."

This announcement was greeted with startled silence, for they could not believe there was no punishment for the theft of Sekou's sword. Sekou tried to say something but found himself unable to speak.

"Yes, the sword," Candlewood said, as if reading their thoughts. "That too was determined by the *cemíes*. By our laws, Heart of Palm was wrong to take it and will have to negotiate with Sekou suitable recompense for the theft and the anguish it caused. Know, Sekou, that you will find your sword safely back with your belongings when you leave here, purified of all contamination."

Sekou couldn't help smiling and bowed in acknowledgment.

"I assure you, your sword was our instrument of deliverance from the evil forces arrayed against us, forces that up to the last minute, as you saw, attempted to gain control. The evil one, embodied in the man we know as Shark Tooth, was armored with the incomer's magic—their sacred cross. The dream determined that he could only be defeated by a weapon forged by the same *paranaghiri*—a powerful weapon, like the sword.

"You, Sekou, were led to us as Heart of Palm was led to take the sword from you and wield it this morning in defense of our nation. Without you all, the Bundle would now be in the hands of another and would signal the heart leaving our nation."

They heaved a collective sigh at this final unraveling of some of the mysteries. Heart of Palm lost his beaten expression and sat up straight, his face shining and expectant.

Candlewood was not finished. "You two," he said, turning to Sekou and Flint, "are matched opposites. Sekou, you are the bringer of the new—you broke away from the enemy to align yourself with us, because you too come from a people who are suffering from their oppression.

"We who are upholders of tradition have resisted what the enemy brings. But the dream tells us we will never defeat them, so our young need to learn and adapt to those things that will make our transition to the new age easier. You bring such enlightenment with you and will be our teacher; I know you have many gifts that will help us in our struggles. We give you this new name by which you will be henceforth known as Guaherí, Gatherer and Joiner of People."

Like the others, Sekou tried to wipe the grin off his face but found it impossible, especially when he saw that everyone was smiling at him, even Heart of Palm, and he felt a sense of belonging wash over him. Never again would he travel alone.

Candlewood took a last sip from his cup and seemed to visibly relax as he looked around the circle. All eyes turned toward Flint, the shy one, who could hardly contain his embarrassment at being the center of attention.

"Flint is a brave warrior like the rest of you, as he has shown on his singular travels, his knowledge of the pathways of our land unsurpassed. Flint has nevertheless been an outsider in our village, with a divided lineage that excluded him from the highest consideration. But the dream has determined for him a different destiny, and he comes to us with the gift of medicine and song, with the ability to heal the broken and find lost souls. In short, to become a *behike*. He is only on the start of this long journey, learning from me as I come to the end of mine. But he will become the last of the great healers in our time. Which is why the new name of Flint the spirit warrior will be Maraka-ti, Great Summoner of Medicine.

"But why Flint? you will ask. Because far from being the outsider, Flint is the bridge, the one who links us all through time. Just as Sekou's pedigree reaches back in time to a land we do not know, so Flint through his mother also has a pedigree which reaches back in time to a land we do not know.

"The Old Ones, we call his ancestors, and by other names as well, demeaning names, disrespectful names. We have scorned the old ways they represent as not modern, just as in future times we Taíno will be scorned as archaic. All that will be found of us is what people will dig out of the earth, the detritus of ourselves. Failing to understand us—or what we have left behind—they too will see us as relics of a bygone, savage age. Which is why we need to ensure that our nation's heart keeps beating, that our blood keeps flowing, just as the blood of the Old Ones flowed into ours."

Candlewood broke into a fit of coughing and held out his cup, which Flint rushed to fill. Sekou could barely keep awake, and through the gloom he could see the others nodding and trying to stay awake also. He wanted nothing more at this stage than to sink into oblivion.

As if reading his mind, Candlewood took a last sip and said, "Enough, friends. Know that the thread that binds you now stretches from the Old Ones descended from the Snow People at the top of the world and our Taíno peoples of the floating worlds through Flint to Sekou, descended from people at the other end of the world, who holds the thread of the new.

"Flint will remain the guardian of this holy place. Sekou and the Taíno warriors Heart of Palm and Night Orchid will be a part of the last stand against those who would seek to destroy us. You will be joined by many others heading for the mountains to establish sites of resistance. You will be given many names by your enemies—Outlaw . . . Guerrilla . . . Cimarrón . . . Maroon . . . But to your dying day, the one you will wear most proudly is Freedom Fighter.

"The dream has spoken. Taíno-tí. Sleep . . ."

Not one of the four saw Candlewood touch the head of Baibrama and disappear, or heard the bats as they streamed out through the hole as night descended, to forage and feast on *guayaba*.

PART V
CIMARRONES

Chapter 71

Sekou and Heart of Palm sat in companionable silence on top of the rock that overlooked the ball court and surroundings. Over the last moon, following the Taíno's healing ceremony, the two young men had bonded. Now they were resting after another strenuous day of learning from each other.

Heart of Palm could be heard yelling "*¡Maldita!*" and other Spanish phrases as he practiced swordsmanship under Sekou's watchful eye. And he laughed heartily when the African fumbled in using the *atlatl* to throw a spear or blew a wrong note on the conch shell as he practiced sending messages. At night, sitting outside, they shared their knowledge of reading the Heavens and star lore. When Flint could spare the time, he showed them how to track and ambush game ("It will work for humans too," he assured them) and how to read the language of the bush. Night Orchid was sharing her skill in turning calabashes into pots, utensils, and water containers, and weaving baskets from different fibers. They'd decided to pool their knowledge. In the kind of warfare they expected, one of quick ambushes and lightning raids by small numbers, each person needed to know how to survive on their own.

Night Orchid gifted them all with new *guaízas*—protective *cemíes* she carved as they sat chatting. She was otherwise

334 ♣ Paradise Once

busy acquiring the military arts—sometimes to the amusement of the watchers when the weapons seemed too heavy or bulky for her tiny frame. But she never gave up and would master them all—enabling Sekou to enrich her vocabulary. "I'll make you eat your words" became her favorite threat, accompanied by a warrior stance whenever challenged.

They were anxious to set off, but Candlewood asked them to stay for a final solstice ceremony when, he prophesied, they would be joined by others. His messages were transmitted through Flint, for the *behike* no longer left the cave, preparing himself for his final flight.

Flint now had help. One day a *behike* had arrived out of the blue, said his name was Guabina, and announced that Candlewood had summoned him. No longer surprised by anything connected with Candlewood, Flint had willingly continued his apprenticeship under Guabina, following Candlewood's instructions.

Guabina brought news of the outside world. Narváez and his men had continued their deadly traverse of the island. Currently on the north coast, they were making their way westward in *kanoas*. Places like Turtle Village had been overrun and their residents were heading for higher ground. Flint's thoughts immediately turned to his friends there and especially to Sandstone and his daughter Pearl. Had their hidden village been discovered? Were they too on the move? Now that he was nearing manhood, Flint had a fantasy of one day opening his eyes to see Pearl standing before him, waiting to be his bride.

Soon, as Candlewood had predicted, other refugees from far and near began to arrive. Some stopped only long enough to rest and receive the holy man's blessing before leaving to establish a new *bohío* in the woods or travel on. Others stayed

in the area and began to put down roots close to the holy
site.

Sekou was amused to see a few of the refugees arriving
with animals the Spaniards had brought, though so far only
a few piglets, a string of goats. No horses or mules or cattle
yet, though he knew it was just a matter of time. The Old
World animals had taken over the New, thriving in the lush
wilderness on all the islands, trampling the native fields and
destroying *konukos*. In time the natives would see the animals for what they were—a new source of food. For now,
like a true Spaniard, Sekou's mouth watered at the thought
of a small suckling pig grilling on a *barbacoa*.

A senior *kacike* who came with his wife took charge, or-
ganizing a council, assigning rosters, and assuming all the
duties of a leader. Families arriving from different directions were happy to find kin and build *bohíos* together. The
women took charge of the *konukos*: the planting, reaping,
and preparation of *yuka* and other crops. Craftspeople set up
workshops to make clay pots and other necessities, for many
of the refugees arrived empty-handed.

Sekou was amazed at how quickly the Taíno, despite
their travails, were able to settle down into the patterns established from First Time. And yet he saw nothing but sadness in their eyes. Was this the end of the road?

There was one joyous event that brought them all together
before the solstice celebrations. When the women heard that
Night Orchid had not completed her initiation into womanhood, the senior matrons took charge. Though her Coming
Out was a subdued affair, Night Orchid, painted and dressed
in gifted jewelry, in shell rattles and beads, was radiant. She
looked completely different with her hair cut short and the
raffia skirt denoting her new status as marriageable. Her

body was beginning to fill out and she seemed to grow in stature.

Sekou teased her: "You know, I am now your eldest uncle, so I'm in charge of finding you a husband of which I approve. Who do you choose of the young men here?"

She smiled sadly, for there was no suitable candidate. Not yet. Most of those coming were older people who had lost their young men to raids and the *encomienda* system. The few young men who showed up were brought by their families for spiritual healing or recovery from the physical wounds inflicted by their masters, including amputation. A child or an expectant woman arriving was a cause for joy. The Taíno had been decimated not only by the invaders; women had increasingly made the decision not to bear children; some resorted to killing their children by poisoning with bitter *yuka* juice rather than see them live under the Spanish yoke. Even when the women were left safe in their villages, few of their men ever came home from enforced labor. Family life was destroyed. The women who were captured and raped by the *paranaghiri* were having children who would then become part of their labor force in the ever-changing *Nuevo Mundo*.

Chapter 72

Many of the new arrivals were startled at their first sight of a Black man, but soon got used to Sekou's presence. Now that he was so much better at speaking Taíno, he could have deeper conversations with some of the newcomers or listen to their talk.

His ears pricked up one day when he overheard a refugee saying he'd heard that the *paranaghiri*'s king said they could bring in lots of Black African slaves to work since there were so few Taíno left.

Sekou sat down nearby, not deliberately hiding but unseen by the speakers, a group of men stripping poles for building.

"What are Black Africans?" someone asked.

"I don't know. People like Sekou?"

"I guess."

"But he's not a slave."

"How did he come then? Someone must have brought him."

Sekou flushed, and melted farther into the shadows. *Black African slave* rang like a gong in his ears. How dare they! He was *ladino*, born in Spain and Christianized; completely forgetting for a moment his rejection of everything Spanish as he fled the massacre.

Despite himself, he couldn't stop listening.

"They say they are people they capture in some far-off country."

"The way they scraped up the Lucayan on the cays and loaded them into their boats and took them away. Remember?"

"I was too young, but I have heard the elders speak of it."

"They say you have to be a different color from the *paranaghiri* to be taken this way. Your dark skin makes you a heathen. So they say their Black Robe told them."

"Like us?" The speaker laughed.

"They say they can work them much harder," said a man from Española. "And it's not just the mines now. They're planting the grass that produces something sweet like honey. They say you have to plant it and reap it and grind it and plant it and do it all over again. Hard work. They say the Black African slaves are best for that kind of work."

"Working for others is not something we were ever used to . . ."

"Not until they came . . ."

"They brought some Africans to Borikén not so long ago, and they ran away as soon as they arrived and took to the hills."

"As did the ones in Española. They're joining our Taíno rebels to raid the *paranaghiri* settlements."

"That's good then. Let them come."

Sekou listened harder when the refugee from Española said that in his youth he had known enslaved Black people who had been brought there during his father's time. He recalled spending time as a child with an old man who herded cattle near his *bohío* and who told him stories of his life. "I could not believe such cruelty until the *guamikena* came to our world. Not even from the Kwaib. It was only when I saw what they were doing to our people that I believed that the old man spoke truth."

Sekou was appalled as the speaker repeated what the old man had told him of his experience. He began to wonder if this was how his own parents had arrived in Spain. *Captured* like animals, *torn* from their homes, *shackled* and *packed* into a ship like sardines. *Stripped* of their clothing and *paraded* like animals to be sold. Sekou cringed as he remembered the conversation between Narváez and Velázquez the day they discussed him. The same way they discussed an animal. Sekou clapped his hands to his head. Why had he been such a stupid youth, so wrapped up in his pride? His thoughts in a whirl, he sat and thought for so long he was not even aware when the speakers moved away.

The few Black people he had seen on his travels he assumed were also *ladino,* servants going about their master's business. He too had spent his life going about his master's business, though he'd left home too young to be conscious of what *Black African slave* really meant.

His parents made sure he knew of their proud Joloff ancestry, and they never spoke about slavery in his presence. Not even when he was handed over to the ship's captain. "Now be good and obey the master," was all his mother said before she fled in tears. He felt sad now when he remembered how his six-year-old self had been so fascinated by the life on the docks, the excitement of being on board a ship, how as it sailed away he hadn't cried for his mother—he had cried for his toy drum, a *djembe*, that was left behind.

He was not Spanish then? Black African. What did that really mean? He spent a long time just sitting there, thinking about his past and all the twists and turnings of his life. He glanced around at his surroundings, at the Taíno holy site and ball court, the *yukayeke* that was growing on the hillsides, and below, the women's beautifully laid-out *konuko* with the high mounds in which they planted the sacred *yuka*.

He sighed and thought of all the Black African slaves and the world they'd left behind. Was it like this one?

You have to be a different color from the paranaghiri *to be taken this way.* The speaker's voice rang in his ears.

He looked at his black skin.

The Taíno were not black. They were red. Did it matter? Red and Black. Dark colors mingling with blood to make maroon. Dark skins hiding in the shadows. Waiting to strike. Waging wars of rebellion. Together. That is what mattered now.

He knew he would never see his parents again, but he could still make them proud. He would be Guaherí, Gatherer and Joiner of People—a leader, a teacher, a warrior, a freedom fighter for all. So Candlewood had prophesied as he pronounced his new name.

Guaherí stood up and squared his shoulders. Embarking on yet another life. This time as his own master.

There were now freedom fighters on all the islands, new arrivals told a fascinated audience, Indian as well as enslaved Africans escaping to the mountains. They engaged in raids to harass the Spaniards who were putting down roots, establishing towns and ranches in addition to their relentless search for gold. Already, the rebels were being called by the name attached to feral animals—*cimarrones.*

How could the little group from Maima join up?

None of them had any idea. Until one day a Taíno named Cedar arrived with two women and a child. They were greeted warmly by the Maima villagers, for they had kin there and often visited. It was Cedar's male companion, though, who electrified them, not least because he carried a long bow and a quiver of arrows, weapons they were anxious to acquire. Although Taíno in some regions did use bows and arrows, the weapons were not commonly used by the people of Maima.

The newcomer was readily identified as Kwaib, from his battle-scarred body, his tattoos, jewelry in his pierced ears, nose, and lips, and the distinctive *caracol* breastplate of a high-raking warrior. He looked as fierce as his people were said to be, though his face broke into a friendly smile at their greetings. He was named Caonabó, he said, after the legendary leader who was half-Kwaib, like himself.

After they fed and settled the visitors, the residents were anxious to hear what Caonabó could tell them. A man of some twenty-five summers, he was happy to talk as they seated themselves around him. He was coming from Borikén, where he had been the second-in-command to Guarionex, leader of the insurgency there, and had escaped when Guarionex was captured and their camp destroyed. Since then, he had spent many moons paddling, first to Ayití and from there to Cuba.

He'd been born on Guaticabon to a Kwaib father and Taíno mother. "I have lived among Taíno for most of my life," he told those gathered, "but my spirit is that of my father's lineage." And he solemnly beat his chest with his right hand.

He'd been taken by his uncle on a trading mission to Borikén as soon as he had completed his initiation. At that, his audience was all ears. On the tips of their tongues were all the questions they wanted to ask about his initiation. If the stories told of the extraordinary endurance required of a Kwaib boy were true. But his next statement kept them quiet.

"My uncle was killed by a shark soon after arriving. What was I to do? I had seen fourteen summers and considered myself a man. I was a newly made warrior. I offered my services to *kacikes* on one island after another, up and down, and that is how I lived. I didn't take sides. I didn't care what we were fighting for." His face was stern. "The battle is everything."

But now, he said, he was totally on the side of his mother's people, "because that is the heart that is beating." And he laid his left hand softly on his chest. "The *paranaghiri* don't fight like men but hide behind shells. We cannot allow ourselves to be conquered by cowards like that." He was on his way to join the remnants of Hatuéy's army that was coming together again in the mountains of Cuba.

When he ceased talking, one listener asked how he'd come to be part of Cedar's group.

His mother, he said, had told him repeatedly that he had a duty to find the daughter she had left behind in Cuba the day she was captured by Kwaib on a fishing trip with her husband. Her husband was killed and she had ended up on Guaticabon as the wife of her captor. But she had never forgotten her daughter. From the time Caonabó was old enough, she had made him promise he would find her. She was anxious for her daughter to know that she had not abandoned her. "Whenever we were alone, that is what she said." Caonabó sighed. "I might never see her again to tell her that her daughter knows."

He related how he'd been on his way to find his mother's *bohío*, not certain it still existed, when he met Cedar's group. They too were fleeing *paranaghiri* raids that now extended into the mountain villages. As they exchanged information, he discovered that, by some miracle, he had found his mother's kin.

Everyone assembled before Caonabó looked in awe at the quiet woman sitting with her sister-in-law, Cedar's wife. She had lost her husband in a raid many moons past. She tried, but couldn't keep the grin off her face as she gazed at her newfound brother.

It was pure chance that had brought them together, Caonabó said.

But the Taíno knew differently. His arrival was a gift from the *cemíes*.

Caonabó was chosen to show them the way.

All the able-bodied joined in the fighting lessons that Caonabó and others gave. The matrons and older men vowed to stay and defend the site. They hoped enough marriages would be arranged at solstice so that young women could leave with the group. Caonabó had warned that the warriors would not succeed alone. While they had to be mobile, they also needed permanent camps that were well hidden for their women and children. The women would cultivate *konukos* to provide supplies for the men and ensure that they and the children would survive.

Candlewood had said the same. That the holy *yuka*, forged by the guardians of fertility, Yukahú and Attabey, had to be kept alive. "Keeping the *yuka* alive wherever you go is a sacred duty," had been his last warning, "so the *cemíes* will not forsake you."

Sekou, Heart of Palm, and Night Orchid, along with others including Caonabó's sister, were planning to travel with the Kwaib warrior when he left, for at least part of the journey.

Beyond that, the path was open. The *cemíes* would show the way.

They made up a new war song. A song that would join them one to the other, breath to breath, even if any found themself alone and on the road to Koaibay.

None of them knew the wind would take that song and hold it breathlessly for another five hundred years, waiting for other voices to bring it to life.

So it was. So it always will be.

Glossary

The preference of linguists now is that in spelling we use the letter *k* to represent the hard sound of the letter *c* when writing Taíno. Thus, many familiar words in the literature, such as *cacique, canoe, caney, casabe,* etc., will be found listed under *K*.

Agouti—a rabbitlike rodent eaten for meat (*Dasyprocta agouti*)
Aguate—avocado (*Persea americana*)
Ajiako—pepperpot stew
Anacaona—or Golden Flower, historical figure (1474–1504); Taíno *kacika* of Xaragua, one of the historical chiefdoms of Haiti; her legacy is memorialized in the contemporary Caribbean
Anana—Pineapple (*Ananas sp.*), also *yayama*
Anki—evil person
Areito—ceremonial festival in which the histories were recited
Atlatl—spear thrower, used by Taíno and other native people
Attabey—Taíno *cemí*, the Great Mother
Ayití—Taíno name for Haiti; referred to by the Spaniards as Española/Hispaniola, the island shared with present-day Dominican Republic

Baibrama—Taíno *cemí*, associated with fertility of crops
Barbacoa—barbecue, a platform of sticks used for roasting and drying meat
Batéy—ball game and the ceremonial plaza where it's played
Behike—medicine man, shaman

Bejuco—name given to a variety of flexible stems, vines, and roots used for making ropes or cord; also medicinal
Bixa—annatto, roucou (*Bixa orellana*), sacred coloring matter
Bohío—the typical Taíno round dwelling house; also means *home* or *community*
Boinayel—Taíno weather spirit
Borikén—Taíno name for Puerto Rico

Caonabó—historical figure (d. 1496), war chief of Santo Domingo, husband of Anacaona
Cemí, Cemíes (pl)—Taíno spiritual entities and their representation in carvings, amulets, etc., often written as *zemi*
Cibucán—long woven tube used in processing *yuka* (cassava)

Datiao—friend
Duho—elaborate ceremonial stool used by *kacikes, behikes,* and other high-ranking Taíno

Encomienda—Spanish system of giving Taíno villagers to Spanish settlers
Española/Hispaniola—Spanish name for the island now shared by Haiti and the Dominican Republic

Guabancex—*cemí* weather spirit causing wind and hurricanes
Guahayona—mythological figure, the first medicine man
Guaíza—*cemí* amulet worn on the body
Guama—Lord; used in respectful address
Guamikena—white man
Guanábana—soursop fruit (*Annona muricata*)
Guanara—temporary hut for initiation, cleansing, and other sacred events
Guanín—Taíno precious metal, regarded as sacred
Guaraguao—a type of hawk
Guataúba—weather *cemí*, assistant to Guabancex; makes thunder and lightning
Guatiao—ritual friend
Guaticabon—Taíno name for the island of Dominica

Guay—common expression denoting pain or surprise
Guayaba—guava fruit (*Psidium guajava*); eaten by the Taíno
dead; Maquetaurie Guayaba was the *cemí* of the dead

Hamaka—hammock—hanging bed made of cord
Hato—(Spanish) ranch
Hatuéy—historical figure (1478–1512), a *kacike* who fled
from Hispaniola to Cuba and led the insurgency there
Henequén—sisal; a type of agave with useful fiber
Hutía—small mammal hunted for food (English coney;
Capromyidae)

Inriri Kahubabayael—Mythological woodpecker who created
women from wood

Jagua—guinep (*Melicoccus bijugatus*), a fruit tree that yields
sacred black dye
Jobo—plum (*Spondias mombin*); fruit that features promi-
nently in Taíno myths

Kacika/Kacike—Taíno chief
Kacikazgo—domain of a chief
Kaney—Taíno large rectangular dwelling occupied by the chief
and those of high rank
Kanoa—canoe
Kasabe—flat bread made of *yuka* (cassava)
Kasaripe—cassava liquid
Kasiri—cassava liquor
Koa—multipurpose fire-hardened stick
Koaibay—Taíno abode of the afterlife
Kobo—seashell (queen conch) used to signal and transmit
messages
Kohoba—narcotic snuff used to communicate with the spirit
world
Koki—frog
Kolibri—hummingbird
Konuko—agricultural plot

Kwaib—Taíno for native of the Eastern Caribbean (formerly *Carib* in English), now known as Kalibri or Kalinago

Las Casas, Bartolomé de—historical figure (1484–1566), Spanish priest who became known as "Protector of the Indians" for his defense of indigenous peoples; he was present at the 1513 massacre of the Cuban Taíno village of Caonao, the prototype for the fictional Maima

Lucayan Taíno—the indigenous people of the Bahamas archipelago

Mabí—fruit tree (*Colubrina reclinata*) and a drink made from it

Mahíz—maize/corn (*Zea mays*)

Maho—mahoe (*Hibiscus sp.*) used for timber, cordage, and nets

Mamí—mammee apple (*Mammea americana*)

Maquetaurie Guayaba—*cemí* spirit of the dead

Maraka—sacred gourd rattle

Márohu—*cemí* weather spirit, twin to Boinayel

Mayohuakan—sacred drum

Naboría—servant, commoner

Nagua—skirt

Narváez, Pánfilo de—historical figure (d.1528), Spanish conquistador involved in the conquest of Cuba and elsewhere

Ni-Taíno—Taíno nobility

Olla—pottery jar

Opía—spirit of the dead

Opiyelguobirán—*cemí* dog guardian of the spirit world

Panol—A Taíno name for Spaniards

Paranaghiri—a general name (not Taíno) for the Spaniards

Quisqueya—present-day Dominican Republic (along with Haiti the island of present-day Hispaniola)

Siba—stone; jewelry made from stone and shell

Tabako—tobacco (*Nicotiana tabacum*), a sacred plant
Toona—prickly pear cactus (*Opuntia sp.*)
Turey—the sky

Urakán—hurricane

Velázquez, Diego de Cuéllar, historical figure (1465–1524), Spanish conquistador and active participant in the conquest of Hispaniola and Cuba

Xamayca—Jamaica (Spanish name—*Yamaye* in Taíno)

Yuka—cassava (*Manihot esculenta*)
Yukahú—*cemí*, the supreme being
Yukayeke—Taíno village

Zemi—see *cemí*

Acknowledgments

I am grateful for various types of assistance during the writing of this book from Allyson Latta, Honor Ford-Smith, Andil Gosine, Ana Chichester, and a special thank you to Johnny Temple for the push start.

Our Caribbean myths and legends are full of tales of revenants—the unquiet dead who cannot rest until they find the means to reveal their stories. Such are the dead in the fictional village of Maima who forced me to bring them to life in *Paradise Once*.

This was not the story I started to tell. Over many years, I tried out different scenarios and approaches, all of them leading to a dead end. It was as if I had to yield to voices that, once heard, held onto me like Clinging Woman or the spirit Death in an Anansi story that once taken up can never be put down. The only release is to answer the call.

The call was from an actual village in Cuba called Caonao (on which my fictional Maima is based), the scene of a massacre by Spanish forces in 1513.

The conquest and colonization of the Americas is filled with images of death and destruction of the native peoples. But this graphic eyewitness account by Bartolomé de las Casas embedded itself in my consciousness (and is the event, incidentally, that led to las Casas's renunciation of his property and conversion to the cause of protection of the native people). Las Casas's description of the Spanish troops sharpening their swords on whetstones in a river as they neared Caonao for a "goodwill visit" on their traverse of the island chillingly foreshadows their deployment on the native people who were gathered to welcome them:

> *A Spaniard, in whom the devil is thought to have clothed himself, suddenly drew his sword. Then the whole hundred drew theirs and began to rip open the bellies, to cut and kill . . . a stream of blood was running, as if a great number of cows had perished.*

This image has been like that invasive object to me, causing irritation until it is expelled or acknowledged.

The genesis of this story, though, lies much further back, in my colonial Jamaican childhood where history books informed us of Columbus's "discovery" of our Caribbean islands. There he found "primitive" peoples called Arawaks and Caribs who were soon airbrushed from the conquest story.

How could a people simply vanish? Thus the myth of Taíno extinction became embedded in my consciousness, even as I made the imaginative leap to discover them. Not to "discover" in the Western sense of "laying claim to," but reverting to the word's original meaning which is to "uncover" or reveal that which already exists.

At the time, I did not know that I could begin this reveal in my own rural Jamaican backyard where we ate bammy or cassava bread (*yuka*) for breakfast; raided guava (*guayaba*) trees for the sweet fruit; drew patterns on our skin with guinep (*jagua*) after we had eaten our fill; used annatto (*bixa*) as food coloring; or cowered in darkness as the eye of the hurricane (*urakán*) gave pause. Yet only the water spirit Ribba Mumma with her comb and long hair magically whispered, "Indian."

Knowledge of our living connection to our indigenous forebears came much later, as the approach of the Columbus quincentennial in 1992 led to an upsurge in investigation of the indigenous world of the Americas, including the Caribbean. Investigation that continues today and informs our writing practice in both poetry and prose.

Paradise Once is a product of the imagination, as are the characters, but the history, background, and culture are based on what has been revealed by the work of scholars to whom I am deeply indebted. I have tried to be true to the knowledge I have gained, but creating a work of fiction gives me that extra privilege of imaginative re-creation. To see the Taíno up to five hundred years ago not as artifacts but as modern people with a well-developed social and cultural life; people like us. Or so they told me.

—*Olive Senior*